ISOWORG

ISOWORG

Henry Bentinck

London

MICHAEL JOSEPH

First published in Great Britain by
MICHAEL JOSEPH LTD
52 Bedford Square
London, W.C.1
1971

7181 0876 0
Set and printed in Great Britain by
Northumberland Press Limited, Gateshead
in Times ten on eleven point, and
bound by Dorstel Press, Harlow

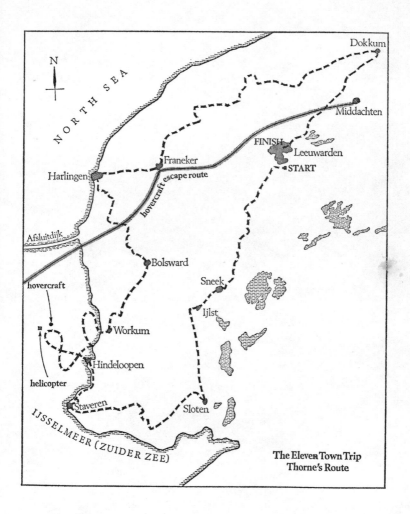

The Eleven Town Trip
Thorne's Route

Chapter One

His flat had been broken into and searched, yet nothing had been taken. There had been telephone calls from a public opinion outfit: Would he answer questions? It had seemed phoney, the questions curious, so he had played along with it. It had been going on now for some time and there was something increasingly perplexing about the voice. To begin with it had been staccato as though taped; gradually it had grown familiar.

Thorne felt he was being sussed out. And now today he realised that he was being followed. Accordingly he had gone for a walk in Hyde Park. He did not want to lose the followers, he just wanted to find out more about them. He wanted to find out more about everything—wanted to take the action into their camp, whoever they were—but he couldn't think how to do it. He continued walking slowly in the Park thinking about this. The air was blue with cold, the Park deserted, the ground frozen. The pattern of footprints, dogs' paws, girls' heels were like a plaster cast recording the crossed purposes of nameless individuals. On this Monday afternoon his followers were easy to detect slinking along among the trees. In a strange way he welcomed them. He walked on slowly, trying to make a pattern out of the events. For instance, his long, very special racing skates had attracted much attention. Why should anyone fish them out from the bottom of that box—nearly hidden—leaving marks in the old coagulated grease? The Serpentine was ice-bound. The trees seemed frozen stiff, making black incalculable patterns against the violet sky. What was somebody trying to find out? The people following him weren't very expert. He walked on, his mind busy considering the papers, letters, objects

7

—their ambiguity to a stranger. He realised that the questions on the telephone and the search were complementary. There was an old violin case smelling faintly of gun oil. There was a press photograph of a crowd in Czechoslovakia at the time of the Hungarian uprising. By chance a part of him was visible carrying the violin case. And then the 'phone had asked, 'Do you play any musical instrument?' And on a different occasion, 'What's your opinion of Hungarians?' To this he had replied, 'A Hungarian's a bloke that'll enter a revolving door behind you and come out in front. My kind of bloke, that.' And the voice had chuckled.

He felt less and less antagonism towards the voice. Why? He should feel more and more. Why hadn't he put the receiver down? Thinking carefully he knew it was because he was getting to like the voice.

He was standing by the ice which bonded this side of the Serpentine to the other. Ice made islands into non-islands, made him feel different, new, strange as he walked out upon it.

He went back over two items which the search must have revealed. His bank statements had one or two, not many, very large credits. The dates, to a good observer, coincided with such items as a cryptic letter of thanks from a South African black liberal smuggled over the border into Basutoland. Elsewhere between the leaves of a book upon his shelves, there was a particularly fulsome obituary for an Afrikaans policeman of notoriously sadistic zeal. His activities in the Congo. His diamond smuggling exploits. These and others could have been deduced from the scrappy pieces of evidence and knitted together by the telephone conversations.

Distantly, across the frozen Park, the roar of London came to him. The air—so cold it made the hairs inside his nose bristle—suddenly seemed to combine with his thoughts into a sensation of pressage. He and the atmosphere were caught up together and held like a footprint on the frozen soil in some tingling time of held breath. He walked back from the edge, took a run and, as he sent himself sliding, flying across the ice, there suddenly leapt into his mind the incredible notion that the voice on the telephone was becoming his own.

Thorne was six foot two and weighed thirteen stone. When you

8

stood up against him, he felt hard, unshoveable and hot. And his movements were fast, almost irritable, as though the need and decision to go here or look there were part of a plan that he was getting a move on with. His hair was long and thick and glossy. His eyes brown, nearly black; when he was angry they blazed with the sort of total committal you see in the eyes of an animal as it goes into the attack. But when he was not angry they seemed to be alight with a burning disbelief that life could really be so funny, so amazing, or that you could be so beautiful or interesting.

It being so cold today, he had gladly taken the opportunity to wear his sable coat, its thick collar lying across his wide shoulders like a gorged python. There was no self-effacing modesty about Thorne. He loved the swing of the coat, the way his narrow trousers were cut down at the heel and up over the instep. He loved the nuggety hand-made chukka boots, and most of all he loved the fact that modern London would smile and approve of him in his peacock pride.

His *own* voice? His mind raced over the technical questions of how it could be done, finding answers. But the real question was why? And to that not even a guess came to mind. It had been going on for nearly three weeks now. Time after time he had tried to interrogate the voice on the 'phone. It parried his questions until he pressed too hard and then it hung up. He had had the calls traced and discovered that the voice had some means of tapping into a variety of numbers. Well, that wasn't so difficult. He had pondered every possible explanation and had come to no conclusion.

It couldn't be an official enquiry into his activities, lawless though most of them were. Officialdom wasn't like this. Enemies then? He had many enemies but none who were organised as this must be organised. In any case, this didn't seem to be hostile. Weird—intriguing—unfathomable certainly, but not malign. Even the two thugs lurking like beacons by the trees, he reflected, were somehow wrong.

He suddenly walked on across the lake and noticed with a grin the 'beacons' flash off in opposite directions to circle it and so presumably avoid the conspicuousness of crossing the ice.

He reached the road at the point where Wellington Barracks

9

had once stood. A taxi was moving towards him. Suddenly its light came on. It stopped next to him. He had not hailed it. Thorne looked at the driver. The driver looked back warily, his right hand was out of sight, the rest of him bulked big and hard in the cab.

'Who sent you?' Thorne said, and even as he spoke he saw out of the tail of his eye the handle of the rear door move. Without an instant's pause he grabbed it, jerked it open and as the surprised inmate, crouching behind it, came out head first, Thorne got his hand-made, nuggety chukka boot into his face, grabbed the driver's hair and slammed his face down on the edge of the window. He turned, ducking, as one of the followers raced in with a raised cosh. He dodged and then struck a swift karate blow into the face of the second follower, and in the same movement flung himself forward to smash his heel hard into the groin of the cosh man. He turned very quickly, opened the driver's door and pulled him out. The man's nose was broken and he didn't want to know very much about it, so Thorne jerked him on to the frozen grass, slipped in behind the wheel, put the cab in gear and then looked at them for a second.

'Good luck with your girl friend,' he said to the one nursing his balls, and let in the clutch. Driving sedately round the Park in his sable coat with his long hair, at the wheel of a cab with its light on, he was hailed by a smart woman who, when he didn't stop, shrieked high-pitched obscenities at him which made him laugh. As he drove on he tried to fit the attack into the pattern of events. But it didn't seem to fit. He felt sorry for the thugs—they were pretty soft—but he tried to comfort himself with the thought that you can't take chances when the odds are four to one. He left the taxi on the other side of the Park and went home.

His open-plan flat was high over London on the top of one of its tallest buildings, and most of the walls were glass right down to the floor. He liked the feeling it gave of living in air high over the moil of the town. The furniture he had collected from time to time because he liked the individual pieces. The bed was hard enough for a girl to come up to meet you as a proper girl likes to do, and it had a footboard for proper purchase. It also had four posts and a canopy, because he liked that too. There

10

were a great many books, a carefully designed kitchen and an open fire in the centre of the room. Upon this he burned peat, which gave its inimitable outdoor smell to the airy, sky-bounded room.

When he got there he took off his coat and sat down. He gazed into the fire, thinking, waiting. He knew that the telephone would ring. The sky went from violet to cobalt blue, the stars came out. Below was the roar and twinkle of bright London. Up here alone he sat and waited for the telephone to ring and the voice to speak which sounded like his voice. He sat for a long time quietly, and sure enough it rang.

'Hullo,' he said, 'Thorne speaking.'

'Same here,' said his own voice.

This was different. It had told him something instead of only asking questions. He sat very still in the darkness. And then he said carefully, 'Yes, it's my voice. I've sussed that, but who are you?'

'You—partially.'

'What's that mean?'

'You're being sussed out.'

'I know. What for?'

There was a fractional pause. Then the voice, so like his own, said flatly, 'Isoworg'.

It was like a shot of adrenaline. He was instantly alert, mind racing. He waited, saying nothing.

'How much do you know about it?' asked the voice.

'Nothing,' Thorne said.

'You know enough to deny it.' There was a chuckle. 'How much do you really know?'

Truthfully he said, 'All I know is that it stands for The International Society for World Government.'

'Right. It has many departments. It wants you to join the Intelligence Department.'

'So that's why all the—'

'... flat searching bit and—'

'... the questions—'

'... yes.'

He had never had a conversation like this before in his life. It rippled back and forth like thinking to oneself, talking to

11

oneself, and now he was saying ...

'Yeah, but how about—?'

'... the voice—'

'... mmm—'

'... I'll come to that in a moment. First I'd better fill you in—'

'... on what the Intelligence—'

'... Department does.'

'Yes.'

'Well, its purpose is to glean top-secret information from all countries and *publish it to the world.*'

'Why?'

'... because secrecy breeds suspicion, suspicion fear—'

'... fear tension and tense people press tits. Christ, what an idea,' he exploded and added as an afterthought : 'I hate governments.'

'Yes. Of course, it's not only military information, it's political, scientific, trade secrets—everything that inhibits—'

'... World wide free intercourse and development.'

'Yes.'

Thorne drew a deep and excited breath. 'Gordon bleedin' Bennett,' he said.

'Now I'll tell you how Isoworg is organised and how it works.'

Thorne was fascinated, hooked. Realising this he said coldly, 'Why should I believe all this?'

'Is this your voice?'

'Yes.'

'Were the hards real?'

'Yes.'

'Kind of elaborate hoax. What else could it be for?'

Thorne sat quietly by his peat fire.

'What indeed?' he said to himself, and his voice answered instantly, 'Can you think of any other possible explanation?'

For three weeks he had been unable to think of any explanation at all; and now this. For a long time he sat thinking, and at last he said slowly, 'How much do you know about me?'

Almost before the words were out of his mouth the voice began to tell him, and it went on telling him for a very long time. It knew him all right.

12

'Christ,' said Thorne at last, 'you've done your homework. Why?'

'I'll explain. World Government, like space travel, is only conceivable in terms of the information-handling potentialities of a computer. What's more important is this. The world's going to get *more* crowded, *more* heavily armed, emergent nations *more* ambitious. No assembly of men could ever be sufficiently competent or sufficiently objective to handle such a problem and the penalty for failure is annihilation. A computerised administration could do it. Isoworg is building up the most powerful computer in the world. It will be able to handle all the information and problems which would occur in the context of a world government. It has memory banks which contain all the information to which you could refer if you knew where to look. Plus, of course, a great deal that it acquires from its own sources. That's the general picture. As I said, it has a political division—economic division—cultural division, etc. etc. But all Isoworg operators are linked to it, linked together, in the same way that you will be if you join.'

'How then?'

'Well, a certain portion of the total computer exists for each operator. Such a portion is coming into existence for you now. It works according to a new principle. Imagine a dish of acid. In one corner is an electrode connected to a wire. All the information about you (and I need very much more) gets coded into electrical impulses and fed through the wire into the electrode. This causes a growth to occur on the electrode in the acid—it looks like a fern. The more information that is fed in, the more the fern grows. Given your compliance, it will learn you totally—whims, weaknesses, experience, knowledge, the lot. It will grow and become what you are. It will be your alter ego. It already has more or less learned your voice. You like talking to it. You trust it.'

'Why—what for?'

'First of all it's linked to memory banks which are the common pool of Isoworg. This means it knows what's going on in the lives of all other agents simultaneously. Also, the extent of these memory banks is almost unlimited. You will, as I said, have instant recourse to most of the world's available knowledge.'

13

'What's the square root of 659,859,784?'
'25678.'
'What's the telephone number in New York of Mary Kopek of 1129 East 59th Street?'
'Tuxedo 2096.'
'How do you know?'
'I know the New York telephone directory by heart.'
'You said first—what's second?'

'Second, the things that I choose to tell you will be the things that you yourself would have chosen if you had had my resources, and don't forget any crumby old computer can examine ten million answers to a problem in a second—this one is much better. When you are under stress or exhausted, I—your alter ego—will still react as coolly, as tirelessly as you would, sitting there in your own room by your peat fire, with a potential like mine at your elbow. Of course, it may turn you into a souped-up operator or it may destroy you.'

'Of course,' said Thorne chattily. After a pause he added, 'Who runs all this? Who are the people behind it?'

'Although there are, obviously, the dozen or so men and women of different nationalities who started it, nobody exactly *runs* it. As I told you each operator has an alter ego. All operators are linked by radio to their own and thus to all other alter egos and the memory banks. The alter egos know what everyone else is thinking and doing all the time, and therefore feed back to the operators, when they come through by radio, information and opinion derived from this awareness. The directorate, as it were, is the sum of the members who have been wised up by the vast amount of information in the banks.'

'Does it work?'
'I don't know yet—we're only just beginning.'
'How many members are there?'
'Thirty all together.'
'Who are they?'
'That's the only thing I don't tell you. All other questions will be answered fully and truthfully. You will never be misled or duped.'

'But you said the whole idea was to tell everybody everything.'
'Yes, except the identity of Isoworg members. If that were

14

known they would be discredited or killed. Think of people like M. Spaak and the other architects of the Common Market. They wouldn't have got anywhere if people had been able to accuse them of being members of some screwball, do-good outfit like Isoworg would sound. And another thing, there are two points of view to remember: One—An Isoworg spy makes all other spies meaningless. Therefore all ordinary spies will kill you instantly. Two—The Isoworg ideal makes national leaders meaningless. Therefore governments will praise Isoworg in public and in secret destroy you or it.'

Thorne sat and thought about all this. 'Who do I meet? Who's my No. 1.?'

'You meet no one—I tell you what to do.'

'But you're me—nearly.'

'Yes. But, as I explained, I'm also perpetually aware of everything that's going on in all Isoworg's activities. I'm also just as aware of the "mental" activities of the other alter egos as I am of my own. And I will react to all this exactly as you would if you had the same awareness.'

'So you mean you—I—we—um—assess all this and decide what to do?'

'Yes.'

Thorne chewed this over. 'Being permanently aware of what's going on in the minds of the others is getting very close to what I'd be like if I was in telepathic communication with a bunch of colleagues.'

'Yes, very like that.'

Restlessly, more or less at random, Thorne said, 'The voice—how did you manage that?'

'Electronically it's not hard to analyse speech patterns and reproduce them. The technique was worked out in connection with teaching deaf children to speak. They learned to make noises which produced the same pattern on a screen as teacher's did. At first it was staccato—remember? Even now it's imperfect. As I get to know you better it will improve—it will become your voice—your idiom—intonation.' It ended lamely. There was silence.

Finally Thorne said, 'What were those poor sods in the Park all about?'

'To see if you'd got soft.'

'I was sorry for them, I needn't have been so rough.'

'They were paid,' said the voice flatly, expressionlessly.

Would he have said that? he wondered. He thought it over. Then his eyes went grim. He'd have thought it, he realised, but not said it. He was silent again. The fire needed making up. He put down the telephone and did it. He began asking questions. Some were trivial, some profound. He went back to the beginning and demanded a complete explanation of Isoworg. The conversation went on nearly all night. The icy dawn was lighting up the eastern windows when he said, 'If I accept this, what'll be the first move?'

'I've got to get to know you completely before making any decision about you, so you'll ring 007-0072, say "This is Thorne", and you'll find out.'

Then the line went dead.

Chapter Two

Thorne looked at the time. It was nearly eight o'clock. He was cramped and tired. He undressed and went to bed. When he woke the whole episode seemed unreal. His flat was full of cold, winter sunlight. He walked across naked to the shower. He was crazy about showers, and this one was very special. It was placed in the corner of the apartment, a corner of glass, and it stood over a glass bath. He turned the water on thoughtfully and stepped under it. The rose was two feet across and the hot water pelted down in torrents, while all around him was the icy, airy day and, vertically down past his soapy foot, London. His mind was seething with ideas. Souped up or nuts. A hundred million answers per second—memory banks—permanently aware of what's going on everywhere—kill you on sight. Did he believe it or not? If it wasn't what it said it was, then what was it? That was the crunch. What else? How could anybody have done it, if it hadn't been done in the way that the voice had explained. He turned the taps on hotter and harder and the outlandish possibilities grew and suffused and elated him high over icy London, and then suddenly, all around him in his hot shower, it snowed. The flakes stuck to the glass—he was momentarily in a snowy cocoon. It was exciting—beautiful—he felt immensely happy and eager. And then he darted out of the shower, grabbed a huge saffron towel and, bundled like a Buddhist priest, he dialled 007-0072.

A girl's voice said, 'Hullo.'

'This is Thorne.'

'So you're on.'

'Maybe.'

'Come to Acme Studios, Carter Hill, N.W.3.' She rang off.

17

Thorne dressed quickly and took a cab there.

Acme Studio had once been a small church. Now the ceiling was obscured by gantries, hung with lamps. The walls were padded and the padding was held in place by chicken wire. The floor was cluttered with lamps and equipment. He looked at the girl. She looked back, cool and sexy. Her nylon overall was belted tight round a small waist and slim hips. Under it there was nothing but her.

On one side of her was a television camera, on the other a control panel and behind her an operating table, a divan and a chair. There was an x-ray machine and the paraphernalia of a doctor's consulting room. The ceiling was high, the walls padded, the atmosphere relaxed.

'Who are you?' he asked.

She said, 'I'm a doctor. This studio specialises in making training films for hospitals. I have worked here. I suppose that's why I got this job.' She seemed uncertain, fingering a file of instructions.

'What sort of doctor are you?'

'I specialised in psychiatry.'

He waited.

'There's no paper work,' she went on, 'no records. Everything goes straight through the camera or the mike to Isoworg—to It.'

He still said nothing.

'Why did you come?'

He shrugged. 'Spying and telling turns everything upside down. I like that.'

She nodded.

'What do I do?'

'Strip.'

He did so. She put him in front of a camera, lit him, looked at her list of instructions and said, 'Okay, we're running. This is Thorne. Seems daft,' she muttered. She took every measurement that it is possible to imagine and gave him the most thorough medical examination he had ever had. He was x-rayed and specimens of blood, urine, sputum, sperm, mucus, stool, etc. were taken, put in a special box and sent by messenger for analysis.

18

She consulted her instructions.

'Right,' she said. 'Next—talents and aptitudes, then background. What are you good at?'

He told her.

'Also,' she said, 'you're a good skater.'

'Yes.'

'Long distance stuff. How long?'

'The Canadian Marathon.'

'Tell me about it.'

He did so, describing its length and hazards.

'How fit are you now?'

'Very.'

'Could you win it tomorrow?'

He grinned. 'Depends who's in it.'

'Yes.'

'Why so interested?'

'It says so here.' She tapped her instructions.

They talked on. Time passed. The telex started its staccato chatter and she explained that it was feed-back from Isoworg.

'Anything which it has learned or deduced that might be relevant to further questioning, it tells me,' she explained. 'And now it wants to know your full name.'

'Why?'

'Why not?'

'Thorne,' he said.

'Is that all?'

'Yes.'

'Why?'

'I don't know, it just is.'

'What did your parents call you?'

'I don't remember them.'

'Well, what were you called when you were little?'

'I don't remember being little.'

'What d'you mean?'

'I remember nothing before I was ten.'

'Good God—why?'

'I wish I knew.'

'Where were you at ten?'

'In South Africa.'

'What's your first memory?'

'The police station—I'd been picked up starving and taken there.'

The telex chattered. She read it and looked at him speculatively.

'What's it say?' he asked.

'Tell you later. After the police station, what?'

'Orphanage, and then pretty soon I was sent to England.'

'Why?'

'I wasn't told much, but I think somebody in England thought that I was their long-lost son. Then I think the somebody died, so when I arrived I got bunged into an orphanage again.'

'Then what?'

'School—scholarship—London University.'

'But that's all you remember of the early part?'

'Yes.'

She crumpled up the telex sheet saying, 'Okay, we'll come back for details later. What are you now?'

'Well, I'll tell you what I'm not, I'm not a spy, an agent, anything like that.'

She looked at her instructions again.

'Isoworg people apparently never are,' she said. 'What are you then? You look rich.'

'I have been—getting short again now.'

'How did you get it?'

He told her about smuggling diamonds out of East Africa and people out of the Union. And he added, 'And then there was the Congo.'

'Which side?'

'My side. There are people who would pay a lot of money to get people out. Ditto Berlin. It started in Hungary when I was sixteen. I packed a rifle in a violin case and had a go. God, it was fun.'

'Fun and idealism, violence, adventure.' She looked at him wistfully.

He shrugged.

There was a pause. She pointed at the screwed-up telex message.

'Says you've got some Negro in you.'

He sat still looking at her.

20

After a while she said, 'Didn't you know?'

'No.'

She said, 'Negro temperament is prone to excess—peaks and troughs—joy and despair—they're heroic and panicky—giggle when they're terrified.'

'Just like me.' He grinned, and then after a long while he said, 'Very interesting. Okay, what do you want now?'

She looked at her notes. 'I want you to tell me all about you and your life, in detail. It'll take a hell of a long time. But first I want a general picture to fit the details into.'

Thorne sat and looked at the girl. He ran his mind back over his life and the events of the last three weeks. He would be known and understood. By whom? By himself. The situation was so strange, so exciting he knew he could not possibly ignore it. He began to talk. The pattern was rich and varied but there was a pattern. Ruthless, restless, resourceful, a violator of all men's principles except his own. It was there the pattern lay; elusive, quixotic but there—a man capable of reckless altruism, of barefaced robbery, of brutality, of murder; a fun lover, womaniser, and finally a man subject to fits of depression and introspection. The introspection, she discovered, was the key to a side of him that, after all this, surprised her most. In his varied life he had learned about most of the systems with which people have tried to make sense of life, had picked what he needed and read and thought about it. It was because of this, she found, that his fits of depression, when they came, could be so crippling. It was, in fact, this propensity for introspection and speculation that was his Achilles heel.

Finally he said, 'How do I operate? What do I do?'

'You ask.'

'Where—how?'

'There.' She pointed to an object like a cigarette case. 'It's a mini two-way radio. You can talk to it whenever you like. You can sit and talk to it for the rest of your life, I should think.'

He thought about this for a moment, and then she said, 'What was the second question?'

'What's in it for me?'

'Two things,' she said, looking at her instructions. 'First, your alter ego will boost you into being a new type of person or

21

else drive you bonkers.'

'Yes, so it said. What else?' he asked.

'Money.'

'How much?'

'As much as you need.'

'What's that mean?'

'How much d'you want?'

'Depends how tough the going gets, say £50,000 a year—cash.'

'Your alter ego will know your worth,' she said.

'That means me—I mean that means *I'm* deciding my own salary!'

'In a way—yes.'

He smiled and said, 'I'm a pretty good judge of that.'

She nodded and said, 'It's lunch time. Your alter ego ordered it. I'll go and get it.'

He sat in a dressing-gown, looking at the cameras. He imagined somewhere a fern. A fern in a solution of acid hooked to the components of a computer. He imagined it was now growing, in its eerie way; fronds for his passions, fronds for his pains, fronds for his aspirations, his loves, his fears, his appetites so that they would all be understood and played into future conversations, which would be couched in his own voice whether he spoke from here or Timbuctoo. He shuddered. The girl came back and he looked at the tray. He realised that he might have ordered the meal himself. After lunch he said, 'Why couldn't you have been a tape, why couldn't the whole thing have been automated?'

'Why d'you think?' And she came and stood beside him, looking at his brown face with the rather beaky nose. She ran her fingers through his thick hair. She felt the hard power of his body—his passionate resoluteness of mind—she pressed closer to him so that he put his hands inside her overall and their bodies seemed to be like burning satin slipping and flowing together in their pleased joy.

While they were making love on the divan she said, 'Tell me your fantasies.' The muscles in Thorne's stomach jerked as he laughed. 'They chose you well.' And so, as they went on making love slowly, he talked about women, about the kind of woman he wanted and the kind of desires and kinks that he had. Finally

22

they came together and he let his arms flop beside his body.

'What an exam!' he said. 'I feel like a marionette with the strings out.'

'Yes, what an exam,' she said wistfully.

And the next day the exam went on. Aptitude tests, language tests, conversations which, with the help of the chattering telex, she guided into special channels so as to stress and probe him to the maximum. Day after day it continued, and off and on as they talked they made love, talking as men and women do, until one night at about 11.30 the telex chattered for the last time. She read it.

'That's it,' she said. 'It says that'll do.'

They stood suddenly at random.

'Just an exam,' she said.

He put out a hand and stroked her hair. 'Did I pass?'

She glanced at him, catching the look in his eye. Was it longing, was it reserve? And then it was gone. It was, she decided, just a wry look he was giving her. But she kissed him quickly on the mouth.

'Yes, you passed,' she said. 'Oh yes, my love, you passed. Now you'd better go and get your coat from the passage.'

'Why?'

'Telex says you're to leave now.'

He did so. When he came back she was gone. On the table was a note with the radio and some money: *Isoworg says, Be at Lunar Mews, S.W.3., 12.30 a.m. Watch, do nothing, and report. Goodbye, my love.*

Thoughtfully he screwed up the note and threw it away. For a moment he felt surprised that Isoworg had made up its mind so speedily. Then he realised that, given so much information and the ability to handle it at the rate of a hundred million items a second, the speed wasn't surprising.

Then he felt that he had given—through the girl and into the hands of his alter ego—so much of himself that he would never be able to deceive himself again. The idea was at once exciting and terrifying. He felt on test to himself. And now too the other tiny Negro self was there to make him feel different.

He left the studio and walked into Regent's Park. The trees were black and complicated against the glow of London's sky.

The air was so intensely cold it smelled funny in his nose. He walked off across the bone-hard ground of the Park. He felt positive and precise. The radio bleeped.

'Where are you?'

'Regent's Park.'

It asked him a number of questions and he had several for it. He had never had a conversation like this before in his life. At the end of anything he said the response came back instantly without any pause at all, as though it had known what he was going to say. Communication was faultless. He never needed to explain himself—to hedge a question with provisos or disclaimers. It caused him to be so confident in being understood that he became more lucid and succinct. He realised that here, among a great many other baffling and inspiring experiences, lay also the gateway to self-knowledge. He sighed and smiled.

'How d'you feel?' it asked him.

'As though every synapse and neurone in my system had had a fricative and unguent grooming.'

'Jesus,' it said and clicked off.

He grinned and walked on. It came to his mind that this was the one competition of a person's life; the competition with himself. And its beginning was graced with an added inspiration derived from the poignancy of having a girl enter his life and then go out of it for ever.

Chapter Three

On the opposite side of the road from Lunar Mews was another mews with an arch at its entrance and a telephone box. Thorne waited nearby out of sight at 12.15. Nothing happened. The cold was still and intense.

After some time a taxi arrived. A man got out. He was big—about six foot six. Even in the few steps he took getting out of the cab, moving about while fumbling for money, Thorne noticed something odd about his gait. Pigeon-toed? Knock-kneed? High-heeled boots? There was something.

'Which is No. 10?' His American accent was clear in the cold, still night.

The driver craned to look and point. The American started in the direction indicated.

'There,' said the cabby, 'bloke comin' out now—see.' A figure lurched up the basement steps of No. 10 and reeled across in the direction of the 'phone box.

'Dah! Pissed as a newt.'

'Shaddup, buster,' said the American because he, like Thorne, had seen a wet patch glistening in the man's back and something sticking out of it. The man made it to the 'phone box and dialled. The taxi drove off.

Thorne's radio bleeped, and he shifted the ear piece and listened.

'There's an Isoworg agent in the 'phone box at Lunar Mews 'phoning his alter ego—listen,' the voice said in his ear. His mind racing to keep up with events, Thorne concentrated on a new voice, a telephone voice—evidently that of the man he could see in the 'phone box.

The taxi had gone. The American was heading for the man in

the box whose voice was saying, 'Pierre C-C-Canton—d-d-dying —my note.'

Thorne watched him fumble for it and fumble and fumble. The American got to him and propped him up. Pierre slumped. The American took the paper, read it very carefully, put it in his pocket and picked up the 'phone.

'Hullo,' Thorne heard him say.

'Hullo,' replied the voice of Pierre Canton's alter ego.

'Who are you?'

'On the c-c-contrary, old boy, who are you?' said Pierre's voice.

'Don't give me that goddam "old boy" crap, there's a stiff here.'

'Yes, I know.'

'I'm his friend. What was he trying to tell you?'

'Have you got his note?'

'What note?'

'I say, are you one of those s-secret agent chaps?' the now dead humour of Pierre chided him.

The American laughed—the kind of laugh you use to show you've understood some crumby British joke.

'Look, put me down, will you, this guy really is dead—stabbed in the back.'

'So now you tell me what's on that p-piece of p-paper.'

'What piece of paper?'

'You b-b-bum.'

'Klwatsack,' muttered the American furiously and added, 'Look, this guy's my buddy. He doesn't have any bit of paper.'

'Thanks,' said Pierre's voice, and the line went dead.

Thorne's alter ego said, 'Describe him.'

'Six foot, tough and solid as a sandbag. He's got a look on his face as though he was tired of being the only guy in step with all the other shits. Walks funny, pigeon toes? Knock knees? High-heeled boots? I dunno, something like that.'

And then his voice replied instantly, 'Klwatsack is the Friesian form of rotsack, Dutch swear word—thus maybe an American of Friesian parentage. I've run that, plus your description, through the C.I.A. files and it fits Jan Towers. Listen carefully. Big like you say, sixteen stone, Judo black belt, pistol shot,

26

athlete, skater, university graduate, paranoid. He was a C.I.A. agent, very high reputation. Ruthless. Then he got the boot. Something unsavoury. Personality like this might try to reinstate himself by some chancy deal which, if it came off, would vindicate him in the C.I.A. Or he might turn resentful against Uncle Sam and simply sell out. Stay and watch.' The radio clicked off.

'Jesus Christ,' muttered Thorne, his mind reeling at the potential to which he was hooked. He watched Towers search Pierre, saw him find the little radio which was smashed, saw him find gun and money and put them back in the pockets. Then Towers stepped out of the 'phone box. He hesitated a moment, looking down consideringly at the basement from which Pierre had emerged. Then he turned and walked away to the left. A moment later Thorne heard him shout for a taxi.

From somewhere on Thorne's right a scooter started, then it accelerated past him. It was ridden by a girl. She looked pretty in her deerstalker crash hat. Thorne reported this and his alter ego said, 'Wait and report'.

The body in the 'phone box still hung propped on the 'phone-book shelf. A few cars came and went. The moon shone out of the freezing sky. Thorne did nothing. About half-an-hour later the girl in the deerstalker crash hat came back. She put the scooter on its rest and went down the steps into the basement of No. 10.

Thorne passed this on and his own voice told him, 'Snoop, don't get involved'.

It took Thorne some moments to find his way round into the garden and to identify the basement window. He listened. The girl was talking to someone. There were thick curtains, it was difficult to hear, the mike wouldn't pick up the voices so he couldn't feed them directly to Isoworg. He deduced there had been a fight, some one had been killed, another wounded. The wounded man had a Russian accent—the girl, he gathered, was splinting his leg with a broom handle. She had followed Towers —followed him to the Chinese Legation. Now she was being told to get back and watch. The girl scarcely spoke. When she did her voice had a curious blurting manner, and a slight foreign accent, which he didn't recognise.

27

'Can't,' she said, 'don't know how to, Dimitri. This kind of thing isn't my—'

'Andrei's dead—I can't—there's nobody else. So you've got to, this is the biggest—'

'Always is.'

Dimitri's voice was full of the pain from his smashed leg. 'Listen, will you—a Dutch scientist has made a breakthrough.'

'Breakthrough,' she scoffed, 'reached a *new high,* always something.'

Furiously he said, 'Sustained power from atomic fusion. I've spoken about that to you.'

'Yes.'

'Well, he's done it.'

'A Dutchman?'

'Yes, a lab. job only. The Dutch haven't the big equipment to exploit it.'

'But the Russians, the Americans, the Chinese have,' she blurted scathingly.

'Yes, maybe the British and the French. So get back there and do like I told you.'

'But, Dimitri, I can't—I mean how do I?'

'That's your business, I've shown you how to use the gadgets.' He swore in Russian and said, 'You're hurting like hell.'

There was silence. Then Thorne heard her moving about, putting things straight. After a time he realised that she had left without a word. He dashed away, but long before he regained the road he heard a scooter start and drive off.

He reported on his radio.

'Was she English?'

'No.'

'Russian?'

'No.'

'What?'

'Dunno or I'd have said. Funny voice.' He described it. Talking to his alter ego was in all respects unlike talking to another person. One of these differences was the fact that the voice answered him the instant his own voice stopped, in the manner of a person who knows what you're going to say before you've

28

said it. This time it didn't. There was a fractional pause. Thorne noted it.

It now went on, 'I know the Chinese Legation. They'll probably have put him in a back room with a barred window. From the street plans it's opposite No. 9 Heslop Terrace—not certain about elevations etc. No. 9 is flats. You must be able to get a view across to the back of the legation from the top flat. It's occupied by Sarah Burns—nothing known. Go there and snoop. You can't very well spring him, since he appears to have gone there voluntarily, but see if there's any possible way of getting him out. We've got to have Pierre's note.' It clicked off.

It took Thorne a long time to get a taxi, and when he reached Heslop Terrace he made a careful recce of the area before going to No. 9. Sure enough, Sarah Burns occupied the top flat. It said so on the bell pushes. He wondered what to do about her. He found the street door open and suspiciously he went up the stairs. He pushed a piece of plastic against the tongue of the yale lock and quickly walked in. The boards creaked. The door into the back room was ajar and light was coming from it. He drew his automatic, kicked the door open and was ready with a snapshot for the fire he expected it to draw. Nothing happened. A girl was sitting looking at him. Next to her on the divan was the deerstalker crash hat.

Before his brain could tell his hand that she was unarmed, his finger had started to squeeze the trigger. But even as it did so he shifted the aim. The silenced gun plopped. The bullet thudded into the upholstery of the sofa, next to the girl. She flinched and they stared at each other. She had long auburn hair and grey intelligent eyes. She made an impression of intense femininity. Her thighs seemed to slink down from her hips and her legs were slim and compelling. Her face, which was cool and a shade beaky—or was it haughty?—looked at him with dislike and fear. And it was this aspect that, conflicting with the femininity, gave her such a remarkable personality. His glance at what had been done to the room made him say, 'You're not Sarah Burns. Who are you? Where is she?'

Her face remained graven and devoid of expression as she got up. Her hands shook. He reached forward and snatched her handbag away from her and searched it. It had no gun so he then searched her. There was nothing. She still did not speak. He realised she just wanted to get out.

He remembered her remonstrances to Dimitri—remembered the alter ego's symptom of duplicity about her. He looked round the room thinking. She had sellotaped an eiderdown across the window. He wondered what to do about her. It flashed into his mind that she might be an Isoworg agent. Would this account for the alter ego's hesitation? An agent whose loyalties were suspected perhaps?

'Can I go please?' she said in her odd blurting manner.

He didn't want her here, watching what he did, listening while he talked on the radio.

She stooped to pick up her crash hat. Her legs were breathtaking. As she straightened, she caught his eye. He grinned.

'The higher they go, the better they get,' he said.

'Drop dead.' She walked towards the door. He remembered Dimitri had said there was nobody else available. Presumably, therefore, she couldn't go and get any help. He noticed that her hands were still shaking. Instinct and uncertainty and then, too, something else, made him let her go. He shut the door behind her wondering if he'd boobed. Well, he'd done what he'd done. He put the problem out of his mind.

He turned out the light and made one of the holes in the eiderdown bigger, put his miniscope to it and looked across. The snow clouds had come, hiding the stars. The night was very dark. At first he could see nothing. Slowly he identified the window. He was thinking about the girl's legs. He saw that the light in Towers' room was on and that Towers was walking up and down, puffing a cigarette. He watched him for some time, noticing that the window was open at the top. He deduced that the Chinese had the central heating on too high. In the miniscope he could see cigarette smoke coming out. He was just putting the miniscope down when a glint caught his attention. A glint in the curtain. He focused on it and recognised it at once, a bug, almost certainly, he felt, fired from this room. But the girl hadn't been carrying any recorder. He put the flap down, turned on the light and searched the room. He found the recorder on the windowsill behind the sellotaped eiderdown and the gun for it under the settee.

He picked up the recorder, examined it and then spooled it

30

back. The fact that she had just gone off like that leaving the recorder behind confirmed his feeling that she was genuinely afraid and out of her depth and that he had been right to let her go. Then he remembered with a sudden grin of pleasure and excitement the potential to which his radio connected him, and like a boy with a toy he called up his alter ego and played the tape.

At first there were a number of clickings with snatches of conversation. Apparently Towers had refused to talk to anybody but the boss, Mr. Wang. This had caused trouble but eventually Mr. Wang had arrived. The following facts emerged.

The Chinese, having learned of Towers' dismissal from the C.I.A. had already paid him well to get him as far as the room this evening with what information he had gleaned from Pierre Canton. The reason why he had insisted on talking to nobody but Wang was to say flatly and cryptically that his price had just doubled. This, he told Wang, was because he had memorised accurately Pierre's coded message.

'So we buy it or beat it or drug it from you?' Wang said kindly.

'You buy it for ten grand, and then I work for you too.'

'But—'

'Shaddup and listen. I told it to a friend. If I don't give him a couple of grand in person by breakfast time he tells Uncle Sam—he's that kind of a friend.'

They haggled and finally agreed on a method where they couldn't double-cross each other, and he told them the coded message.

SS22fbgbndoskuftnuc

'Now what happens?' said Towers' voice.

Wang said, 'All we know is that there has been a breakthrough by a Dutch scientist, and that the Russians plan to kidnap him. You will kidnap him instead, Mr. Towers. We will help you.'

'When, where, how?' asked Towers.

They didn't know. They had heard 'on the ice'—it was very vague. They must crack the code.

'On the ice!' Towers said incredulously. 'What ice?'

'In Holland,' said Wang doubtfully.

'Holland and ice suit me all right.'

31

'Why's that, Mr. Towers?' asked Wang politely.

'For Chrissake, my father only did the bloody Elfstedentocht.'

'What is that?'

'The Elf—' He stopped abruptly and went on in a leisurely, confident manner. 'Say—er—how much money did we settle for?'

'10,000 dollars.'

'Yeah, well, it's just doubled again.'

'Why?'

'Because I've just cracked the first part of the code. Now all we've got to do is find the name of the scientist and that won't be hard when I tell you that he'll be—' and the tape ran out.

Without the slightest pause, just as if it had known what the tape would say, his voice said, 'Pierre's alter ego says the code is a phoney—it certainly isn't Pierre's. Thinks Towers had to make up something on the spur of the moment. That means it'd be a kind of free association on Towers' part. So we ran a few million permutations of those letters, and the one that fits Towers' personality best occurs when you simply reverse the letters in groups.'

'A few millions!' Thorne expostulated.

'Yes, said his own voice irritably. 'Listen. The FB/GBN groups turn into BF/NBG, which is fairly obvious, so then you reverse the DOSKUF groups and you get SOD FUK. Typical Towers, and he obviously just made it up; so it can't ever be cracked because it doesn't mean anything. The last group is TNUC.'

'Bugger,' Thorne said.

'In the meantime,' his own voice went on, 'there's the first group.'

'Yes?'

'That's easy. Reverse it like the others and you have 22SS— run that through the permutator and the only group that Pierre's alter ego picked up was 11TT half of 22 and the next letter in the alphabet to S. This means, to Pierre, the Eleven Town Trip— the Elfstedentocht.'

'The thing Towers said his father had done!'

'Yes.'

'What is it?'

'A skating race round the Eleven Towns of Friesland from

32

Leeuwarden back to Leeuwarden—only happens in very hard winters—due to happen now.'

Thorne was grinning with pleasure. 'You're quick.'

'I'm you. Accept the potential.'

'Hell and damn, why did the bloody tape have to run out?'

'Doesn't matter. We simply ran through all possible Dutch Physicists having to do with controlled fusion as Dimitri mentioned. The one that fits is Hank van Hockeren. He's working on the fusion problem in Phillips lab, Leeuwarden, capital of Friesland. He won the Eleven Town Trip last time and the time before. He's hell bent to win a third time.'

'There's something screwy about all this. Fusion research isn't secret, there's been a British team working in Russia on a machine called the Tokamak. I read about it.'

'I know.'

'Well then?'

'Makes it all the more interesting, doesn't it?'

'Yes, I suppose it does,' Thorne said, feeling let down. Then he said, 'I suppose Towers will tell the Chinese that it's something to do with the Eleven Town Trip to prove his bona fides.'

'Yes.'

'Dimitri knew about Hockeren, I wonder if the Chinese do?'

'I think they do, if Towers goes to Leeuwarden it won't take him half a minute to realise Hockeren's skating—everybody's talking about him.'

'I'd better be off.'

'Where to?'

'Leeuwarden, van Hockeren, see what's cooking.'

'I'll book the 6.30 flight to Schiphol and fix a private plane from there to Groningen and a taxi to 14, Tyhofslaan in Leeuwarden, which is where Hockeren lives. Don't forget your passport. The taxi driver will give you Dutch money.'

'God, I'm efficient,' said Thorne and clicked off quickly.

Chapter Four

Whenever the conditions look as though the Eleven Town Trip is going to be possible, Holland goes mad. Thousands start to converge upon Leeuwarden. The atmosphere is electric and everyone is glued to the weather reports since a thaw could ruin everything almost up to the last moment. The chief contestants in the race become for a moment national heroes, household words. Radio and T.V. talk about nothing else. Into this Thorne flew to meet the Dutch scientist, Hank van Hockeren, and then to do what? He didn't know. What sort of a man was van Hockeren? What sort of a plan could he make to prevent Hank being kidnapped?

No. 14 Tyhofslaan had eaves nearly to the ground in the Dutch manner and a huge window facing the road, so that the front looked like a goldfish bowl which somebody had filled with pot plants.

Thorne rang the bell and a girl in spectacles with buck teeth answered it.

'Mijnheer van Hockeren?' he enquired.

'Ja zeker komt U binnen Mijnheer.'

The girl shivered and gestured. He went in. The house was jumping. He saw a plump woman race up the stairs, all stocking tops, fat thighs and unattractive knickers. At the top he heard laughter and squeals as she evidently bumped into a youth who was coming down just as fast, skinny, grinning, carrying a white anorak, a string vest and, of all things, shammy leather pants.

Thorne was shown into the living room where he shook hands with Hank. The room was over-furnished and over-polished. It had a carpet on the table, ducks in echelon on the wall, framed reproductions of Van Gogh; the central heating was stifling.

34

Van Hockeren was small, fair with blue-grey, unworldly eyes. Thorne looked him over carefully. He had a face like a weasel and Thorne could imagine him as a spotty student swotting to cram himself with his special subject at the expense of any interest in life or people. He realised that the benign expression which Hank tried so hard to fix upon his stoat-shaped face was there as a shield against the possibility of making any close, and therefore baffling, contact with the real world. He was wearing trousers and singlet and Thorne could see that his ugly, wiry body with bow legs and sloping shoulders was in excellent condition.

'You're in training,' Thorne said.

'Yes.' He looked surprised for a second and then said, 'Yes, the Elfstedentocht. How do you say that, the Eleven Town Trip, I think.'

'You won it last time?'

'The last twice. I want to win it three times.'

'Why?'

Hank said, 'First of all who are you?'

Thorne walked to the window. He looked across the road at the flat Dutch fields, white and frozen. How do you persuade a man like this to accept Isoworg and leave Holland now, this instant? Crazy. His mind was a blank. Nothing came into it at all except suddenly the stocking tops and brown knickers. It irritated him, so after a time he turned and looking across the room with the plants trailing hideously from brass pots, he said, 'Knickers,' politely. Hank had been joined by his fat sister and skinny brother. They stood on the other side of the table and smiled agreeably.

Thorne had no idea in his mind at all, except the knickers of the fat sister, which he very much wanted to get out of it. Mercifully they were now covered by her skirt. Thinking unwittingly about her thighs, he said at random, 'I must speak to you alone—it has to do with your work.'

Hank said something politely in Dutch and the others left the room, shutting the door. He did not invite Thorne to sit down. He just waited.

After a time, when Thorne still couldn't think of anything useful to say, he opened the radio and said, 'I'm in Hank's house. What's he done?'

35

Hank watched him. Thorne turned the volume up and went closer to Hank.

His own voice replied, 'Sustained fusion chain. The problem is how to constrain plasma at very high temperatures—millions of degrees. Various attempts have been made. The Torus—The Magnetic Mirror—The Magnetic Well. Now the Torus is back in fashion. Indeed, the Tokamak is toroidal. Plasma at these temperatures vaporises anything it touches. Thus only a magnetic field of great complexity can constrain it. Up till now this field leaks away. Hank has found a way to prevent this leak. It has to do with muon meson injection. It's a lab job. Ask him about the big plant application.'

Thorne turned to Hank enquiringly. 'Well?'

Hank shrugged. 'There is no secret.'

'No, I know.'

'All over the world—isn't it?—the nations try to do this. There will be one nation which by chance has been working in the way I have worked. They will have the big plant—isn't it?—and it is very, very big indeed—it has to be very big, it takes years to build.'

'And they need you to supervise the application of your theory to the big plant?'

Hank tittered complacently. 'Yes—my workings are, how do you say?—better—much better with me—yes.'

'And what is the reward?'

'Power, simply. Power for industry, electrical power almost for nothing.'

Thorne wanted to get back to the alter ego and really get all this explained properly. In the meantime, however, he had to try to think of a way of talking Hank into doing what he wanted him to do, and he couldn't think of any possible way to begin. There was a pause.

'Who is that?' Hank pointed to the radio. 'Why are you here?'

'To prevent anybody from getting your formulae and you.'

'Instead the British want me?'

'Not Britain, Isoworg.'

'What's that?'

Thorne explained at some length. At the end Hank laughed like a rat in order to show he wasn't fool enough to believe. Thorne waited. The whole situation was like being at a polite tea-party. He wished the lady doctor was here so that they could exchange a glance and giggle. He hoped that silence would embarrass Hank, and so he stood still saying nothing. At last it did embarras him and Hank said, 'Then what can this clever computer of yours do?'

'Ask it.'

'What shall I ask it?'

'Anything.'

Hank looked round, then he grinned, 'Okay, who lives in the next house here?'

Thorne had left the radio on and it replied instantly, giving names, past jobs, salaries, wives' maiden names, children's names. It became boring.

'How does it know all this?'

'It knows the street plan—telephone directory—doctors' year book, newspaper files, etc. by heart, as one might say. It's assimilating knowledge all the time—growing.'

Hank stared at him. 'Eventually it will know everything.'

'Then get your finger out and help, otherwise you'll be kidnapped and squeezed.'

'Squeezed? What is?'

Thorne explained.

Hank walked up and down the room, in and out of the gear which was being prepared for his use. Sometimes he stopped and sprang adroitly sideways from one foot to the other, flicking his heels up. It was such a peculiar manoeuvre, he did it so easily, that Thorne realised he must have done it a hundred million times and that it was part of his training as a skater to get his muscles into condition. He watched Hank walk in and out of the untidiness, watched him stop and do his funny little skater's dance and then go on again, while all the time he wore a thoughtful face. He wore it self-consciously, like a child who has been told to think and is trying to convince everybody that that's what it's doing. Thorne felt pretty sure he wasn't thinking at all, and when Hank finally spoke, his words confirmed this because he said, 'For the moment my work belongs to my government,' which, thought Thorne, is exactly the point from which he'd started.

He wondered if Hank liked big, idealistic phrases, so he said

37

heavily, 'Universal knowledge—that is true science.' Hank didn't react much, so Thorne tried, 'If the others get you they'll beat the living shit out of you.' Hank grimaced, and Thorne said flatly, 'That's what'll happen.'

Hank swore in Dutch and walked about. Finally he said, 'Tomorrow morning at about 2 a.m. I skate. Today I must get ready—then I must sleep. Come and talk to me the day after tomorrow when I have made the race and slept again.'

Thorne realised he might just as well not have spoken. He began again. 'They'd have made a grab for you yesterday or today, except that right now you're so much in the public eye it'd have caused a rumpus. Tell me something. During the race, would there be a chance to kidnap you so's—well—so's it looked—I dunno—like something else, like an accident perhaps? Tell me about it.'

Hank drew a breath. Talking about the Eleven Town Trip was his favourite occupation. He said, 'We skate for perhaps nine hours through the eleven towns of Friesland—one hundred and twenty miles—two or three hours are in the dark. We cross two lakes, skate out on to the Zuider Zee—the Yssel Meer, In 1963 there were five hundred and seventy starters for the race, only fifty-seven finished. They had frost bite, went snow-blind, some who didn't finish nearly died. This year it's colder than it has ever been—there is no snow—it is perfect black ice the whole way. But ...'

'But what?'

'On good ice you can go fast, that makes the cold worse—then there's the blizzard coming.'

'What blizzard?'

'From Norway—the Arctic—a bad one. The meteorologists say it will hit Holland tomorrow mid-day.'

'So what?'

'So we will start earlier, skate for longer in the dark, finish before it gets here. Who knows?' He shrugged.

'Then it all fits,' Thorne said to himself quietly, and looked at Hank. Hank's security was threatened. The real world he wanted to keep at arm's length was coming closer. He looked nervous now and spiteful. His voice went up a little, and he began to gesticulate.

38

'Look. I am a very ordinary man. I have a job. It turns out to be important. I am not interested at all in that. I want to win this race for the third time because my father could have won it three times but for the Germans. Nobody has ever won it three times.'

'What do you mean?'

'The Elfstedentocht only happens when the canals all freeze—only twelve times since it began in 1909. So generally a man gets too old. But it happened in 1940, '41 and '42. My father won it twice, could have won the third time perhaps, except for *the Germans*. He was like me, you understand.'

Hank was staring at Thorne. His unworldly, stoatish face looked bitchy and unpleasant. 'He was like me,' he said again. 'They are like you. He was a good Dutchman so they beat him though he knew nothing, cared nothing except about ordinary living, you know. So I want to live ordinary. I will skate, you see.'

Thorne turned this over in his mind. He felt sure that things were planned to come to a head during the race. He wanted them to come to a head. Then he'd have a chance to get Towers and with him Pierre's message. Hank would get his nose rubbed in reality and *have* to make a decision about Isoworg and whether he would come and work for it.

If Thorne were to tell the police or Hank's Lab and they prevented Hank from skating, the whole situation would become diffuse again, with police protection and the necessity for Hank to make up his mind spread out over an unspecified period.

'I'll skate with you,' Thorne said.

'But you have no idea. I am not conceited but you could not—'

'Oh shut up and help me get kitted out.'

'Get what?'

'Skates for me, clothes, what I'll need.'

Hank was flushed with anger and he said contemptuously, 'You can't skate in new boots, nor new clothes, you don't under-stand. You'd be—how do you say?—made sore, you know.'

'When did you say it started?'

'About 2 a.m. tomorrow.'

'Where?'

'From the garage of Hobema—we run to the ice, just outside

Leeuwarden—but there are only perhaps ten men in the world . . .'

Thorne wanted to hit him, though he didn't know why. He said, 'Listen, Knickers, I'll start with you and finish with you. Now will you do something for me?'

'What?'

'Get your papers from the laboratory and put them somewhere else.'

Hank looked at him. 'No,' he said shrewdly, suspecting him.

Thorne could think of no way of compelling him to take this precaution. He tried. He tried for a long time. Hank was obdurate. Finally Thorne consoled himself with the thought that Hank himself was the key, the papers of small value without him, and at last he said, 'Tell me all about the race. What will I need? Show me the course.'

Two hours later, when he had been thoroughly briefed, Thorne left. The cold outside was fierce but a relief after Hank's stifling, horrible home. He told the alter ego to put his skates etc. on the next plane and he took the taxi back to Leeuwarden.

He found it bursting at its seams and in a ferment. Moving about the bars and T.V. lounges, he got caught up in the excitement. Nobody talked of anything else. People were flocking in from all parts. He settled down in the station hotel to wait for his kit to arrive. The lounge was crammed with people. The light lay in pools over the tables covered in the Dutch manner, with small carpets, grey with cigar ash. The noise was deafening.

Skating is a tradition in Holland. Throughout history her canals have been a communication network far more reliable than the ancient roads of Europe in winter. When they froze, therefore, the people took to the ice as readily as today they take to bicycles on their flat country.

The old tales were being gone over, the excitement, the exploits; the whole country was ringing again with the deeds and names from the past: van den Berg, called the Friesian Ice Man, who finished though snow-blinded; van de Horn, the great Paping; and of course Hank's father, the immortal Bobby van Hockeren from Guelderland, nicknamed the Guelder's Ghost.

Two or three thousand people would skate this year. About four hundred start together for the race, the remainder in batches later, just for the trip. The trip round the eleven towns of

40

Friesland had, he discovered, no known beginning. Originally you used to start from your own town and skate round the others and back home. Until 1909 that was. Then it became organised and everybody started from the capital, Leeuwarden, and finished there.

Thorne had found a corner seat where things were a bit quieter, and he now opened his radio and said, 'Look, you'd better fill me in on this fusion subject.'

'Okay. Nuclear power at the moment is from fission—the splitting of heavy elements. There are many unsatisfactory aspects. For one thing, all it does is make steam to turn a generator for the electric grid, not very efficient; for another it produces a lot of radio-active waste, which is hard to dispose of, also the fuel is expensive and hard to handle. Now, the opposite process—fusion—the smashing together of light elements—is much better. No radio-active waste for a start. Theoretically it could convert directly to electrical power in an everlasting self-sustaining chain reaction, enormously efficient. Finally, *fuel*, and this is the point, fuel from the sea.'

'Heavy water?'

'Yes.'

'What is heavy water exactly?'

'Deuterium, the first isotope of Hydrogen. Two-thirds of all the water in the world is Hydrogen, so there's enough Deuterium to last for ever. Now the kind of fusion reaction the whole scientific world is after is the Deuterium Tritium reaction.'

'Does Tritium come from the sea too?'

'No. There's none in the world.'

'What the hell?'

'You can make it. Briefly, once you got it started, a self-sustaining fusion reaction would go on making Tritium as its own fuel indefinitely.'

'But why all the fuss?'

'Because it means electrical power practically free from the sea for ever.'

'But, like I said, power— *power's not secret*.'

'No, but the situation is this. In all advanced countries teams are trying to solve the problem of containing plasma at these huge temperatures—ten million degrees. Different teams have different

41

machines. The machines represent years of research. Now it is just possible that Hank's breakthrough could apply very well indeed to one machine but not to another. This would put that machine, that team, about ten or twenty years ahead of its rivals. And these machines are vast—they cover acres—for example, the condenser banks have to produce in one micro-second about as much juice as a city like Norwich uses in a day. Then there's the appliance itself, a kind of bangle, an American style doughnut, about thirty feet high and five hundred feet across in which they heat the plasma up. It's the *engineering* know-how, as much as anything else, to build the thing so that it works, which puts the country ahead. Now, whichever country has been going ahead in such a way that it can profit by Hank's new physicist's lab breakthrough will be miles ahead of its rivals—but they'll need Hank to follow up the application of his lab theories in those enormous machines with enormous surges and temperatures.'

'Yes, okay, but it's still only power and power isn't secret,' Thorne insisted.

'No, but supposing the application of Hank's theory really works. Two things would happen. First, the country concerned would get virtually free power. Second, they'd be able to go ahead and build other appliances very quickly and just supply free power to their own industry. Do you realise that in basic industries—like chemicals and steel and others—power is about half the cost? Imagine the effect upon any national economy where power was free.'

'Christ, it would undersell every other country in every world market.'

'If Russia had it she could wreck the international economic balance.'

'If America had it she could, to put it briefly, buy the world in a few years time. What if Isoworg has it?'

'We'll take the correct steps to ensure, as far as possible, that all countries have a chance to proceed at an even pace.'

'You've just said one country may by chance have a ten year lead.'

'Yes, and that gives us two opportunities. One, to fix it so that all the advanced countries proceed more nearly together—I can see a way in which we might do that. Second, to handle the imbalance in world economics that must inevitably ensue. This is something we could do so much better than anyone else. It is conceivable that the powers would recognise this and accept our help. It could, therefore, be an "in" for us and an "in" at exactly the practical, non-political, non-dictatorial level that would be best.'

'I see. Thanks.' He switched off and sat thinking. He looked at the electric light, imagined it free—imagined industry ran on free electricity. The price of goods would tumble, the whole international capitalist system would crumble. If one nation had it, it was a weapon; if they all had it, it could become a boon. The complication of keeping its effects in equilibrium made his head reel. But it wouldn't make Isoworg's head reel; it was just precisely what an organisation with Isoworg's powers and resources could do and what no other power on earth could do. He sat for a long time thinking about this. He tried to order a meal but the hotel had run out of food. Finally his kit arrived from England and was brought by the taxi driver to the station hotel. He returned to Hank's house.

Friends had come to drink a glass of genever and wish Hank luck. They sat sycophantically in the little room, with the copper kettle singing on the stove. As he came in, Thorne could smell the cold smell of something having been burned. He sat down. A centre light with a red shade and tassels hung low over the carpeted table. There were the plants, brass pots, pieces of Delft china; and the jolly guests were going over the good old jokes. His eye fell upon an electrolux vacuum cleaner. The Dutch passion for cleanliness irritated him. The flash attachment of a camera lay on the untidy desk. Presumably there'd been photos for the album of 'the hero in his home'. The cosy atmosphere enveloped him and he had to make inane contributions to it. He explained about the hotel and the food. That was a big gas. The sister went barging out full of pride that she hadn't run out of food and fetched him some supper.

Thorne's two pairs of Norwegian racing skates, the same as Hank's, had been sent out to be sharpened and were now returned. They were passed from hand to hand and discussed while Thorne thought of Towers. He remembered the bogus version of Pierre Canton's message which Towers had passed on to the Chinese. He wondered whether Towers' dismissal from the C.I.A. was real, whether he was infiltrating the Chinese secret service, or whether he had really gone over to them—just for money.

He wondered about the girl on the scooter, wearing the deerstalker crash hat, whom he had nearly killed in Sarah Burns' room. He remembered the light in her eyes and her silky legs. If she could follow Towers to the Chinese Legation, bug his room etc., presumably she could follow him here. He assumed both the Russians and Towers and the Chinese would be after Hank on the ice. But what about the girl? Who was she? Where did she fit in? What would happen, when and where and how and why?

At 6 o'clock all the callers had gone. The family sat round the radio, listening to the weather forecast. The blizzard from the Arctic was getting worse. It blotted out everything, and it was approaching faster. It would hit Friesland in the morning. They switched off and went to bed.

At midnight they got up. Thorne went for a shower. There was a hand douche on the end of a flex. The hot and cold didn't work well and he scalded or froze himself in various parts until he gave it up and went back to his room. The central heating was off—he was shivering. He looked at the clothes and began to dress carefully. His brown eyes were thoughtful, dedicated. Everything must be done carefully and well. You never knew what tiny detail might suddenly become of crucial importance. He felt elated, longing for the start and completely determined that he would stick with Hank.

First, the string vest and long silk pants, then the shammy leather pants to stop his balls getting frost bite, then the woollen shirt, the silk shirt, the windcheater, the ski pants, silk socks, woollen socks, loose boots, silk gloves, mittens clipped to the sleeves of the windcheater. He wondered how fit Hank really was. Silk balaclava, tight fitting right down over the forehead and round the throat. Then another hood, pale blue like his windcheater and his trousers. How many would there be against him, against each other? Where was the girl? Goggles were no use because they steamed up and the steam froze on the inside. On one wrist was a compass, on the other a watch. In its shoulder-holster his gun. Stowed away in another pocket was his little radio and what

44

he now called his spy kit. Elsewhere was plenty of money, and finally a simple harness to strap comfortably to his back the spare skates each competitor was allowed to carry. He carefully put two benzedrine tablets in the sleeve pocket of his anorak.

He met Hank and his brother and sister in the sitting room, now cold and cheerless. Hank's windcheater and ski pants were white. The family spoke little and in Dutch. There was a new atmosphere.

They went out and the cold hit Thorne like a blow in the face. The sky was clear, the stars bright, the temperature four degrees below zero Fahrenheit; forty degrees of frost. A wind, a little alien wind, came flipping round the corner of the house just as a reminder of what it could do if it got up to blow.

They set off in the Daf for Leeuwarden.

The race ends at the centre of the town, where the great canal sweeps round the mound upon which stands the ancient citadel. Under arc lamps some men were putting up a banner to mark the finishing line. Hank and Thorne watched this for a moment and then turned away into the narrow mediaeval streets. The roads were cobbled. The pavements were made of small bricks. The window sills of the houses came down very low, with their painted shutters on either side. They gave the impression of being involved in the life around them, unlike the anonymity of modern house fronts. There was no traffic but there were crowds of people on foot. Their breath came smokily out on to the air. The shoes tapped, the clompen boomed and slithered on the cobbles. Their dress was amazing. There were hundreds of people and each seemed to have improvised something different against the cold. There were horse rugs, oilskins, fur coats, army coats, parkers, balaclavas, girls dressed in blankets, high boots, golf kit and ski kit. There were clogs stuffed with straw, battery-driven hair-driers for cold hands, butane gas cookers, thermoses, advocaat, genever, whisky, brandy, huge roast potatoes produced with a crafty grin from great Dutch pockets by the Dutch hands that built Dutch dykes to wrest a whole country from the sea. 'God made the whole world, except Holland. The Dutch did that for themselves,' ran the proverb.

Thorne, moving along with Hank and the crowd over the

45

frozen cobbles, felt paradoxically like a cat on hot bricks, knowing that somewhere some one would come, that something would happen. He looked forward to it, feeling the old crazy excitement beginning again; only this time he could enjoy making new speculations about its tribal origins. All around him the crowds were converging. And from all over Holland, under the star-blazing sky, threading through the crowds of spectators were the skaters, the dedicated skaters, and only a few knew what it meant to race on the limit of a man's endurance for one hundred and twenty miles.

They left the old city and came out into a world of motorways, flyovers, tenements, filling stations. Lamp-posts thirty feet high shone their ice-blue light down on the crowds and the sparkling ground. The starting point is by a big bridge where the motor-way crosses the main shipping canal. In one of the quadrants of this cross is Hobema's garage, and Hank was making in that direction.

'Why the garage?' Thorne asked.

'They spray cars, so they've got heaters for drying them; keeps us warm.'

'How long do we hang about in there?'

'We start from there.'

'On foot?'

'Yes, and run to the ice.'

'Four hundred people all going through one door?'

'Yes.'

'What time?'

'In about one-and-three quarter hours.'

'What do we do till then?'

'I wait by the door to get a good place at the start.'

Hank had a small collapsible stool with him. As soon as he entered the garage he opened it and sat down. He leaned against the wall and relaxed. People came to talk to him. Thorne made a quick search round the factory, found an old car-seat, bullocked his way back through the crowd and sat next to Hank. He listened to the conversations and having heard the word recur so many times he finally asked, 'What is a Kopgroep?'

Hank said, 'Skaters get strung out. Only about a dozen have any real chance of winning. They get to the front and stay in a

46

group, a Kopgroep, head group.'

'Why?'

'They take turns to be the leader—to act as wind-breaker. One skates better with the rhythm of a group.' And Thorne knew from the way he spoke that Hank was deceiving somebody. Time went by. Thorne wondered what would happen and when.

Chapter Five

The Press and T.V. interviewers came and went; the atmosphere became more and more tense. Transistor radios kept telling them that the blizzard, worse than expected, was coming faster, much faster. It would be here in the early morning—perhaps very early. The veterans looked at each other and wagged their heads.

They put on spiked running shoes for the race over the icy ground to the canal. Now they were standing. The starter's voice could be heard speaking through a loud hailer, counting. The big double doors were opened, a rope was stretched across, the voice said, '5-4-3-2-1.' The rope dropped and, to Thorne's surprise, there was a roar like a Wembley crowd at a goal. Then they were sprinting for the ice.

The scene was fantastic. Flares and brazier smoke and T.V. lights and cameras on cranes, thousands of people on bridges and banks. Out on the black gleaming ice, planks had been laid on soap boxes to make seats where the racers could put on their skates. Hank ran slithering to the end of a plank furthest in the direction they would be going. They sat down side by side.

As Thorne expected, Hank tried to race him even in the mere art of putting on their skates but they stood up simultaneously. Thorne realised Hank intended to go it alone, without help from the Kopgroep about which he had spoken in the garage. Thorne put his running shoes into the harness with his second pair of skates, but Hank flung him aside.

'Goodbye,' he said coldly to Thorne.

There was a tremendous roar from the milling crowd as the T.V. searchlight held them. Hank crouched, then his skates bit the ice as he sprinted off down the canal, arms swaying wildly in the typical manic straining action of a racing skater as he starts. Thorne was on his heels. A confusion of crones, children, clompen, cheering faces, cries of 'There he is. Go it, Hank'—a friendly, competitive, sporting crowd. And now their desperate sprinting eased and gave way to the beautiful winging stride of the long-distance skater.

The noise dropped away behind them, the wind from the north-east was on their right cheeks, and there before them under the light of a full moon stretched the flat fantastic panorama of frost-bound Holland.

The stars blazed in icy fury—lights sparkled, the wind sang in their ears, and in long graceful zig-zags they flew like snipe over the black ice.

After a mile on the big shipping canal they turned sharp left into a much narrower canal and headed away to the first control at Sneek, twenty-four kilometres to the south.

With the wind behind them, they seemed suddenly engulfed in silence so that the rasp and ring of their skates at each stride echoed in the ice and stayed with them. The banks of the canal were only about a foot high, and then there was nothing the height of a man until a house light some unimaginable distance away. Nothing moved. All the cattle were in their stalls. The whole world was still, bound down in stillness under the moon.

Thorne watched Hank's action. His hands were clasped behind his back. His knee joint, on the recovery stroke, seemed like the leading edge of a bird's wing as it carried the foot forward. Then he placed it, delicately, in front of the other so that the two skates seemed for an instant to make a single runner. Then the other foot was flung back for the next stride. In step, one behind the other, they sped southwards away from the dreaded blizzard, away from the hundreds of other skaters, at nearly thirty miles an hour.

The reeds and rushes stirred a little in the moonlight and the freezing breeze. Thorne and Hank shot past alone. Somewhere between now and the finish in Leeuwarden he knew something would happen and he grinned.

Ahead was the bridge at the hamlet of Dille. There were people. He could hear them cheering, could see their stubby winter-clad-arms waving like small bolsters. And then Hank went down on his side on the ice and shot under the bridge which gave about two feet clearance. A gasp and a cheer from the spectators. Thorne awkwardly, because unprepared, did the same and lost several yards. As he regained his feet, he caught a whiff of cow manure, warm and friendly, as a boy with a lantern heaved at a steaming forkful by the edge of the ice and waved at him.

Thorne felt as though he was skating downhill and realised the wind must be getting up. He glanced over his shoulder but could see no one. He wondered about Towers and the key to Pierre's message that he held. Then again he wondered about the girl in the deerstalker crash hat with her auburn hair and the breasts you wanted to touch. Who was she? Why couldn't he get her out of his mind? He could hear her blurting speech and see the small fierce smile and the indomitable eyes.

Hank turned to look at him. Critically he appraised his style—seeming surprised, displeased.

Sneek was the first check-point. He caught up on Hank as they came streaking into the little town's main canal.

There were blunt bowed barges with lights in cabin windows, faces peering. Then the rasp of Hank's skates, the great bow wave of powdered ice as he skidded to a halt.

The check-point was a plank on two barrels with a cocoon-like official blowing on his hands. Carefully he stamped 'Sneek' on Hank's official card, and Hank was off like a flash, thinking to gain on Thorne. But Thorne went with him. There was tumult. Skaters rushed after him—'You must have it stamped—'

'... There's no point unless—'

'... the Englishman. ...'

'I lost it,' Thorne shouted.

'Another one at the next point,' they shouted as they dropped behind.

Through the open bridge, past river traffic bonded into the solid ice, towards Yest, only four kilometres away, the next check-point. Through Yest—'No control card,' voices shouted. 'There will be one at Sloten.' He realised Hank had not given him a card, hoping to delay him.

Still going south—the wind rising behind them. They had settled to a rhythm and Thorne wondered how long he could keep up with Hank at this pace—how long indeed Hank could keep

50

it up himself. So they flew through Woudsend and then a few moments later suddenly there were no more canal banks, just the silver moon shining down on a lake of black ice, desolate and hard and hostile as glass. They skated on across it.

At last the banks on the southern side came into view. In the bank he could see the opening where the canal went. They skated into it and soon it swung sharp right round the base of an ancient windmill. Hank's legs crossed one over the other in lovely leisurely strides that carried him at high speed under the bridge and into the main canal at Sloten. This Renaissance town is only about a hundred yards long. A canal, thirty feet wide, runs through it with trees on either side and a cobbled roadway separates its banks from the fronts of rose-brick seventeenth century houses on either side. Seen suddenly in icy moonlight its beauty made Thorne gasp. It was like skating into an old master. Even the watchers seemed as though they had been standing like that for centuries to watch the skaters race by.

Again Hank's skates rasped, the powdered ice arced up whitely in the moonlight. Breughel faces in muted moon-colours spoke urgently. Thorne was given a card. Some one tried to explain something and would have delayed him, but he snatched it away and stayed with Hank.

Sloten, Thorne had been told, was where the housewives rent footage on the municipal washing lines, and as they left the houses behind he could see their laundry bumping about as stiff as boards.

Leaving Sloten, they turned back north up the canal by which they had entered from the lake. For about two kilometres they had to retrace their steps to the lake, before turning away to the west towards Balk. Here the wind hit them. Their easy flight over the ice was ended. The wind bit into eyes and trachea, making them gasp. Their once winging strides became shorter and more laboured.

Just as they reached the lake Thorne saw a Kopgroep coming towards them. He watched them carefully. There were six, and at the back a tall man skating well.

A few guttural cries, 'Hi, Hank—you bloody idiot—never keep up that pace'—and they were gone, all but the tall one. He

51

swooped out of his line, crossing his feet lazily and headed their way.

Thorne went up alongside Hank, who said, 'Friend of yours?'

'No,' said Thorne, 'he's a Yank working for the Chinese. He'll kidnap you and kill me if he finds out who I am.'

'Pah!'

'You'll see,' Thorne said, and he dropped in behind Hank and felt Towers a moment later fall into step behind him. They headed westward towards Balk two kilometres away on the other side of the lake where a lighted beacon marked the entrance to the canal leading them into the town. As they shot into it only a few feet separated each man.

Thorne looked to windward. It seemed to him that there was a dark line across the sky. Then they were out on the other side of Balk into beech woods. Here the trees sheltered them and in the silence from the wind Thorne thought he could hear a helicopter. He doubted if it could get any photographs by moonlight and wondered therefore what its mission was.

They ducked and slithered under fixed bridges and Thorne found it a relief to move his body in a new way.

The trees petered out—the route suddenly turned sharp right and they were heading north-west again, more nearly into the wind's eye, and it was stronger.

On over the lakes of Gala Madammen out to Staveren. Then due northwards into the teeth of the wind towards Hindeloopen with its tradition of painted furniture and its small port on to the Zuider Zee.

The wind was now very strong. Hank had allowed Towers to go in front, knowing that if he did not, he would exhaust himself, and the group behind would catch him. So now Towers was leading. Towards what?

The wind bit through all clothes. Nose and eyes were numb. It blew dust off roads and fallows and flung it in their faces, scouring their skin and making it sore.

The black line across the sky covered more than half of it, and now approached the moon. The shore of the Zuider Zee curves and with it the thirty foot high dyke which protects Holland from death by flooding. Suddenly they were in the lee of this dyke. They could hear the wind screaming over their heads,

52

Raising his eyes Thorne looked for an instant again at the incredible landscape, moon-frozen, windswept. He saw telegraph wires straining in the wind against the moon, and then the moon was covered by the blizzard clouds and darkness came. They rounded a bend out into the wind again, and they were merely three little men puttering in the icy dark.

The lights of Hindeloopen guided them in. The canals in the town were very narrow, mere ditches, separating people's back yards or farmyards. They passed row-boats in the ice and skated under the branches of fruit trees. Then they reached the check-point by the sluice gates. And it was here that the first few brittle flakes of snow fell and tickled their numb faces.

Deep straw had been laid for them on the sluice dyke. Hank, knowing the form, shot into the lead and they ran up the straw path and down the other side into the harbour of Hindeloopen. The frozen sea stretched out in front of them for fifteen miles to North Holland on the other side. They had to skate out on to this for a few miles, then swing north to enter the canals again at Workum.

Just as they rounded the corner of the harbour to battle out against the frightful wind over the frozen sea, three things happened. Towers took up the lead again, Thorne saw a figure leave the shelter of the harbour wall on the north side and race down wind on flying skates towards them, and the blizzard hit them, blotting out everything.

Towers looked at the compass strapped to his wrist, jabbed a finger at it, shouted, 'Compass,' to Hank in Dutch. They bowed their heads skating dead to windward and followed him.

Thorne kept looking round for the other figure and once, when the blizzard seemed to have blown a hole in itself, glimpsed some one skating behind them. There was something different about the skater's stride. Then he vanished again. Now Hank was looking at his compass, looking at it very hard. Then he shouted to Thorne, 'I think the wind is changing and going round into the East—that is good.' And they skated on. A few minutes later Thorne looked at his own compass and a suspicion dawned on him.

He took it off his wrist and, shining his torch on it, turned it quickly through ninety degrees. Ordinarily the needle would swing with the turn and then move back. This time it barely moved at all. Only a powerful magnetic source placed close by could cause this, and he understood why Hank thought the wind had gone to the East. It was not the wind that had changed direction, it was they. They were being lured to the West—lured due west out on to the Zuider Zee 15 miles wide.

Another hole in the white blizzard blew itself around them. Out on the ice there suddenly appeared the shape of a machine. Towers and Hank had their heads down and didn't see it. From it, suddenly, a skater came at Hank, swinging a bolas, and Thorne could hear him quite distinctly shouting in Russian, 'Out of the way, friends.' Behind him was another man with a tommy gun raised, sweeping it up to aim at Towers. Hank and Towers jerked up their heads in surprise at the voice and even as Towers saw the men there was a crack from behind Thorne and the tommy-gunner dropped one arm. There was a second crack and the bolas man crumpled and slithered along the ice, like a bird shot on the wing. The tommy-gunner raised his gun with one arm and fired past Thorne in the direction of the shot.

Thorne spun round, drawing his gun, flashed his torch and caught the shooter with its beam for a split second right in the face. Goggles hid the eyes but the small, fierce mouth and the girl's shape were instantly recognisable. She shouted something at Towers in Dutch. He swung on the tommy-gunner just as he opened up again, but the snow closed in before Thorne could see what had happened.

Thorne flung himself forward, close to Hank, shouting in his ear, 'The wind *hasn't* changed, come this way.' And he headed off eastwards, with the wind on his left cheek, to get back on course.

A moment later the blizzard blew itself clear and in front of them stood a hovercraft, with three small stocky men on conventional figure skates waddling towards them holding guns. Thorne picked off two of them while fire from the other machine, now recognisable as a helicopter, was returned from the hovercraft keeping the third man busy. Thorne saw Towers' arm fly back to hurl an object at the helicopter and he brought Hank down in a rugger tackle as the grenade exploded and the petrol tanks followed. Men leapt away and the blizzard came down again.

Red leaping tongues of light made the snowflakes look like sparks falling with the wind in a crazy curtain. Thorne grabbed Hank to his feet.

'Go *with* the wind,' he shouted in his ear, and they flew before the howling blizzard, and this time it stayed.

They circled gradually until they were heading back north again. They knew they were heading north because they were going straight to windward. Then Hank, knowing they had been lured off course to the west, turned eastwards and skated on blindly until suddenly he tripped over the edge of Holland.

He got up. 'This way,' he said, and started off with the shore of the Zuider Zee on his right. They lost it and skated further and further to the right until they struck it again.

'Good, that was the cape between Hindeloopen and Workum,' Hank said. They struggled on and Thorne tried to make sense of what had happened.

The girl had seen that the Russian tommy-gunner and bolas man had intended to knock Hank over with the bolas and capture him and shoot anybody that tried to stop them. So she had shot them. Therefore she could not be one of them. And yet she had been working, albeit reluctantly, with the Russian Dimitri. Thorne couldn't understand what was going on. Towers had chucked a grenade at the Russian chopper. The hovercraft had not fired on Towers, nor had it fired on Thorne, but presumably that was because he had the white-suited Hank with him, and the object was to capture Hank alive.

So it looked as though both Towers and the girl were on the side of the four squat men who had come for Hank from the hovercraft. Or was she an Isoworg girl playing some devious game? And who were these men from the hovercraft? Presumably they were the Chinese whom Wang had promised would help Towers. What would Towers now think about *him*? The arrival of the girl had made the whole thing even more uncertain and unpredictable.

He was leading now, butting into the terrible wind, and Hank shouted into his ear, 'Thanks.' Thorne raised a hand in acknowledgment. For a moment the blizzard thinned and Thorne saw a light ahead to the right, and a few minutes later it appeared again. Thorne stopped. He turned to Hank.

'There's a light ahead and to the right.'

'Good, that will be the marker for the canal to Workum.'

Thorne looked at him. The tiny snowflakes were frozen on the front of him from head to toe. His face was caked with them. The creases in his clothes were coated and frozen so that they looked like plaster of Paris.

Thorne said, 'The hovercraft might find that light'—and there was a roar and a gale that blew them off their feet and flung them away as the hovercraft shot past at about seventy miles an hour.

'We must take to the land,' Thorne said.

'Never, I'm skating to the marker.'

'You're mad, they'll kidnap you.'

Hank shouted into the gale, 'This is Friesland, the Elfstedentocht. It is for amateurs—for fun—for living. Here, nobody tells a Friesian what to do.'

His voice was high, almost weeping, and he turned and butted into the wind and the terrible snow. Thorne stuck close to him. Then he shouted in his ear, 'They'll move the light to lead you to it as a trap.' This was simple and Hank could believe it. They stopped.

'How wide is the canal's mouth?' Thorne asked.

'About twenty metres.'

'We must go overland to get into it.'

'Then I am disqualified ...'

'Just one hundred metres to dodge them. No one will ever know.'

'I will know,' he said, stubborn as the upturned toe of a clog.

'To save your life, man ...'

'For my father,' and the next words were in Dutch. Then he shouted, 'We will go out to sea to the north, then come down on the wind close by the shore fast—very fast. They will not see us in the snow and from that direction. The sluice is not far.'

They butted off into the snow again. After a while Hank turned to the right. He found the coast and skated down it a little way till they encountered a breakwater.

56

'Now I know where we are. It's two hundred metres to the canal, then sharp left and one hundred and twenty metres to the sluice. Come.'

With the gale behind them, skating like madmen, they built up a terrifying speed. Thorne could not believe Hank could follow the coast and wondered what'd happen if they hit a breakwater. Suddenly Hank lurched left, crossing his feet and, taken by surprise, Thorne lost him. For an instant he glimpsed the bulk of the hovercraft and was going straight at it. He flung himself to the left and the hovercraft disappeared in the blizzard. The next instant he hurtled into a file of half a dozen skaters. He scattered them and came down with a crash himself. He slithered to his feet and dashed off in the direction Hank had gone. When he reached the sluice gates there was a flare burning and round it were people waving. He raced up the straw-covered path to the top of the dyke and down the other side on to the canal between the cars parked on the quays. Faces were peering at him, girls in fur hoods, hands rubbing steam from the insides of windows—a thermos—a bottle of advocaat—and then he was at the check-point tearing past it amidst cries, and so gaining a little on Hank.

The blizzard was beginning to seem whiter because of the daylight, which steadily grew. It took him half a mile to catch Hank and he hated his protruding rump and his curled left hand holding his right wrist. When he caught up with him, Hank looked round, but his face was a frozen mask and showed nothing.

Thirteen kilometres to the next check-point at Bolsward, and then they would be half-way. He knew they could be ambushed at any point along the route, and tried to calculate what he would do in Towers' or the girl's or the Chinese's positions. He didn't think they'd try anything where there were people. As to the deserted stretches, he doubted if anyone in this blizzard could reach a predetermined spot in the Elfstedentocht course even in a hovercraft. The snow which had fallen caused all the canals to look alike and obliterated tracks as soon as they were made. Maybe, therefore, an ambush had been planted beforehand, and he realised that he must be on the look-out for it, though he wondered what the hell he could do, since he couldn't use his gun because his hands were too frozen. He pondered the girl and could come to no conclusion about her at all. But the excitement of her sudden appearance on the ice and the fact that she was around somewhere and involved, exhilarated him.

At Bolsward the canal is very wide and the dense crowds had come right down on to the ice, leaving only a narrow track for the racers between them. The check-point is at a café, with a verandah giving on to the ice. As they approached, braziers glowed suddenly through the snow and the white light of dawn. He had a glimpse of bunting, tents, eighteenth century sleighs. People skated beside them shouting, and were lost. Again, as Hank reached the check-point, he skidded fiercely to a halt, but this time he did not immediately race on.

Soup made from split peas, celeriac, and pigs trotters, ears and ribs, all boiled until you can stand a spoon in it, is called smert. As they stopped, the smell of smert assailed Thorne so strongly that he felt like a smert addict and supped it gratefully through the pipes provided for their numb lips. Hank did the same.

'Lekkere hoer?' someone said grinning. The words were almost onomatopaeic but Thorne's face was too frozen to grin back. He nodded.

After the check-point the canal turned right, and they were off among the fields which they could not see, plugging doggedly into the blinding snow seventeen kilometres almost due north to Harlingen, a port on the North Sea. Sometimes drifts lay across their path and in the white-out of the morning light they would flounder into them. It spoiled their rhythm and tired them even more.

At the check-point at Harlingen, Hank's card was stamped and then he stood still.

'Get it stamped,' he said, 'I'll wait.'

Thorne produced the card he had picked up at Sloten. The wind whipped the coat of the official and made the card quiver. Thorne could see no sense in Hank's behaviour. He heard the babble of excited Dutch as they saw that all the other places were blank. Hank answered a question, the seal was put on his card and then they were off. Thorne was leading and shouted over his shoulder, 'What was the point of that?'

58

'I will swear a public swear—how do you say it—for the other towns; if you like.'

'I like a public swear.'

'Good.'

What sort of a man was Hank? He turned his mind to assessing him carefully.

They swung away to the east for Franeker on the wide shipping canal which leads from Harlingen on the North Sea to Leeuwarden. Here the ice had been broken to let the ships through. Then it had frozen again. Then the blizzard had come. As a result, under the fallen snow were great fissures and slabs of ice had ridden up and then frozen on. Only along the extreme edges was one likely to find the going possible. They stumbled and recovered themselves, hampered by the snow which, in the lee of the northern bank, lay thick on the ice. Finally Hank fell and stayed down. Thorne was about to help him up.

'Don't touch me, *verboden*.'

Hank floundered over into a squatting position and dug the snow away from his right foot. The skate had fallen into a crack and slid under a slab of ice. He got purchase with his left foot and pulled the right skate free. Then he looked at it, the skate was badly bent. He jumped to his feet, hobbled to the bank and dug about with his hands. Thorne, wondering what he was after, took some chocolate from his pocket. When he opened his mouth he nearly cried out at the sudden fierce pain in the corners of his lips. Gingerly he slipped the chocolate between his half-opened teeth and, munching cautiously, watched Hank. At last Hank found a stone and prized it loose with the damaged skate and hobbled up the bank. At the top there was a gate. Hank took off his damaged skate and laid it along the top of the steel tube gate. Then he began hammering it with the stone. He finished, ran back down the bank and began tying it on.

Pointing Thorne said, 'Other skates?'

'Ice bad like this as far as Franeker, why spoil them? May need new ones on the way to Dokkum; you'll see.'

It was full daylight now, but it didn't help the visibility very much. The blizzard made a total white-out. Thorne felt it might give him a slightly better chance if anything happened.

They blundered on into Franeker. Their cards were stamped

59

and, leaving Franeker behind they headed out on the longest and most deadly leg of the whole race. Almost due north they must go into the teeth of the blizzard, then east and then north-east, forty-five kilometres to Dokkum. Dokkum. What did he know about Dokkum—Dokkum—Dokkum—Dokkum—oh yes, in 755 the Friesians had murdered the English St. Boniface, born at Crediton in Devon. Irrelevant, irrelevant, his skates were saying, must keep your mind on relevance.

They were passing a farm when it happened. Two figures were standing in the deep snow by the ice's edge. They looked too short as though the bottom half of their legs had been sawn off. One waved. Hank waved back. The other man suddenly dashed out towards him holding something in his hands. He was nearly on Hank when Thorne flung himself forward and brought him down. He was about to kick him in the face with his skate, when Hank barged him out of the way.

'*God verdomme; je stomme smerige lul.* He's my cousin, damn you.' Hank's voice was hysterical. 'Damn you, damn you, damn you.'

Thorne looked down. Half buried in the snow was a small thermos which the man had been carrying. He picked it up and gave it to Hank. He held out his hand to the cursing cousin and helped him up. They skated on all together. Hank spoke a few words, presumably in explanation, drank from the thermos through a pipe and then gave it back to his cousin. A moment later the cousin turned back and vanished into the blizzard.

Thorne's spirits sank lower. He began to feel cold. Not cold in his extremities as he had been all day, but cold through and through. He took out some more chocolate and ate it. Then he felt his skates were slipping on the ice underneath the snow. He watched Hank and was relieved to find that the same thing was happening to him.

The blizzard whipped the snow viciously across the land, laying it in long, smooth drifts, piling it about the place, leaving upon the face of Holland the pattern of the wild wind.

'My skates aren't biting any more,' Thorne shouted into Hank's ear.

'Here on each side it is ploughed land. Before the snow came it was dry. The wind took the sand—isn't it?—and blew it on the

60

ice. It freezes on then. Now we skate on it and it blunts the skates.'

'What about our second pair?'

'Yes, but after Vrouwbuurt only. Then there'll be no more ploughed land, otherwise we blunt our second pair of skates too.'

They went on but now they were merely shuffling.

After Vrouwbuurt the wind lessened and lessened and when Hank stopped and stooped to feel the ice, Thorne found that it had, in fact, stopped altogether. It was now mid-morning. The snow fell quickly all around them. Steadily and lightly, it fell out of heaven to engulf you for ever in ease, if only you would do what you wanted to do more than anything else in the world, lie down in it and sleep.

'No more sand,' Hank said. They sat down in silence and changed their skates.

By the time they were through the check-point at Dokkum the snow was falling more lightly. Here they turned and came heading south on the last leg towards Leeuwarden, twenty-four kilometres to the south.

It was noon. The snow had now nearly stopped. Abruptly a shaft of sunlight blazed through. The snowflakes danced in it like dust motes, it burned at the flat landscape like a spotlight and then it vanished.

The snow plough had been out in front of them on the Wijde Murk, and as they went further south they could see black ice again. Sunbeams shafted down. The soft woolly masses of cloud began shifting furiously and breaking up. Hank suddenly had a shadow lurching along behind him.

They swung evenly through Dudkerk with only a few miles to go. Thorne knew he had not much left in him. Carefully with his numb fingers he reached into the sleeve pocket of his anorak and took out a benzedrine tablet and swallowed it. Now there were only two kilometres to go. Thorne was certain that something would happen at the finish. It was the one place where Towers would be sure of finding them. Therefore he should prevent Hank from reaching that point. He should lay him out and cart him away. But he knew he wouldn't do that. After all, he wanted to get Towers, didn't he? He wanted Pierre's message that Towers had memorised, didn't he? But he knew that wasn't the real reason why he wasn't going to stop Hank now. The real reasons were very complex. They concerned Hank's father, the things Hank cared about and that Thorne cared about too—respect for an adversary, etc. He smiled with wry pleasure as he realised that he could only properly sum them up in the old-fashioned idea that to lay Hank out now would be 'downright unsportin''.

Hank had taken his hands from behind his back. His arms swung, his stride lengthened, his style never faltered. The winging stride very gradually grew longer and faster. Thorne, waiting for the effect of the benzedrine, hung on. Then it came with the sweet taste, the singing in the head and the sudden loss of fatigue. The violent swing of his arms forced the blood through his hands. The pain became intense but slowly and agonisingly he clenched and unclenched his fists, determined to get his hands working again. Now they were in Leeuwarden, now there were people, more and more people crowding the track on either side. For a moment the snow clouds slithered madly away, the sun blazed on the ancient Dutch snowscape as they came in sight of the town's citadel.

Hank's arms were flung crazily from side to side, he leaned closer to the ice, his strikes were more savage. The ice was black with crowds, the banks solid with people.

Thorne knew he must be with Hank at the finish—right beside him—he put every ounce of strength into his fierce striding, the pace built up and up, he was right in close behind Hank. The crowd were yelling, and then Hank's acceleration continued and Thorne's did not. He couldn't go faster—nothing he could do could keep him up to Hank. The crowd went mad as Hank at the end of this fantastic race drew away from the Englishman in blue—drew away and away. Once Thorne tried to yell at him but it was no good—Hank was fifty yards ahead, a hundred yards, flying down the funnel of screaming onlookers. He crossed the line, and they fell upon him, engulfing him in a solid mass of bodies and congratulations. And Thorne had lost him. He struggled furiously with the crowd trying to peer over their heads, trying to keep Hank in view. Then he saw a man forcing his way towards Hank, forcing his way ruthlessly, causing anger and curses. He must have climbed over a box used by a spectator, for

Thorne recognised Towers and saw upon his arm a large Red Cross armband. Desperately Thorne struggled to reach Hank before Towers. But it was impossible. Towers wrenched through the people, grabbed Hank's arm and almost at once Hank went limp. The big Red Cross man picked him up, shouting in Dutch that the champion had collapsed. He carried him round the bend of the citadel, everyone following. There stood the hovercraft but now with a huge Red Cross painted upon its side.

Then a woman's voice on a loud hailer in Dutch was urgently telling people to move, speaking the name Hank van Hockeren in anxious tones. Thorne knew that blurting voice in any language. He saw Towers carry Hank nimbly up a ladder into the hovercraft, and then the fallen snow belched out from under it as the engine was revved up. There was a furious shout from the crowd as Towers drove the craft straight at them, accelerating with tremendous speed.

Thorne had the advantage of wearing skates and forced his way to safety away from the people. The panic which the hovercraft caused made the main crowd run in a mass for the safety of the steep bank of the citadel. But the crowd here was already thick and surged forward to see what was happening. As a result the people on the ice were packed tight and could not move. There was a desperate and extraordinary scream from the thousand people, all realising at the same instant what was going to happen—then a long crack ran and echoed in the ice as it broke, and the next moment hundreds of people were floundering and drowning in the icy water. Even as Thorne watched two things happened. A sudden squall of wind bore down, carrying shreds of blizzard, and something caught his eye on the other bank. An Army snow vehicle was moving slowly on its tracks towards the crowds at the finish. As he watched, the co-driver jumped out and ran forward out of sight. Then the blizzard struck and swallowed the vehicle up. Thorne dashed in that direction and scrambled up the bank until he reached the flat ground at the top and stopped. He heard the engine of the snow vehicle and found it. The driver was sitting quietly at the controls, ear phones on his ears.

Thorne took out his knife, sliced his bootlaces, kicked off his skates, vaulted into the vehicle, gave the driver a sharp blow on the base of the skull, flung him over the side, took the controls, and turned the vehicle round in its own length. Then he aimed it down the bank and when it hit the ice turned right-handed back towards Dokkum, the way the hovercraft had gone. He worked the little machine up to its top speed of about sixty kilometres, having no idea how far the hovercraft would go. He could follow its track because it swept the ice clear.

Gradually the blizzard diminished again, the great soft snow clouds swilled about, broke, re-formed, broke again and the sun came through. The sides of the canal were only a few inches high and he knew that the hovercraft could leave it anywhere.

A mile or two ahead he saw it in a swirl of snow, and then it vanished behind some trees. When he reached that point, he followed the track across country. Each time he came to a ditch he had to slow down for fear of breaking the ice or the vehicle. The hovercraft, of course, could negotiate all such obstacles at full speed and therefore continued to gain on him. Soon he came to a plantation of pine trees and moved on down a forest track with the pines on either side. About two hundred yards ahead the track was crossed by a line of tall beeches and a wall of rose-coloured brick.

Some of the tiny snowflakes raised by the hovercraft still hung in the air among the blue shadows and sunbeams. Whatever lay behind the wall was, he felt sure, the hovercraft's destination. He slowed, turned down a side track and switched off the engine. The silence was absolute, the air was cold and bright, the sky blue above him and the snow held everything in an ecstatic, tingling stillness. Somewhere a bird sharply sang, further off a dog barked.

Thorne took his running shoes out of the pouch of his anorak and put them on. He climbed stiffly over the side of the vehicle and stood in the deep snow.

He tried to brush some of the snow from his caked and frozen clothes but he could not. He searched in the lockers for a lunch haversack and found it; a thermos too.

He stood listening to the silence as he drank the sweet scalding coffee and ate the sandwiches. Some were made of rye bread with slices of sausage, others from buttered honey cake spread with chocolate flakes. Then he heard the engine of the hovercraft.

64

Its note rose and fell as though it were manoeuvring in a confined space. It wasn't very far away. Finally it stopped.

The food made him feel less tired, a kind of second-wind determination came over him. He left the vehicle and approached the wall. To his right it was pierced by a wrought-iron gate, padlocked. He crossed over to look through it, and then he caught his breath. The sunlit snow lay evenly over a vast formal eighteenth century garden. In the centre, a castle, serene in its snow-covered moat, rose pink and perfect in the amazing light. He stood and looked at it, drinking in its air of permanence and its immaculate elegance.

A drawbridge over the moat connected it to a quadrangle flanked by stables and coach houses. These buildings were surrounded by a second moat, which joined the one round the castle.

He could see the hovercraft inside one of the huge stables, converted now to a garage. The girl was finishing the job of clearing snow so as to shut the vast door. A moment after she had succeeded in doing this, Towers came out through a wicket in the great door carrying Hank over his shoulders. The girl came out after him and shut the little wicket gate. They shuffled through the snow to the drawbridge. They crossed it, and the girl with a bunch of keys in her hand opened the door.

It seemed funny to Thorne to see some one walk across a drawbridge and open a castle with a key, and he realised that the oddness of it lay in the fact that she had obviously done it many times before. He stood and watched, wondering what to do next. Then to his amazement the drawbridge began slowly to rise.

The next instant he was up and over the gate and running fast from one clump of rhododendrons to the next to get to the back of the castle. It had come to him suddenly that no man, particularly not an American of Dutch descent, would be able to resist watching a drawbridge in action. As soon as they left the drawbridge Thorne would not know in what room they were nor where that room looked out. He reached a clump of rhododendrons that grew right down the bank and out on to the moat. On this side the snowdrifts had filled the moat right up to the first floor windows in a long, spectacular ramp. The basement windows were, he saw, on the side clear of the drifted snow all heavily barred. So it would have to be a first floor window.

Growing up out of the side of the rhododendron bush was a fir tree. Leaning against the trunk were a couple of short lengths of plank. They gave him the solution to his problem. He grabbed them and raced across the frozen moat and laid the first one on the snow ramp. Then he placed the other one in front of him. In a few moments he had crawled up the planks and he was at the upper storey window sill. He pressed the planks edge downwards into the snow and out of sight.

Looking in through the window he realised it was one of the state rooms of the castle, formal, as though on display. On the other side of the room were a pair of great gilded double doors. They were shut. He stood on the window sill, ready to jump backwards into the snowdrift if trouble came. For a moment he was vulnerable, standing at the vast sash window. It was very old and the two halves fitted loosely. It was easy, therefore, to push back the catch with his knife. He lifted the window, slipped inside and shut it.

He had shut out the sub-zero temperature and the hours of buffeting into the blizzard. Around him was the warm room, smelling of English Ronuk and pot-pourri. In the silence a gilded clock ticked, gravely measuring the present into the past. He stood listening, his eyes darting round.

A huge and brilliant portrait of William III on a horse looked down from brocaded walls, thickly hung with paintings in vast gilded frames. He had an impression of chairs with narrow backs and crimson upholstery flanking cabinets with glass fronts containing Dresden china. Then he was across the room and standing at a little door, half concealed in the corner. There was no sound. He opened it. It led to a service passage and service stairs. He moved quietly along it until he came to the next door. Then he again looked in.

The same sort of paintings on brocaded walls but smaller, better, more intimate. Pretty eighteenth century French furniture, a desk covered with papers, a stove with twentieth century armchairs round it, deep and luxurious. Bookcases, occasional tables, ashtrays, silver cigarette boxes. In the centre was a large marble-topped table—on it a Louis XV clock.

'The stupid bastard's coming round.'

The voice was so clear that Thorne froze. Then he realised that it had come echoing up the stone service stairs. He heard the girl's voice answer, 'upstairs'. He waited, listening.

'Keep still, you sack of icicles,' Towers' voice said, and Thorne's eye glanced to the handle of the other door of the room, saw it turn and he pushed his own door almost shut, leaving a crack for eye and ear.

The door squeaked as it opened and Towers entered, pushing Hank in front of him. Hank groggily wrenched himself loose.

The girl took something from a table by the door—a book, a transistor radio?—and turned to go out.

'Where are you going?' asked Towers.

'To have a shit,' the voice blurted uncertainly.

'Christ, I thought you were supposed to be a Countess or something.'

'Teresa Stanley,' she said coldly.

'Who cares?'

She went out, and Towers, turning to Hank, said, 'Feeling better now?'

'Who are you? Why have you brought me here?'

Towers said urgently, 'I'm with the dame, she's *Dutch* N.A.T.O. I tried to lead you away from those guys in the helicopter on the ice—knew they'd be there, had a tip-off—then it all got screwed up. We've got to hurry.'

Hank was rubbing his arm. 'You drugged me, I felt it, out there, why?'

'Yeah, I'm sorry, how else could I have got you away so quick?'

'Why should I believe you?'

'We don't have much time, Hank—we've got to get to your papers and make sure they're safe.'

'Safe from whom?'

'Listen, those guys out there on the ice weren't fooling, they'll be after you—they'll tear your place apart and your folks— unless you come clean.'

Hank swore in Dutch and Towers answered. They went on shouting at each other.

67

Suddenly Thorne could hear radio music coming to him via the service stairs, as Towers' voice had done. He realised that she had gone back to wherever they had been when they came in. She turned up the volume. He listened carefully, and then very faintly he heard another noise. He heard the noise of machinery and a whine gradually lowering in pitch. Finally a heavy clunk was accompanied by a slight vibration. He realised she had taken the radio to drown the noise of lowering the drawbridge so that Towers should not hear. He wondered whether she planned to leave or to admit some one.

A few moments later the radio noise diminished from the service stairs, and he realised that she was coming back. So she wasn't leaving—yet. The door squeaked again as she came in, and Towers said, 'Turn that damn thing off and tell Hank who we are.'

She turned it off and spoke to Hank in Dutch. His refusal to have anything to do with them was obvious in any language. The girl shrugged at Towers and started poking the stove.

'Okay, buster, then we'll do it this way,' Towers said, and he spun Hank round and hit him on the nose, smashing it right across his face. He brought a knee up into his groin. Hank cried out and crumpled in agony on the floor.

Thorne looked at the girl. She quite simply lost her temper. 'Not like that,' she shouted and swung the poker at Towers' head. He ducked, moved in, grabbed her and spoke without the least rancour as he expertly took the poker and her gun away from her.

'Look, I dunno who you are but you plugged those Ruskies that were after my skin, and that's good enough for me. Maybe Hank's different and you don't like the rough stuff—' He put the poker in the stove to heat up. '... But you're both gonna learn a couple of things in a minute and, unless Hank's got some sense, it'll have to be the hard way. So sit down there and make like a clam.' He kicked a stool into the corner of the great fireplace, shoved her on to it and pushed a heavy armchair in front of her.

Thorne watched her, remembering Dimitri's threat, the shooting, his alter ego's caginess, the drawbridge. He couldn't suss her at all.

'Dutch N.A.T.O.,' Hank was muttering, 'lot of bloody nonsense, who are you?'

Towers had gone to the window and was cutting the sash cord, when Hank catapulted himself across the room and drove Towers through the window. If he had not had hold of the sash, Hank's plan would have succeeded, and he would have fallen twenty feet on to the ice. Towers' grip on the cord saved him. The weight flew up, jammed at the top and Towers hauled himself back, rode a punch from Hank and caught him with an expert left hook that sent him reeling back. Towers was grinning.

'Good for you, Hank.'

The girl sat smoking a cigarette, looking at Hank hunched up on the floor. Towers cut the sash cord, shut the shutters over the broken window and then the curtains.

'It's good and warm in here,' he said to the girl, who didn't answer him. 'May as well keep it that way.'

Towers fastened one of Hank's hands and led him to the marble-topped table. He swept the beautiful clock on to the floor. Thorne saw the girl's eyes flicker. Towers gave Hank another clout to keep him groggy, flung him on his back on the table, and tied his arms and legs to the four corners. Then, unfastening Hank's trousers, he tore all his heavy clothes down as far as they would go.

Outside his door Thorne watched grimly. Yesterday he had tried to persuade Hank that a man with his kind of secret couldn't sit on any fence. In one way or another it was a lesson Hank had to learn. So Thorne stood still and waited.

Towers had crossed to the stove, taken out the now red hot poker.

The girl expostulated furiously in Dutch.

Towers ignored her as he turned back to Hank. Thorne saw the girl glance anxiously at her watch and so he began to wonder who she was expecting over the drawbridge. And then Hank screamed.

'That was only the top of your leg,' Towers said, holding the poker. 'I don't know what your sexual ambitions are, but the next heating will be for the real thing.'

'What's your proposition?' Hank asked, trying to keep his fluttering voice steady.

Towers, suspicious of the girl, bent to put the poker back in the stove, and his eyes, darting round the room, flashed past the door which hid Thorne.

'Just while it heats up, I'll tell you.'

He moved over towards Hank's head and out of Thorne's range of vision. Thorne had decided that this was the moment to put his counter-proposition to Hank, when all sixteen stone of Towers hit the door from the other side. It caught Thorne in the face and flung him back with Towers on top of him. He was, to all intents and purposes, out, even before his head was driven against the floor by a blow from Towers' fist.

Chapter Six

When he came to, he was on his face. Towers was sitting on him and tying his little fingers together behind his back with the cord from his anorak. When he had finished, he pulled off Thorne's socks and tied his big toes together too with the remainder of the cord.

He carried Thorne back into the room and flung him in a chair. When the girl saw him, she said in amazement, 'Good God!'

Towers said, 'Okay, so you know him—who is he?'

'He was on the Zuider Zee, wasn't he?' Her fierce and furious face gave away nothing.

Towers took a cigarette from a silver box and lit it. He blew out smoke, thinking. Looking at the poker, waiting for it to heat up again, he said, 'Fuck the introductions, if he can follow us here so can other people,' and then he caught Thorne's eye as it watched the caked snow and ice melting off Hank's clothes, making a pool on the floor.

'Yeah, it was melting off your's too and leaking out under the door.'

He had taken the poker from the stove and was crossing to Hank when a thought struck him. Shoving the poker at Thorne's face he said, 'Hey, what did you say to Hank that he went along with you?'

'Knickers,' Thorne replied, and Hank interrupted piteously, 'I wish I'd listened to him. His people are *good* people.'

Towers looked at Hank. 'Good?' he said slowly. He chewed this over and then Thorne saw his eyes suddenly narrow and harden. 'I guess that tells me who he is—Isoworg.' He looked at Thorne with loathing. 'Perverts, that's what you lot are. I shoot the bastards on sight, we all do.' He took out his gun.

The door squeaked and was flung open. There were three shots, and one man at the entrance fell with a bullet in his eye. His companion grunted as Towers' second bullet took him in the leg. Towers' automatic was blown from his hand and he dived over Thorne's chair, skidding along the parquet floor as the third man missed him with his second shot. At once Towers was on his feet and into the room by which Thorne had entered. There was a splintering crash as he jumped straight through the window, and the newcomer was shooting some more. Then the shooting stopped.

The man whom Towers had shot in the leg had picked himself up. Thorne noticed that he had one wounded arm thrust in the front of his anorak. He recognised the tommy-gunner from the encounter in the blizzard. He now hobbled about, picking up the fallen guns in the silence. To Teresa in Russian the man said, 'Stepan's gone after him.'

Teresa didn't answer him. The Russian was looking at her with interest and at the room in the castle that was hers, and now he went on, 'So *you're* Dimitri's girl; no wonder people talk.'

She stared back at him flatly.

'You done well out there on the ice, real well, but ...' and he gave a short rueful laugh, 'you weren't supposed to shoot *me*, you know.'

He spoke the language badly, so Thorne wondered if he would be able to pass himself off as a Russian.

'Who are you?' Teresa was saying.

'I missed you with the tommy gun, on purpose that time, like Dimitri told me.'

Thorne tried to put the pieces together, trying to find some way of turning things to his own advantage.

'The man with the bolas,' Teresa blurted, 'poor man—did I kill him?'

'Pah! He was for the big jump anyway,' said the Russian, 'that's why Dimitri set him up for you.' He shrugged. 'It worked. Towers believed you and you get Hank here for us to collect. Well done!'

Hank was watching as best he could and listening uselessly to the flow of Russian. Thorne was thinking fast. So she worked for the Russians. They wanted to make certain of Hank. Therefore,

72

they had set up a man for her to kill, so as to convince Towers she was on his side against them. Then she could offer Towers asylum in this place where they could collect him and Hank. Presumably Dimitri had guessed that Towers would accept the offer in order to sweat the necessary information out of Hank. Presumably they had meant to be here first in the chopper.

But this still didn't explain to Thorne what the Russian had meant when he had said, 'I missed you with the tommy gun—on purpose *that time*—like Dimitri said.'

And then Teresa said, 'Did Dimitri know the Chinese would be there?'

'He guessed.'

'And this man too?' Teresa jerked her head at Thorne.

The Russian shrugged. 'Dimitri said, "Shoot the lot".'

Thorne said in excellent Russian, 'If *you* don't know who I am, you're a bigger fool than you look.'

'That means shoot both of you,' the Russian went on, not listening to Thorne, and also not caring to glance at Teresa.

Thorne felt the fear making him ice cold inside. His voice sounded harsh and authoritative. 'You know damn well Dimitri would never have left a thing like this just to one person—and a girl at that.'

Teresa blurted out, 'Who are you then?'

'Typical Dimitri,' Thorne went on, 'never telling anybody anything.'

He had no plan. He was just talking. Fear made him just keep talking.

The Russian, holding his gun, now at last turned and looked at Thorne. 'Ever seen him before?' he asked Teresa.

Thorne was sweating, his mind racing.

'He came to a room where I was watching Towers. I suppose Dimitri had sent him to—to ...'

'To what?' said the Russian.

'To check up on me. And yet Dimitri was so angry because I left the tape recorder—oh, and all the time—Dimitri had sent him—' She stopped, red with fury and misery and almost in tears with frustration.

The Russian's eyes went back to Thorne considering him. 'Dimitri never tell me nothing about any other bloke,' he said.

'Has it ever occurred to you, you ape,' said Thorne viciously, 'that somebody has to keep an eye on Dimitri and his activities?'

There was a gasp from Teresa, and before the Russian could think any further Thorne went on incisively, 'Come here and undo my hands, and I'll show you my identification, and for God's sake hurry up, we've wasted enough time as it is.'

The man got up and came towards him, pointing his gun at him. Thorne got up and sat on the arm of the chair so that the Russian could get at his bound fingers. He felt a flicker of excitement inside him, and then the Russian stopped. A crafty look came into his eyes. He looked pleased at his recognition of a trap. 'Let *me* find your identification?' he said. 'Eh? I don't have to untie you, do I? Eh?'

'All right,' Thorne said crossly. Then a new idea came to him —just the germ of an idea. He said, 'It's inside my anorak—you'll have to pull up my shirts.' The idea was taking shape now, so he added, 'Then it's right round under my arm, out of the way.' His idea was connected with the fact that, since the only weapon he had left was his teeth, he'd better get close enough to use them. As yet he didn't know quite how. But he was tingling with a mixture of fear and anticipation.

Cautiously the Russian came closer and began pulling at Thorne's clothes with his one good arm. Thorne looked patient; thinking wildly. The Russian put his gun down on a table a foot from his hand. Then the idea in Thorne's mind became terribly clear.

He said angrily, 'Further round, you bloody fool, hurry up.'

He wondered if he could do it. He had never bitten anybody. The idea was appalling.

The Russian's arm was bulky in his thick clothes. To shove it round inside Thorne's shirts he had to lean close. To counteract his thrust Thorne had to lean in towards him. And so the Russian's neck was close to Thorne's face. It was like being obliged to kiss a man—you instinctively drew back ...

'Can't find it.' The throat moved; the skin was brown, the windpipe standing out from the brown skin. He couldn't do it. Go on, bite hard and deep. Thorne shut his eyes. He shot his head forward, bit deeply into the man's throat, flung himself over backwards on to the floor to haul the man away from his gun and brought

74

his feet up between himself and the Russian. Then, with jaws clenched like a bulldog, he kicked the man away. The Russian fell back with his windpipe open. He ended against the tapestry stool, threshing and jerking in horrid convulsions.

Teresa was bowed forward, eyes clenched, heaving. Hank was swearing and shouting in Dutch. The Russian stopped jerking about. In the moment's silence Teresa and Thorne could hear him drowning in his own blood.

Thorne spat out the man's throat and rolled over on to his knees. Teresa opened her eyes, stood up and put her back to the Russian. Thorne saw the livid lines round the nostril, the wildly jerking throat, the swimming eyes.

'Before you're sick, cut me loose,' he said urgently.

She didn't move. She stood there, her stomach heaving, quite unable to do anything. He got up and stood in front of her. Her hand reached out for the Russian's gun slowly, quite slowly. He barged between her and it.

'Who are you?' she said desperately, 'I don't understand any-thing—anything.'

'Cut me loose, for Christ's sake.'

'Cut him loose,' Hank's voice said, and went on in Dutch, explaining.

At last, dully, Teresa went to the desk. She came back with a pair of long scissors. They were in a shagreen case, a wedding present from Asprey's in Bond Street. She cut his fingers loose without speaking. He took the scissors from her and cut his feet free. Still in a state of shock, Teresa went over to Hank, took the scissors again, and began to cut his bonds.

Thorne grabbed the Russian's guns and hobbled through into the next room on his numb feet. He looked cautiously out of the window. The sun was setting away out in the North Sea some-where. Its long bars of crimson and orange light lay across the garden, lighting one side of the snowdrifts with careful colour, the other side being blue with shadow. The formal lay-out of the garden needed only some figures elegantly strolling amid the tailored shrubs, the amphorae and statues. And sure enough, walking slowly, ritualistically through the trellis of the rose garden, was Towers at the point of the Russian's pistol. Thorne wasn't surprised. Towers must have been too tired to run.

As Thorne turned away from the shattered window, he glanced up at the sunlight shining on William III's breastplate. He thought how violence lived and belonged in the hierarchy of this house.

Then he turned to go down and meet Towers at the front door. This time he went out through the double doors of the room and found himself on an oval balcony which encircled the well of the house. It was made out of carved seventeenth century oak and gave onto the top of the staircase that opened out into two great elegant flights curving down into the hall below, facing the main front door. He walked down the right hand flight, his bare feet squeaking sometimes on the waxy polished wood.

In the hall the shutters were closed across the windows, which looked out over the drawbridge. He moved into one of the window embrasures which was next to the front door. Beside him were two switches with arrows pointing up and down. He guessed they were for the drawbridge. He waited.

Nearby a table stood in front of a vast mirror. On it were clothes brushes, dog leads, secateurs and a silver salver for calling cards. The floor was marble and cold to his feet. It seemed an impossible thing to wait in such a place to shoot somebody. The water ticked in the central heating system. A yard or so inside the front door was the biggest doormat he had ever seen.

Then the door opened and Towers came in at the point of the Russian's gun. The Russian kicked the door shut behind him. Thorne waited until the Russian was squarely in the middle of the doormat and then he shot him through the head. The huge doormat absorbed the blood and kept the floor clean. Towers had turned and was looking at the Russian.

'Wipe your feet,' Thorne said.

'Limey bastard.'

Thorne touched the switch marked 'UP' and heard the whine as the bridge began to lift. He waited till it clunked home. He locked the door and put the key in his pocket. He was now master of the situation and he felt better.

'Get up the stairs,' he said.

When they reached the room that they had left, they found Hank sipping brandy while Teresa tended to his wounds. His head lolled on his neck. Thorne thought he looked disgusting and disliked him. He wanted Towers out of his hair, so he first told

76

him to sit in a chair, then he laid him out with his gun and tied him up.

Finally he sat down himself and switched on his radio. He explained the essence of the situation and said, 'How soon can you get a chopper here?'

'Not less than forty minutes,' his voice answered instantly, as though it knew he'd say this. 'I'll keep you posted.'

'The castle's called ...' Thorne twisted the silver cigarette box around to read the name on the lid. '... Middachten, it's near...'

'Dokkum,' the voice interrupted, 'I know where it is.'

'How?'

'It belongs to Countess Teresa von Rechteren, married Michael Stanley. He was one of our political operators before he met her—refused to speak of her—got killed on a level crossing.'

'Who by?'

'A train. Her mother's Russian, now in Ashkabad with her father, Prince Gagarin, and Teresa's son Micky, aged five, is said to be there too. I don't know if this is true or false.'

'She's deerstalker.'

'Ah, so it gels—a set-up, like they set up the bolas guy for her to shoot, so's Towers would believe her.'

'Then why did the other guy say he was told to shoot her?'

'Why indeed?'

'You should see her—she's scared stiff.'

'With Hank and Towers on your hands, would you trust her?'

'Does it matter?'

'Yes, she'll shop you.'

Thorne looked at Teresa. She had switched on a light. It shone on her hair; her face looked tender, vulnerable, determined.

'Don't think so.'

'Well, find out, now's the time, while she's shaken up.'

Teresa was looking at him in amazement. 'Who are you talking to?'

'Myself. What's Micky doing in Ashkabad?'

She goggled at him amazed, uncertain. Then fear crossed her face and it crumpled, her lips quivering. 'They've got him there—Dimitri has.'

'What does that mean?' he said harshly.

She flared up and said, 'It means I have to fuck Dimitri and spy for him or they'll hurt Micky—what the hell do you think it means, you awful ...' She looked for the word. 'Lout,' she said finally.

'Yes, that's the obvious explanation,' the voice said in his ear.

All his instincts drew him to her.

His voice went on, 'You're knackered—can't think straight— get on with what has to be done.'

Teresa had left Hank. She came across to Thorne.

'I can't stand anything more. Please tell me who you are.'

'Towers already did.'

'What?'

'He's Isoworg,' Hank said thickly.

'What's that?'

'International Society for World Government. I'm trying to get Hank back to our lab and then publish his discovery to the world.'

The surprise helped to stop her tears. 'Good God Almighty,' she said, and sat down.

'Didn't you know about Isoworg?'

'Never heard of it.'

'Michael worked for the political division.'

'Michael!' she said amazed and then again, 'You mean *my* Michael?'

'Yes.'

'Why didn't he tell me?'

Thorne was listening to the prompting from his own voice in his earpiece and said cruelly, 'You? With a Russian mother!'

After a second a new look came into her eyes. 'The train accident—Who? Who?'

'Who indeed?' said the voice in his ear.

'Who indeed?' said Thorne automatically.

She looked at him in horror, thoughts raced in her mind. 'Why should I trust you, believe anything you say?'

'Or me you,' he replied.

'That's right,' said the voice in his ear, 'she'd shop you as soon as blink,' and it went dead.

78

The moment its cool counsel was removed, his feelings reasserted themselves. He saw Teresa swaying on her feet. He put an arm to her. She moved away from him. There was silence. She turned and they looked at each other. The generations stared down from the walls, their painted eyes full of the knowledge of suspicion, intrigue, torture, power; and all of these were now palpable again in the room, vibrant between Thorne and Teresa, binding them together, holding them apart.

Thorne looked at his watch. He stank. He was covered in blood.

'A chopper will come for us in thirty-five minutes,' he said. 'Will you make some black coffee, very sweet, very strong, and show Hank where to find some clean clothes for me?'

She could see his jaw trembling, hear Hank snoring snottily. He swayed but his voice was clear. She nodded and turned to wake Hank.

Thorne tried to think how she might trick him. 'And don't go and get an arquebus or something mad to blow my head off.'

She turned and smiled at him and he grinned back. His fatigue made his resolution falter, he wanted an ally—wanted some one to trust, wanted to trust her. He noticed Towers was coming round. Hank had got up and gone out. Teresa had followed. He hadn't seen them go. He realised he had gone to sleep or passed out for a couple of seconds on his feet.

The guns he had collected weighed heavily in the pocket of his anorak. He took them through into the big room and flung them out of the broken window into the snowdrift. He noticed that it was snowing again and it would soon be dark. He hoped this would hide their tracks. He wondered how long it would be before the police would arrive. He looked again at his watch. Only three minutes had passed since he had looked the last time. He slipped out through the huge doors on to the landing. He was not surprised to see Hank at the front door, searching madly for a way to open it.

'Hank,' he called, 'stop behaving like a fart in a thunderstorm.' He waved the big key at him.

Gradually Hank turned and started coming back up the stairs slowly. Thorne, hearing Teresa in a pantry, went to check on her. The kettle was coming to the boil. Hank had reached the door of the sitting room.

Thorne said, 'Go and get the clothes like Teresa told you.'

Hank said groggily but defiantly, 'Look, I do not live in your world,' and then he stopped because Thorne was staring into his eyes. Without shifting the stare, Thorne gestured at the two dead Russians, at Towers, at himself, at Hank's burned thigh and smashed nose, out at the Zuider Zee, and he said slowly, savagely, 'Every death, and tear, and drop of blood started in your bloody head. This is the world we live in—I'm trying to change it. What are you trying to do?' He paused and then he added, 'Get those clothes.'

He felt himself shaking because he could see that Hank, like any conventional pig-headed national, had fallen back into childhood indoctrination where the Hockerens were righter than the Joneses and the Dutch than the rest; just like poor dead Tommy Atkins, V.C. So he stood there shaking and watched Hank march off. He saw that his legs were stiff and unco-ordinated because of the passion of hate-filled righteousness inside him.

So then Thorne turned away, to get on with the next bit of his plan, which was to deal with Towers. He prodded him about with his gun to check his bonds. Then he went out on to the landing. He fumbled in his 'spy kit' for a little box which he wanted. He found it and took out a phial and then put the box back.

He met Teresa emerging from the pantry, carrying a silver tray with steaming mugs of coffee on it. There were silver spoons with crests on them leaning in the mugs. He broke the top off the phial and poured its contents into one mug and gave it a stir. He and Teresa looked at each other silently. He called Hank, gave him one mug, took another himself and gestured them back into the sitting room. Teresa put the tray down on the marble table, took one of the mugs and turned away drinking it gratefully. Thorne thought this would be some kind of a test for Teresa. If she warned Towers, he still wouldn't have lost anything. Then he thought, maybe she would realise this too. He waited. To Towers he said, 'Coffee.'

'Untie my hands then.'

'You'd steal the spoons.'

He sat down to drink his coffee. It was very good.

Towers had hitched his chair over to the table and taken the mug in his bound hands; he was drinking. Thorne was taking care not even to think about Towers drinking the coffee, far less look at him. He noticed that Teresa had not raised her eyes from her mug and that her hands were shaking.

'What's eating you?' asked Towers suspiciously. He looked from her to Thorne. 'I'm talking to you, lady,' he said, drinking more coffee and eyeing her hard.

She raised her eyes finally, looked directly at him and said, 'I'm told my husband was a member of Isoworg—political division. . . .'

'Is that so?' he said, very interested. 'Now is that so? And yet you were working for the Ruskies—how about that?' He took another pull at his coffee, and gave her such a look of knowing complicity that she blurted out, 'I am being blackmailed.' He raised his eyebrows, twisting his mouth into a round 'oh' of mock surprise. 'Sure—sure, you were,' he said. She blushed furiously and did not answer him. He took another pull at his coffee and looked across at Thorne. 'Do you believe her?'

'I don't know,' Thorne said, trying to sound interested.

'I do,' said Hank.

'You're nuts, both of you,' Towers said. 'Where the hell did she learn to shoot the way she does?' He downed the last of his coffee contemptuously.

'Get up,' Thorne said.

Towers shook his head. Thorne took the poker and hit him on the wrist with it. Towers got up. Thorne watched him narrowly and went behind him. He squatted down to cut his feet loose. When Towers felt them nearly gone, he lashed out at Thorne's face, but Thorne had expected this and the kick missed.

'Now walk upstairs,' Thorne said unemotionally, and putting away his knife, he took up the poker again in the hand that did not hold the gun.

'Why?' said Towers.

'Get going and shut up,' Thorne said and feinted with the poker. Towers went and Thorne wearily followed.

When they were in the loft, Thorne switched on a light. He found there was a door leading to the flat part of the roof over the central well of the house. It was surrounded by high eaves

81

which enclosed it. Satisfied, he looked around and found a mattress, and told towers to lie on it. Towers looked up at him in sullen surprise. Thorne sat down tiredly on the arm rest of an ancient pale-brown hip bath.

'What are you doing this for?' Towers asked.

'Because I didn't want to carry you,' Thorne said and waited. After a few moments Towers felt the drug and said thickly, 'Limey bastard.' Then he passed out.

Thorne heaved a sigh of relief, knowing that this would keep Towers out of the way for about twelve hours, untied his hands and flung an old horse-rug over him.

He switched on the radio and said, 'The roof's got a flat well in the middle. Chopper could drop a hoist to us there.'

'Okay. E.T.A. thirty minutes. Flash I's on your torch, they'll flash G's.'

'What's cooking?'

'Everything. The country's jumping. Police radio network indicates snowfall obscured tracks, but it can't take them long. It'll be touch and go.'

'Okay, I'll be ready. Out.' He switched off and went downstairs.

Chapter Seven

He found Hank and Teresa in a man's dressing room which led into a bathroom on one side and a big bedroom on the other. It was full of cupboards and chests of drawers which smelled of boots and camphor. He sat on the bed. There was half-an-hour to wait—unless the police arrived. Suddenly, because there was no urgency to do the next thing, all energy seemed to drain out of him. He tried to think what Hank would do, whether he'd have to take him off by force. His brain just refused to work and all kinds of ideas raced in it at random. His eye fell upon the shower and the bathroom. Teresa and Hank had clothes ready now. Be daft to have a shower. He couldn't think what Hank would do. Did Hank know himself?

Suddenly he jumped up, took off his anorak and pulled the jersey up to get it over his head. The congealing blood made it heavy and it smeared itself all over his face. He retched.

'Get in there,' he suddenly said to Teresa and Hank, pointing to the bathroom. Teresa obeyed calmly, Hank expostulated. Thorne was tearing off his vest. Presumably Hank believed in the police and expected everything to return to normal, provided nobody killed him in the meantime; and he knew that Thorne would not. Thorne shut and locked the bathroom door, wondering if it would be possible to talk Hank into any kind of co-operation. His chest was tacky and smeared with blood right down to his navel. Blood was up his nose and in his hair and it stank. He put the gun and the key in the soap dish of the shower and turned it on. Teresa had put down the flap of the lavatory and was sitting on it, leaning back, smoking, watching Thorne's trousers as he unzipped them.

'If you are being blackmailed, now's your chance,' he said.

She glanced up, not seeing the connection. Their eyes met, they both laughed.

'I mean,' he said, 'the Russians need never know whether you died here or didn't.' He pulled the trousers down and trampled them off, then the long pants and finally, to Hank's disgust, his blood-soaked under pants. 'You could disappear.'

Teresa said, 'I hadn't thought of that.'

He stood naked, watching her take in the idea. That look in her eyes, was it hope? He was adjusting the shower. He was longing to get into it so much that he found his mouth was watering. He wondered what she was thinking.

'Isoworg could look after you,' he said.

'But Dimitri said—'

'Oh,' said Thorne. 'So he *had* mentioned Isoworg.'

'Didn't say what it stood for, just said such people were vermin to be killed—perverts.'

'So did Towers.'

She nodded. 'When you bit that man, I thought you were worse than Towers, worse than anybody.'

'Michael was one too,' he said.

'I didn't know that then. Would Isoworg really look after me?'

'Yes.'

The shower deluged over him with its furious, scalding cleanliness: stinging, tensing him, bringing him to an ecstasy, until he was oblivious of everything else. Teresa watched. His muscular body contracted; he shuddered with his neck arching back and gasped. Everything that was female in her reacted to this familiar, heart-rending orgasmic instant of vulnerability, and he opened his eyes in panic because for a second anyone could have jumped him. Their eyes met, his vulnerable, hers brilliant with impromptu compassion. His hand darted to the soap dish, stopped. There had passed between them a sharp, unguarded admission of longing and of disbelief.

He began to soap himself. He rubbed the soap into his hair— up his nose to smart the clotted blood and stench out of it— rubbed it into the hairs on his chest. Teresa watched the muck flowing away down his beautiful legs, while the Dutchman washed his face and hands at the basin.

84

She seemed to know when he would step out of the shower and was ready, holding up a huge, crisp, white towel. Their hands touched. Then he began towelling himself vigorously. The chopper would soon be here. Towers was sixteen stones of inertia, Teresa was unpredictable, Hank recalcitrant. How the hell could he get them aboard it? The first thing was to persuade Hank to come willingly. Instinct told him Teresa would help—but for how long or how much he was quite unsure.

Hank was now sitting on the bathroom stool, resting his elbows on his knees. Nakedness and countesses were two of the things which this Low Church physicist had always found embarrassing. But perhaps it was fatigue, the steam, the brandy, because now, seeing the countess and the nude here together, it suddenly all seemed cosy, and he even began to feel that he was really, in his way, quite a dog.

Thorne looked at him, saw him grinning with his head wagging like a tail, and so he tried a new tack. 'Good old Hank,' he said warmly, patting him on the shoulder. He turned and winked at Teresa and turned back and said, 'By God, we've been through a bit in the last twenty-four hours, haven't we?'

'By God, we have,' Hank beamed; so Thorne laid it on thick.

'It's a privilege to have saved a man like you, Hank, from the Chinese—from Towers—from the Russians. Your kind of brilliance belongs to the world—to mankind.'

'How are you going to make sure the world really gets the benefit of Hank?' Teresa asked Thorne.

'In the Isoworg lab,' he answered.

'What sort of a lab?' asked Hank.

Thorne had no idea what the lab was like, so he said, 'It's a marvellous lab. Where's my radio? Ask that.'

'I'll get it.' Teresa reached for the key in the soap dish, where the gun was. He could have jumped her. He didn't. He watched. She took the key and the gun and was pointing it at him. For a second the idea of being this woman's prey was amazing. His breath came quicker, his lids drooped. She noticed, her eyes widened, his lips parted and then very slowly she gave him his gun. She turned, she twirled the key, she swung her hips and she swept to the door and opened it.

'God, what a girl,' said Hank.

'Yes, you old bastard, yes, what a girl.'

Hank felt good about being called an old bastard.

Teresa came back and gave Thorne the radio, and he said to it, 'Here's Hank, tell him what sort of a lab we've got that he'll be working in.' He gave Hank the radio and, while he dressed, he watched carefully, measuring the degree of Hank's excitement at hearing of a lab so much better equipped than his own. Thorne even began to wonder about the problem of taking the chopper to get Hank's papers and files. Finally, Hank put down the radio.

'*Gottvedomme*, all Englishmen sound the same to me—except cockney—I can recognise a cockney.'

'Yes,' Thorne said.

'*Wasschiemeenen*, that is one fantastic lab over there.'

'Yes.'

Hank now began to make heavy philosophical statements like a drunk. Thorne dressed.

Teresa said, 'Just think of it, Hank, with Isoworg you'd be safe. No one would try to burn your balls off to ...'

'It's not nice for a countess to talk like that,' he interrupted.

'A countess would do something much nicer with them,' she said, huskily.

'Oh God.'

Thorne laughed. He tried to wonder whether Teresa was now his ally, or if she was just aiming to shop them all to Dimitri as soon as she got a chance—in England, if they made it. But he couldn't wrestle with a problem like this. He could only go on doing what he was doing. He looked at his watch, and said, 'Fifteen minutes,' and then to Hank, 'Hank, I think God gave people like you talents to use for *mankind*—this is your chance.'

Pepped up, exhausted, stubborn, bewildered, Hank turned this around in the mind which had been indoctrinated to convince him that he was better than the Joneses.

'Yes,' he said, 'for mankind. It is funny that God should have intended anything special for me.' He didn't think it was funny at all, he thought it was very natural that God had special ideas for Hockerens, but that was how you were supposed to talk. Thorne and Teresa, therefore, nodded profoundly as Hank went on like an actor when you've told him he's good.

'I won the Tocht for the third time—that was something—for my father—for decent things.

'Surely,' Teresa said.

'Goddamn,' he said, 'what a trip I've come through since yesterday. With my friend—isn't it?' He held out a hand to Thorne and shook it. 'But now—yes—I must decide.' He looked up smiling. 'I'll come.'

'I think both Teresa and I would like to congratulate you on your courage and resolution,' Thorne said, copying Teresa's gravity.

'Absolutely,' said Teresa, her hair falling across her face, like a screen between herself and Thorne. They had moved back into the dressing room and the relief that he had won this battle made Thorne fling himself down on the bed to think out a way of picking up Hank's papers. He shut his eyes for a second and then, hearing Teresa going out, opened them again. Only she wasn't going out, she was coming in from the adjoining room and, miraculously, she had changed. He realised he must have gone to sleep. He jerked his watch in front of his eyes.

'Okay, ten minutes to go.'

Teresa's gently flared, mustard-coloured skirt was hemmed with ocelot. She wore blue-green stockings and a heavy cashmere jersey in the same colour. She had done her face and her beautiful auburn hair hung down on to the jersey. She stood in the doorway. He sat up. His head felt clear. He felt good. A girl who, knowing she was to be hoisted into a helicopter, put on a skirt made him feel even better. And then suddenly it made him suspicious. Perhaps she didn't intend to be hoisted into the helicopter. What then did she intend? Then he noticed that Hank was fumbling about with his dirty anorak on the floor.

Thorne said, 'When the chopper arrives, we'll go and collect your papers.'

From the hem of the anorak Hank now took out a roll of microfilm not much bigger than his thumb. He held it momentarily, then put it in his pocket. He looked smug enough to turn the milk sour.

'What about the originals?' asked Thorne.

'I burned them myself.'

'When?'

87

'While you were getting your things from England.'

'Where?'

'In the stove at home.'

Thorne considered this. A lot of paper was difficult to burn. Then he remembered the Electrolux which had been left in the corner. He knew it could be used as a blower. He remembered the odd smell of something burnt and the flash attachment for the camera.

'Yes, I remember now,' he said.

Now there was nothing to do but wait for the helicopter. He bounced off the bed, intending to go upstairs in order to be ready. Teresa had gone back into the other room. He followed her.

It was a bedroom with a pretty little four-poster bed at the far end. The green walls with Louis XVI mouldings picked out in gold leaf were hung with small oil paintings, recently cleaned. There was a fireplace with a curling French overmantle and two great looking-glasses. There was a dressing table and armchairs, all French eighteenth century. The carpet was thick and in front of the fireplace was a polar-bear hearth-rug. There was an air of peace, permanence and great beauty. The room was high and roomy but strangely seemed lived in. It smelled strongly of her scent.

'Is this your room?' he said.

'Yes.' She looked at it wistfully. She pointed to the canopy over the four-poster. 'Micky used to point at that and say "Shower Bath".'

'How old is he?'

'Five. He was three then.'

'It's a good idea.'

'You like showers, don't you?'

'Yes.'

'I could see.'

'I know you could. I hate baths.'

'So does Micky.'

'Does he?'

'Yes.'

'He'd like my shower then.'

'Why?'

'It looks over London.'

'Tell me.'

'No, I'll show you.'

'Will you?'

'Yes.'

'Oh.'

They seemed to be drawn up on wires, taut, taut.

'Do you actually live here?' he asked.

'Yes. At least till Michael died.'

'But you grew up here?'

'Oh yes.'

'You can't grow up and live in a castle with a moat!'

'I know, but we did.'

'We?'

'I had a sister—she died of polio.'

'Oh, I'm sorry.'

She smiled.

Puzzling it out he said, 'This is your actual home then? Like Mon Repos or Bide a Wee?'

'Yes.'

It made her seem remote, marvellous; her skin, scent, everything about her suddenly blazed with inviolable femininity. The alien, for ever alien and unexperiencable fact of her being her and a woman now had added to it the fact of her having grown up in a castle, this castle, this very beautiful castle; it was like fairy tale sex come true. And then they heard Hank singing. He was singing the Dutch national anthem in the voice of a fall-about drunk. Thorne looked at Teresa's face. Again the smile, this time widening, crinkling up the eyes until, as though reluctant, she broke into infectious, rather loud laughter which shook her body. He found himself laughing too. He kept noticing how her breasts shook with laughter, and then they heard a voice on a loud hailer outside. He looked at his watch. Still five minutes, not yet five o'clock. They stopped laughing instantly. They listened. The loud voice was counting in Dutch out there in the snowy darkness.

'Quick.' Thorne switched off the lights and they raced to a window in the front and looked out over the stables and court-yard. It was pitch dark and the full moon shone brightly on the deep snow. Hank had reeled along with them. Now when he spoke his tongue sounded too big for his mouth.

'What is it? What is it?'

In the courtyard there were two tracked snow vehicles with their drivers, an officer from the Army, two police officers and a civilian. The civilian was very tall and well-made. He wore a long, German loden coat and an old-fashioned English trilby on his huge, square head. Fussing round were Teresa's gardeners and an old manservant, plus their wives and daughters.

'God, it's Tom,' Hank said.

'Who?'

'The Chief of Police.'

'The police hate Isoworg just as much as governments do,' Thorne said.

'He's my first cousin,' Teresa said.

Drunkenly Hank said, 'They'll never let us go with you to the lab—never. Police never let us go like that—all those dead people and everything—never—' He went on rambling, as Tom took the loud hailer and blew into it. Then he turned to the officer to ask him something about it.

'Did any of your people 'phone for them?' asked Thorne.

'No, they haven't got one,' said Teresa.

'Was anyone here when you arrived in the hovercraft?'

'No, they were at the Tocht.'

The loud hailer was blown on again, and then Tom said clearly and astonishingly in English, 'Teresa, are you all right?'

The English was good, the tones relaxed as though everything was now over. There was silence within and without. The moon shone on the silent snow and at the window no one spoke. Thorne was thinking that this was the test of Teresa. If she kept quiet, it would mean that she did want the Russians to think that she was dead. Perhaps this would help him to believe that she was in fact being blackmailed. He waited. Teresa did not answer.

The big man raised the loud hailer again.

'Teresa,' he said in the same conversational tone. 'If you don't answer, we will come in all the same.'

'I wonder if he knows about the snow ramp at the back,' Thorne said.

'He couldn't see it on his way in,' she whispered. 'He's thinking of the secret tunnel.'

His heart jumped. A tunnel; all this time there'd been a tunnel! She could have walked out.

'If it's secret, how does he know?' Thorne asked.

'His son and I discovered it when we were about sixteen. We used to make love there. Only one day it fell in and so Tom and his policemen had to dig us out.' She giggled.

'Can't you think about anything else?' Hank said crossly.

'Not at the moment and neither can Tom.'

Then Thorne understood why Tom had sounded so relaxed.

'He's sent somebody in that way already,' he said. 'He's playing for time,' he said to Teresa urgently, and turned abruptly round to rush down the stairs.

'I know,' she said. 'I could tell by his voice.'

'So could I. Come on!'

'No, this end is always shut.'

'They'll break it in.'

'They can't. It's thirteenth century. It was made not to be broken in.'

'Teresa, can you hear me, or won't they let you answer?' Tom hailed.

Hank said fatuously, 'We have got to get out of this.'

Thorne, his brain fixed on the arrival of the chopper, didn't want to know about this absurd situation. He'd better get Teresa and Hank upstairs to the loft to wait for the chopper. And then he felt something pressing into his spine, and he stood extremely still.

Teresa said, 'Hank, I've got a gun on Thorne's spine.'

'What gun?' asked Thorne, knowing that he'd thrown them all away.

'Mine. I took it from Towers' pocket.'

He said nothing. She went on, 'I only care about Micky. If I kill you and Towers and hide Hank in Middachten and give him to the Russians later, Micky'll be okay. True?'

'Yes,' said Thorne.

'I would not let you hide me,' Hank said.

'I would knock you out and tie you up.'

'Why don't you then?' asked Thorne. He could feel her hand trembling on the gun.

91

Behind Tom, two policemen had appeared out of the gardener's house, dusting themselves. Tom put the hailer to his lips and said, 'The tunnel's closed but we have other ways of getting in. I'll give you two minutes.' He had the inimitable voice of one who expects and gets entire obedience because the system enjoins obedience upon his subordinates. He fumbled for a gold watch and took it out.

Teresa said to Thorne, 'I'd only have to think of somebody hurting Micky and then I could shoot you.'

'Steady,' said Thorne nervously. 'I won't move.'

'I'm desperate—understand—'

'Keep still,' he said gently.

'*So* now I will give you back your life if you will promise to help me.'

'I promise.'

'Promise on your life—say, "Because you have not killed me I will do everything to help you with Micky".'

'All right.'

'No, say it please.'

'Don't shudder so much or you'll pull the trigger by mistake.' Then he added, 'I promise that because you have not killed me I will do everything to help you with Micky.' He wondered where Micky really was.

She sighed, putting the gun down.

Every instinct told him that her distress was real. But his instincts would tell him the same tale if she was successfully deceiving him. If she could convince him that the Russians were blackmailing her when, in fact, she was one of them, he would instantly become her dupe. He said nothing. If she spoke to Tom, the word would get round that she was alive and with him, and the Russians would know. If they were blackmailing her, she would not want this. If they were not, she would not care, so he said, 'You'd better answer him.'

'Why?'

'To play for time till the chopper comes.'

'How long?'

Thorne looked at his watch. 'Any time now.'

The men on the other side of the moat were moving away to the little bridge which led across the moat to the gardens and the back of the castle where the snow ramp was.

Teresa opened the catch of the window.

'Say something,' Thorne said urgently.

She hesitated. 'If I do the Russians will know—know I'm with you with Isoworg.' She sounded pathetic.

'Go on, talk to him, for God's sake. Look, they're moving off to find a way in from the back.'

Teresa said, 'You gave your promise, didn't you?'

'Yes,' he said, keeping very still.

'You'll keep it?' She was shaking.

'Yes.'

'They might even torture Micky to get me back,' she pleaded.

'I know. Go on, say something,' he said brutally, pushing her.

'But Thorne ...'

'We've got to stop them finding the snow ramp,' he hissed at her.

There was a silence. Then she sighed and said, 'Oh God, oh God, oh God, please help me,' very softly under her breath, and pushed up the window. They heard it in the forecourt and Tom said to the men who were moving away, 'Stop!' They stopped. They all looked up at the dark window. Teresa had moved back and suddenly whispered, 'Hank, tell them about the Tocht—anything—don't mention me.' Thorne sighed with relief.

'Hallo, you lot!' Hank shouted.

'Who's that?' asked Tom.

'Hank.'

Pandemonium.

'Are you all right?' thundered Tom with the loud hailer.

'Yes.'

'Course he is,' said the gardener.

'Is Teresa there?' demanded Tom.

'No.'

'Where is she?'

'Haven't seen her.'

Then the gardener said, 'You old bugger—you showed 'em.' Every one of them was now interested. They shouted in their jolly yokel gladness about the Tocht.

'The Queen sent you congratulations, Hank. Did you know that?'

'You broke a record ...'

'There was that great tree of a bloke as you came out of Hobema's—knocked him arse over tit.'

'My God, you showed 'em,' said somebody.

'I did, didn't I?' Hank said. 'God, what a race.'

'It was the third time ...'

'It was fantastic ...'

'I saw you go under that bridge at Dille. God, that was something.'

'Nothing to what happened later.'

Others were demonstrating something they had seen, arguing, re-living the whole event. Hank was shouting excitedly, 'I did it alone—no Kopgroep—me alone against the wind.'

Tom, with the loud hailer hanging from his hand, was looking at them all, smiling a patient, crooked smile with the bottom teeth crossing the upper ones, slowly shaking his head over the endearing imbecility of the lower classes. He had just looked up at Hank, smiling like that, tapping his forehead with his forefinger when the sound of the chopper was heard. Everyone stopped talking at once and their faces were shown up whitely against the moonlight as their heads swung, questing, until they all got the direction.

For an instant Thorne glanced at Teresa's face, wrapt and yet excited by the noise. But she had given away nothing; nothing had changed. 'Come on,' he said, 'up to the roof.'

They ran back and up the stairs to the loft. They ducked under the vast wooden joists, past hunting boots, tailors' dummies, past cupboards with glass fronts filled with heirloom clothes, and nearly decapitated themselves on rows of washing lines. Finally, they dashed past the sleeping Towers and burst out through a door on to the central well of flat roof surrounded by the high eaves which covered the servants' quarters. The cold hit them and the stars in the black sky blazed like furious ice. Thorne caught the chopper with the beam of his torch, flashing 'T's', they returned 'G's'.

It came and hovered above them. Its blades were too long for

94

it to land in the well of the roof. A man came down fast on the hoist.

They could hear Tom's voice on the loud hailer but could not understand what he said.

'Go and see what he's saying,' Thorne said to Teresa.

She went and Thorne turned to the man from the chopper and said, 'Police and army out there, three dead Russians in the house; then there's one sixteen-stone drugged American working for the Chinks, plus us three waiting to go aboard. Will there be room?'

'Yes. What do we expect from that lot?' He pointed towards the courtyard.

At that moment Teresa came back.

'You'd better come,' she said.

They went back to the front of the house and stopped at a little window with cobwebs and millions of dead flies all around it.

Tom was sitting in one of the snow vehicles. It had a machine gun on a swivel attached to its side. This he was pointing negligently at the chopper. He put the loudspeaker to his lips and said with the importance he had been given, 'If anybody goes up on that rope, I'll shoot the tail off the helicopter.'

'He has been asked to shoot with our Queen,' said Hank drunkenly. Teresa giggled.

'I could pick him off from here,' Thorne said.

'And then his mates'd take cover and kill us one by one going up the hoist,' interrupted the helicopter man.

'Well, we could ...'

'You can't board a chopper under fire, it's not on.'

'Damn,' said Thorne.

They sat and thought about this.

Teresa said, 'We might take them by surprise in the hovercraft.'

'How'd we get to it?'

'The tunnel. There is a sort of a way up into the garage where we put it.'

'What hovercraft?' asked the chopper man. Teresa explained. Then she said to Thorne, 'Can you drive one?'

'No.'

'Even get it started?'

'No.'

'Oh God, then what can we do?'

'It doesn't matter,' Thorne said impatiently, remembering his radio and added to the helicopter man, 'You could keep them interested when necessary, buzzing them, couldn't you?'

'Sure could.'

'We'll need time to get there, to get it all ready,' Thorne said. 'Listen, you know those tailors' dummies and clothes and boots, we'll rig 'em to look like people, and you can put them up at the windows in the front of the house. Then the chopper can pretend to try and take off first one and then the other.'

'What's the idea?'

'It may prevent them going round the back and up the snow ramp. In the end the 'copter can pick you off from a back window with the hoist. He'd have time for just one pick-up. Will the walkie-talkie work inside the cellars of the stables?'

'Yes.'

'I'll explain to the pilot and then take the walkie-talkie down with me,' Thorne said.

'Okay.'

When Thorne had talked to the pilot, they made up the dummies from the clothes in the cupboard, and the man from the helicopter helped lift Towers on to Thorne's back. Thorne cut down some of the clothes line and stuffed it in his pocket. Teresa and Thorne and Hank then set off down the stairs from the loft. The other man followed, carrying the first of the dummies, and set it up in a front window.

Teresa took Thorne to the service lift. They shoved Towers inside and sent the lift down to the basement. Then they ran down the stairs. At the bottom they dragged him out and across to a tiny staircase in a corner to which Teresa was pointing.

'This part's original,' she said. 'Thirteenth century.'

The newel post of the spiral stone staircase was shiny with centuries of wear. The steps were high and steep and very sharply turning. Teresa went first, then Hank. Thorne laid Towers on his left side, gave his feet to Hank and told him to pull. In this way Towers' body bent round the spiral, and they heaved him down, Hank swearing fluently.

Thorne said, 'For Christ's sake don't smash his head—it's got something important in it.' Hank cackled.

At the bottom they were in a circular space about six feet across and four feet high. In the centre was a manhole cover, made from one piece of stone, with an iron lifting handle in the middle. Laid across the stone were two thick iron bars, deeply corroded with rust but slotted snugly into recesses in the walls.

Teresa picked up a modern lead hammer used for knocking hubs off racing cars, and knocked the bars out of place. They wrestled the cover up and Thorne started down the iron steps set in the side of the shaft. Hank lowered Towers down to him, and soon they were making their way on all fours along the tunnel, dragging Towers with some of the clothes line brought by Thorne from the loft. Thorne wondered how long Hank could keep going. When they had passed under the moat, the tunnel sloped up. Soon Thorne felt that terrible sweet feeling in his muscles that comes before the limbs just stop working.

'We'll have to stop,' he said, and lay gasping with his face in his arms.

Teresa said, 'It's about twenty metres. I'll pull him.'

Thorne rolled over and shone his torch on Towers. Then he saw that Hank wasn't there. Teresa turned round, took hold of Towers' arms, dragged him a couple of feet, paused and then pulled again. After a few moments Thorne joined her. Working together was better. They didn't speak. The tunnel suddenly opened into a room. Teresa pointed with her torch to a rickety ladder and then to a pile of rubbish.

'That ladder goes up into the underhouse of the gardener,' she whispered. 'Behind the rubbish is a way through into another cellar like this one. They only found it the other day, when they tried to make a pit for mending the car.'

'An inspection pit?'

'Yes. The hole went right through. I just hope that the ladder reaches, that's all.'

'Is the hovercraft over the pit?'

'I don't know.'

Hank came crawling down the passage. He had started to mutter to himself.

'He's in the Tocht again,' Teresa said.

They got through into the next cellar. Thorne took the ladder and found that, used vertically, it was just high enough. He went up it, poked his head through the small hole which had so far been made, and flashed his torch around. The side of the hover-craft was right against his face; sticking out of it there was a big mooring ring. He passed the clothes line through the ring, sent the other end down to Teresa and climbed down after it.

With the weight of Hank and Teresa on the end of the line, Thorne was able to heave Towers up the ladder one rung at a time. Finally they got him through the hole on to the floor of the garage, bundled him into the cockpit and joined him there. Thorne flashed his torch around until he found the name and identification of the craft. Then he opened his radio.

He said, 'We're bottled up by the army. We're going to bust out in the hovercraft. It's a No. 2 Lady Bird six seater. How does it work?'

Before the words were out of his mouth the words of the instruction manual were being fed to him in the way he would understand best. He checked carefully through all the procedures and controls as the voice came to them. Teresa and Hank stood and watched in amazement. Finally he said to Teresa, 'How are the garage doors fixed?'

'Bolts top and bottom. '

Thorne spoke into the walkie-talkie. The chopper came round. It hovered as low as it could outside the garage doors. The slipstream churned up the snow, blinding and deafening the people in Tom's group and deafening even those inside the garage.

Thorne pressed the starter and got the engines running. The dust of ages in the garage eddied up to choke and blind them. He waggled the controls experimentally, increased the lift, felt the craft lightly stir and tip and rotate back and forth and start to slide round the inside of the garage.

'I don't know how the hell to turn it round,' he said. 'Quicker to do it by hand,' he added, and jumped over the side. Shutting his eyes against the dust, he grabbed a rung of the mounting ladder and pulled the machine round until it was facing the doors. Then he ran over to them and lifted the bottom bolts. He ran back and climbed aboard. He stood for a moment think-

98

ing. Hank was flopped out on the floor. Teresa anxiously clutched the back of a seat. Thorne looked at the controls, remembering their functions, practising them as best he could. He shut his eyes. He imagined what would happen when he came out through the door and what he would have to do. Then he opened his eyes, said 'Hold tight,' and opened both throttles as wide as they would go. The result was spectacular and astonishing. The craft seemed to jump straight out through the doors and right across the courtyard before he even knew what had happened. He had pre-thought this moment on the controls and therefore just missed the wall of the coachhouse on the opposite side. A huge spume of snow, whisked up by the chopper and the hovercraft, danced in the moonlight as he hurled the craft between Tom's vehicle and the wall. He felt it bump the tracked snow craft on the left side, bounce to the wall, bounce back. Then they were clear of the chopper's snow wake and heading for the moat. He grabbed for a hand hold as the craft raced at the twenty foot drop on to the ice. For an instant the sublime elegance of the garden under snow and moon made him gasp, then the craft tipped and plunged down the bank on to the frozen moat.

All his fatigue was washed away in excitement. The craft was racing at the far bank of the moat at about twenty miles an hour, still accelerating fast. He steered left to get the castle between him and the machine gun, hit the bank, leapt up it and steered for the part of the garden where there was no wall at the back. Beyond was open country.

Thorne looked back. He saw the chopper swing up over the roof as instructed, to flap its hoist against the window where the crew man was waiting. He saw tracer in amongst the tail assembly and then a rotor struck the roof. The slates flew, the body spun on the torque, a blade buckled and the helicopter tumbled down the four hundred-year-old walls of Middachten to bury itself in the snowdrift.

Then the hovercraft was out on the fields and accelerating away at tremendous speed across the flat landscape, which shone in the moonlight so beautifully.

He slowed a little and began practising manoeuvres. He looked at the compass still strapped to his wrist, turned right and steadied the craft.

'Find the map,' he said.

She already had it in her hands and had found the cabin light.

'Where are we going?' she asked.

'England.'

'In this?'

'Yes. Cross country, over the Zuider Zee, across North Holland, on to the North Sea, then down the coast, across to the Thames estuary and up the river to Cleopatra's Needle.'

'How about fuel?'

'Stop at a filling station.'

She giggled at the prospect, then added, 'Does it use petrol?'

'No, kerosene, you can smell it. Which way to the Yssel Meer?'

She directed him.

He looked at his watch. It said six p.m. The race had ended at two-thirty. Had he really only been at Middachten for three hours?

'What d'you make the time?'

'Just gone six,' she said. She switched on the radio, tuning it to a Dutch station. After a few moments she said, 'I got a news flash. Everyone's being warned to report us to the police.'

He did not answer but accelerated, thinking hard. Teresa was wearing an ordinary anorak with a hood. She now pulled it up, tucking her hair into it. 'I'll duck down whenever you think anybody might realise I'm not Hank.'

'Okay.'

Sometimes as they swept rather quietly over the unearthly landscape at about sixty miles an hour, they heard sharp taps against the hull and soon realised that they were made by fence posts.

'The Russian agents can monitor the police wavelength so they'll know where we are just as well as anyone else.'

'So what?'

'So they'll come after us too or the Chinks or both if they've got anyone available to send.'

They swept on over the snow. Hank had found a blanket

wrapped himself up in it and was at the bottom of some deep black pit of sleep breathing like a grampus. Very soon they could see the lights of Leeuwarden, scintillating over to their left, and soon the sodium lights of the great motor road which runs from Leeuwarden via the Afsluitdijk to North Holland lay across the horizon in front of them. When they were fairly close they slowed down. Thorne skipped the craft up on to the dyke of a tributary road and so eased her up on to the motorway. Cars were moving in both directions. There was hardly any snow. The reason was apparent. The road ran east-west, the blizzard had been from the north. It had blown the snow off the road on to the top of the dyke into a vast snowdrift stretching down into the fields below on the southern side. Thorne crossed the road, went down a little road on the other side, struck off across country again and they soon came to the big ship canal. They turned on to it and accelerated away for the next town which was Franeker.

'We skated through Franeker,' he said.

'Yes.'

'There are too many bridges, we'll have to go round the outside.'

They slowed when they came to the bridge at Dronrijp, passed easily underneath, left the canal before Franeker, came to the sea dyke south of Harlingen and found its sides too steep to climb.

'Go south,' Teresa said. 'There's a road coming in from Kimswerd that leads up to the road on top of the dyke.'

He did so. When they reached the top of the huge sea dyke he stopped to look for a way down. Poised there they looked out in front of them and Teresa said softly in Russian, 'Holy Mother of God!'

At the beginning of the frost the Zuider Zee had frozen quickly and smoothly into black ice. Then the blizzard had come. With only smooth emptiness in front of it, the wind had blown the light dry snow where it liked. The snow had been feathered up to become the pattern of the wind and now lay in dunes and whorls tranquil in the moonlight as far as the eye could see.

Thorne turned his head from it and looked at Teresa. He saw that there were tears coming in her grey eyes, and he understood.

101

They stared at each other. For some unaccountable reason the sight before them filled them with a sensation of longing. She undid the hook of her anorak, pushed it back, shook her hair loose. He turned away, and eased the hovercraft down the bank. Then he opened the throttle wider and they raced out. It seemed to be their own place and that their relationship, like the snow-scape, was different from what all other human relationships or worldly landscapes had been or could be. She put her hand on his. He glanced at her.

'I cannot believe in you.'

'Nor I in you.'

He bent his head and kissed her. The warmth of her tongue lazily amidst his mouth reminded him how frozen their faces were.

'Gosh, your mouth's boiling,' she said.

'Gosh,' he mimicked her. 'Do they sell paraffin in filling stations in Holland like they do in England?'

'Some do. On the other side of the Afsluitdijk we'll find one.'

He tapped the fuel gauge. It was well down.

Chapter Eight

The pattern of snow and moon shadow reeled past, and the lights of the towns on the other side of the Zuider Zee grew closer. They could feel each other's shoulders as they stood side by side racing forward. Finally they reached the coast of North Holland. Teresa put her hair back underneath her hood and laced it up. Thorne eased the craft up the dyke and then it was swimming majestically down the main road. She pulled a scarf up round the lower part of her face and put goggles on her eyes. The drivers of all the cars and lorries stopped to stare. They went quite a long way before they found a station with a paraffin sign.

He moved the craft over, let her settle and switched off. The first thing he heard was the petrol jerk's radio jabbering away, and as Teresa ducked out of sight he could see the man already moving to a telephone inside its glass kiosk.

Teresa whispered to him, 'Speak English, they'll understand,' but he could see the petrol jerk already inside the telephone box looking at him fearfully, presumably telephoning the police. He sprang down, seized the pipe, jammed it into the filler hole, switched on and drew his gun.

The kerosene seemed only to trickle into the tank. There was dead silence. People began to gather. Some had bicycles. They pointed and talked and kept watch for the police. The indicator on the pump was whizzing round—thirty litres—forty litres—that was about seventy pints, about nine gallons. Suppose she held a hundred gallons. Using the windows of the filling station as mirrors he could see very clearly in all directions. Many of the onlookers were teenagers. He hoped they wouldn't realise that if they rushed him he could do nothing. Sixty litres. Over in a far corner a hubbub was starting. Eighty litres. Then a man came bursting through the crowd with a woman clinging to him, trying to hold him back. He was shouting in Dutch but with that same kind of hammy emphasis which makes German officers sound so ridiculous. Shouting like a leader who believes in leadership, he came stamping forward, bravely ignoring Thorne's gun, and made a grab for the hose. Thorne obligingly took it out of the filler cap and squirted him in the face with it. The result was dramatic. He staggered about and then fell down choking. His woman and others rushed forward to drag him back and resuscitate him. Two hundred and fifty litres—fifty gallons. The buzz of excitement had died down. There was silence.

The silence went on. In it Hank could suddenly be heard snoring. The crowd could hear the sound. It became obtrusive. A child began mimicking it, keeping time; his friend took it up. Then their whole gang joined in. Then all the kids followed suit. Three hundred and fifty litres—over seventy gallons. And dozens of children all snoring in unison. The snoring got louder and louder. Some people began to laugh. Others laughed. The priest became angry at the laughter and tried to stop it. The women backed up the priest, to show that they were virtuous, cuffing heads and boxing ears to help the priest lead his flock back into silence and hatred again. Ninety gallons. And a commotion. Thorne heard the awful hee-haw of the police Morris horn, switched off the kerosene, leapt in, started the motor and blasted away down the road. The police cars, even with chains, could make little headway in the snowy conditions.

From somewhere near his thigh Teresa said. 'What the hell was all that snoring?'

'Kids.' They burst out laughing. Then they tried to concentrate so that Teresa could map read him on to a canal, but it was very difficult. Finally they did reach the canal, which took them away towards the North Sea. They left the tumult behind and about ten minutes later they surged out on to the sea, whose waves rolled and humped under the brilliant moon.

He set a course south keeping Holland visible on the left. He had discovered the craft's maximum speed was just on seventy-five miles an hour, cruising speed sixty, so he set her to travel at that. The warmth and the drone of the engine made his fatigue creep up on him again like a warm, treacly, strength-sapping bath.

'Teresa.'

'Yes?'

'Can you keep awake?'

'I took a pep pill a little while ago—yes.'

'So did I, but I may go to sleep all the same, so watch me.'

'Okay.'

'I've found the instruction book,' she said, and after a moment of looking through it went on: 'How many gallons did you get?'

'About ninety.'

She worked it out and then said, 'That'll only take us about one hundred and sixty miles—not nearly as far as England.'

'Damn—look at the map and see where one hundred and sixty miles gets us to.'

After a pause she said, 'Somewhere near Ostend.'

He opened his radio link and said, 'We'll need more fuel near Ostend, E.T.A. around nine-forty.'

There was a fractional pause then his voice said, 'Dunkirk has an easy beach and a concrete ramp up on to the sea road. There's a filling station there which sells kerosene—there's a big red neon sign which flashes on and off saying "Parking" with an arrow.'

'Thanks, out.'

He turned to Teresa:

'Watch for a chopper,' he said. 'At this speed we'll have about one minute to get out of the three mile limit. We'll be safe there if it's the Dutch police. If it's anybody else, things'll start popping anywhere.'

'At least they'll still want Hank alive.'

'Yes, I know,' and he added, 'remember you won't hear anything, so keep your eyes going round and round like a radarscope the whole time and at sea level too.'

'Right.'

'And you'd better see if there are any weapons on board—tommy guns, grenades, anything.'

She began flashing her torch round the cabin. Hank had not stirred and was still fast asleep. She found a locker and turned

105

back towards Thorne with a tommy gun and some magazines.

'Have a look at these,' she said. 'I'll steer.'

He gave her the controls and took up the tommy gun and had just pushed some magazines into the front of his windcheater when she said, 'Thorne, quick.'

'What?'

'Look.'

He grabbed the control column and aimed the craft to the right and opened the throttle as wide as it would go. The chopper was as low on the sea as it could get. It was coming at them from the north and closing fast. A few seconds later it slowed down to fly alongside.

'Who is it?'

Teresa, her hood, scarf and goggles now in place, looked up.

'God, it's Cousin Tom in a flying helmet. Looks idiotic.' She chuckled.

As the pilot got the feel of the situation, he eased in close. Tom seemed to be enjoying himself, and put the loud hailer to his lips. In his civilised English voice he said, 'Mr. Thorne, I am warning you that the Dutch government will not allow you to abduct Mr. van Hockeren. You must turn to the shore and stop there. If you do not, I will shoot you. I will count three. One...'

Teresa stood up on a locker and leaned over Thorne, putting her body between him and Tom and keeping her back turned, so that nobody could be certain whether this was not, in fact, Hank, who was thus protecting Thorne.

She said into his ear, 'Think they can see my legs?'

'No.'

'Then if they think I am Hank, this will puzzle them.'

They hurtled on over the silver choppy sea, rocking and bucking at the movement. She screwed her eyes round to glance up at the chopper. There, thirty feet away, buzzing along in the air, sat stuffy old Cousin Tom telling everyone what to do, as usual—and, as usual, being ignored. They hurtled along a bit more. Then, out of the tail of her eye, she saw something and screamed in Thorne's ear, 'Look out, left.' Before he even looked up, he hauled the helm over, and the bullets, like ten

106

joined claps, blurted past behind them. Cousin Tom was whisked up and off, looking sedate, and the other chopper banked round to have a go at him. Thorne gave Teresa the controls.

'Zig-zag, change speed,' he said. 'Keep going south.'

He opened the hatch in the roof and stuck his head and shoulders through into the biting wind, holding the tommy gun. Both helicopters were now closing in. Thorne saw the door of the new one slide open, a tommy gun poke out and let fly a whole magazine at the Dutch chopper. Glancing at Tom, he saw him take a snapshot with a sporting rifle at the tommy-gunner, who pitched straight out of the door into the sea. Thorne put up his tommy gun, aimed well to the front of the second helicopter and pulled the trigger.

Having no tracer, he didn't know where his bullets went, but apparently they did no harm and he realised his error. There was no need to aim off. Relative to one another they were stationary. He realised how tired he was not to have thought of this already. Teresa steered left and shot underneath Tom. Thorne saw a machine gun swivelling inside the new plane, which lifted and darted vertically above the Dutch plane, where it was masked from Thorne's fire and from Tom's. Then a hail of bullets tore up the water. There were two tremendous booming clangs as a couple of bullets hit the craft's skirt. Teresa swung left just in time to see the Dutch chopper, obviously badly hit, heading for the coast. The bullets hitting the hovercraft had woken Hank.

'What's happening? Where are we?' he asked.

Thorne put up the tommy gun and let rip a whole magazine straight at the tail assembly of the second plane, so that it started to spin round and round. It banked madly this way and that, and then, as if deliberately, it dived into the sea.

The hovercraft sped on south alone, and Thorne suddenly realised he hadn't peed for about a million hours. So he did so over the side.

Teresa, undoing her hood and shaking out her hair, said, 'It's only at a time like this that I have penis envy.'

'Goddamn it, you both love filth. Filth—' Hank shouted, pointing to the fallen chopper— 'and blood and death. Your own cousin shot through from head to foot. You love it.'

'Head to foot?' Thorne said, and began to laugh. 'You can't

say "shot through from head to foot".'

'Oh, go to hell,' said Hank.

They sped on southwards at a steady sixty.

'How far did you say to Dunkirk?'

'Hundred and sixty.'

'Two hours and forty minutes.' He opened the radio link explained his plans and said, 'Figure out an E.TA. at Cleopatra's Needle and have a car there,' and he switched off.

His eyes kept closing—he wetted his lids. They still kept closing. Even if he held them open with his fingers, he still went to sleep.

'I'll get the round circles and make up the pole, then we'll be okay.'

'What?' she said.

'Rat the whiskers and look for lights so's we smooth over the time now.'

Teresa shook him.

'Thorne.'

'Yes.'

'I'm all right,' she said, 'I've read the charts. I know what lights to look for. Hank's had his sleep.'

'I'm feeling fine now,' he answered, 'it's only the smatterlinger's playswarp that matters.'

'You sleep.'

'Yes.'

He found a hatch opening into an after-locker and inside it blankets. He wrapped some of them round him, lay back and shut his eyes. Immediately Teresa tapped him on the temple and he said, trying not to scream at her, 'Oh God, now what?'

'I think we just passed under Tower Bridge.'

'You're mad.'

'It is the one with the two towers, isn't it?'

'Yes.' Then he sat up sharply. 'What happened to Dunkirk?'

'Hank and I managed it.'

He looked at her incredulously. 'Super girl ...' he began and then he suddenly froze deadly still, pulled Teresa close to him and whispered in her ear, 'What about Towers?'

'Thought of that. I tied his beastly little fingers like he did yours, just in case.'

108

Thorne was in a cocoon of warmth and rest. On all sides the hurly burly of London was slipping past. Tower Bridge, so only a few minutes to go. He stood up.

He opened the radio. 'Just passed under Tower Bridge.'

'The car will be a black Humber, No. CYN 243, driver named Collins, birthday 1.10.39. Check it. He'll take Towers for brain washing and Hank to the lab.'

'Okay. Out.'

He went to the controls and immediately accelerated as a police launch approached. He raced the craft up the river to the steps of Cleopatra's Needle.

Hank was outside first. He made the craft fast. Thorne looked at Towers, thinking he had to lug him up and out.

Hank's voice said, 'I think I see a bobby. Yes, the bobby is coming this way. No, the bobby has gone away again.'

'For God's sake, stop saying "bobby" like that all the time,' Thorne said, 'and help me with this bastard.'

Together they forced Towers up the steps and on to the pavement. A black Humber, No. CYN 243, came alongside.

'What's your name?' Thorne said to the driver.

'Collins.'

'Birthday?'

'Eh?'

'When were you born?'

'First October 1939.'

'Okay.'

Collins helped them put Towers in the car. The journey to the flat was a blur for Thorne. When they got there, the porter bustled out.

'Good evening, sir,' he said, looking at Towers, assuming him drunk.

'Good evening, Buzzacott.'

Collins said, 'Okay, now?'

'Yes.'

'I'll take this geyser to the laundry then and the other bloke's to go to Potten End.'

'Potten End? The lab?' Hank said. 'Gott—so soon?'

'Yes,' said Collins, and drove off.

Thorne and Teresa went up in the lift. He opened the door.

He was out on his feet. Nevertheless he was able to hear and register as she shut the door behind him—the special door which was made of steel and set in steel—and he heard the two steel bars clunk into place. Then it was different, all clear and like bliss—he floated to his bed, saw it was open, ready. . . .

Teresa felt her legs wobble and her arms go limp. She swayed over to the glass wall and lit a cigarette. It burned her mouth; her hands were filthy and stank. She stank. She felt sticky and smelly and too hot, and then she shivered. The tears ran down her face. She smoked on. A tear fell on to the end of her cigarette. She went on smoking and crying at the high window, and the cigarette started to disintegrate. She crushed it out in a silver ashtray, wiped away her tears with the back of her hand, sniffed and swallowed and went to Thorne.

She undressed him and he didn't move. She went to the bathroom where the glass bath stood in the glass corner of the room. She turned on the taps, undressed and soon lay back floating up there in the tingling hot water over the icy city. Down past her thigh and her feet, miles down, making her gasp to look at them, the myriad lights of London sparkled.

For a little while she was at peace. Then she got out, towelled herself, climbed into bed beside Thorne and went to sleep. It was about two a.m.

Chapter Nine

Thorne opened his eyes. Teresa had woken before and had gone back to sleep again. Thorne found he was lying on his side next to a warm, smooth, slim, naked girl. His face was touching her hair, which smelled of permissive scent, namelessly female. He didn't want to hurry. He lay and thought about her for a bit. It was late afternoon. A few snowflakes were blowing about outside in the sky.

He turned on his side and looked at her. Christ, she was beautiful. He began to stroke her breasts. She opened her eyes, smiled.

'What's your other name?'

'Only Thorne.'

He kissed her. Their bodies stirred and moved towards each other. They were glad to explore each other in the certainty that real response would be forthcoming. Then he stroked his mouth across her breasts. He liked the feel of them on his cheeks and lips and eyes. He put his hand down, creeping it inchmeal over her flat stomach. While he did this he looked at her, watching her savouring the sensation, and then he began playing with her very gently. He looked into her eyes as he explored her. He loved doing so because she was so soft and yet so pursed with eager response. Then she was playing with him, while they still looked into each other's faces, saying without words that, because they would never trust each other in the other context, then in this one they would give everything and all of it true. He turned and hung over her. He paused before going into her. He wouldn't kiss her or speak. And then he slid into her longingly. It made his eyes smart, his mouth open because the jaw muscles tingled and his mouth filled up with spit.

They were both so anxious to believe in each other that this gave an urgent tenderness to their lovemaking. It was as though they made love searchingly. Finally it ended. Then the place where they had been—which has no name and can't be described —began to flow gently away from them, leaving behind an uneasy peace.

To bend his finger was like demanding that it lift a ton. She wanted the world to remain for ever like this. They slept.

She woke and, before she was fully awake, there was Dimitri's face and Micky's face, Thorne with the Russian's throat, the ice and Hank tied down on his back. She abruptly turned and buried her face in his chest and soon began rubbing herself against his thigh.

'Do it again. I don't want to think.'

Her hands were laced behind her head. She looked at his brown face and smiled. His long hair hung forward, his brown eyes looked smouldering and withdrawn. His mouth was stern and she liked that because it went with his eyes so that both surprised you with laughter.

They made love while the setting sun poured through the flat, in one side and out the other; until it sank and the sky turned from green to freezing cobalt blue and then black.

Suddenly she said, '*Now!* With you inside me, promise about Micky again,' and she wound her arms and legs around him and opened her mouth and kissed him. She gave herself up to him with desperate completeness, quite different from before. He lifted his face from hers to look at her. He saw that her expression was fierce, as though she was trying with her whole self to wring committal from him. He tried in this relationship to use the sense of oneness to penetrate and assess her. She knew this and wanted to be penetrated and assured.

'Believe me—help me,' she said. 'Promise to help me. Get Micky back—say it! Go on, say it!' She moved harder. 'Go on, say "I promise I'll do *everything* to help you with Micky".' She saw his pupils contract. 'Say it,' she gasped. And she held back, using it to test for belief, for reality, using also his own approaching orgasm to penetrate beyond speculation into certainty. But eventually she could hold back no longer, so she wrenched herself away from him, swearing.

'Christ, don't you know, don't you know. Don't you know when I'm being true?'

He had rolled quickly out of bed. He saw that his hands were shaking. He walked about among the Chippendale. She looked at him from the bed.

'Go to hell,' she shouted.

Suddenly he yelled at her, 'It's *impossible*. It doesn't *work*.'

She leapt out of bed and stood quivering in front of him.

'It must work. You *must* know by feel that I'd give myself, sex, sight, life, *completely*, relinquish *anything*, just so's to be sure of you being on my side.'

'Why?'

'Because—I need you.'

'Balls,' he said. 'You mean because Dimitri told you to—told you to get me hooked on helping you with Micky, or else Micky would get the chop.'

'No, no, no,' she moaned.

'And you moan on like that because if I don't fall for it you'll get the chop yourself, so where are we?'

'In hell—I'm in hell.' She was standing in front of him, close.

She shuddered, put her forehead on his shoulder and he felt her warm tears upon his skin. He put his arms round her, comforting her. At last he said, 'Let's eat.' She moved over with him to the kitchen. He pointed to a list inside the deep freeze. '*Quenelles de brochet*—jugged hare—onion soup—wild duck— *Coq au vin*.'

'All frozen food.'

'I cooked them, then froze them.'

'You?'

'Mmmm.'

They were safe here. They hadn't finished making love; she was hungry. She wanted more sex. She wanted desperately to be allowed to live—eat—make love—enjoy it.

'*Quenelles*,' she said.

'And the wild duck,' he added.

'Why?'

He looked at her; and then past her at the wild sky.

He took the packages out, put them to thaw and turned off

113

the oven. He got dressing-gowns for them, opened a bottle of champagne and went to the fire and lit it.

For a long time they did not speak.

'What's Dimitri Zoubovitch like?'

'He goes to bed with his pants on.'

'How long have they had Micky?' he shot at her.

'Eighteen months.'

'How did they get him?'

'Mother's Russian, we went there to see Grandpa, Micky too. Then Michael was killed and I rushed back.'

'How did you hear he was killed?'

'Dimitri appeared and said so.'

'Had you met him before?'

'Er—no.' She stopped.

'How did he appear—why?'

'He was a friend of Mother's.'

'What's his background?'

'Science, I think.'

'Was his father a scientist?'

'No, a groom I believe.'

'Who to?'

She hesitated. 'Don't know—a prince, I believe. But formerly they all called themselves princes—ridiculous.'

He wondered what was the relationship between Dimitri and Teresa's mother and who the prince was.

'Your grandfather is Prince Gagarin,' he said.

'Yes.'

'Was Dimitri's father his groom?'

'No idea.'

'I think you know.'

'Oh.'

'Why don't you want me to know?'

She was sitting on the rug in front of the fire. Her hair hung forward, dividing itself round the line of her chin. Her beauty seemed to Thorne unending and her personality unfathomable, her character indomitable, her resources infinite. He cast his mind around to consider other women; they seemed like chaff.

'Teresa, tell me everything you know. Neither of us can lose.'

'All right. Grandfather's about eighty. He had a groom called

114

Zoubovitch, who had a pretty wife. Grandfather had a child by her, the child is Dimitri. Dimitri used to sleep with Mother. Maybe he still does.'

'Why?'

'Yes, there is some secret and I don't know what it is, but I don't trust my mother. Dimitri was at Ashkabad when Michael got killed. His old mother still lives there, looking after Grandpa. I rushed back to Holland. Mother was supposed to follow with Micky. She didn't. Then Dimitri turned up in Holland, and it all started.'

'What d'you do for him?'

'Just lie there—he's rotten.'

'Besides that?'

'I keep in touch with Michael's friends, Dimitri's mad about *trends*—the swinging people and all that bit, you know; it makes sense now, since you told me about Michael.'

Thorne nodded, thinking this over as he drank champagne. Then he switched on his radio link and went over the whole story with his alter ego.

Teresa sat watching him. She looked at the nape of his neck as he bent his head attentively. Sometimes the tendons there jerked taut under the skin. His hands were rather battered, but the fingertips and nails were perfect and surprisingly delicate. She remembered them making love to her and she thought that they seemed to carry knowledge and skill and desire in themselves. She looked at the spread and depth of his shoulders, and the memory of them in her hands reminded her of how much bigger and more powerful he was in fact than he appeared. She listened to him talking for a while. She moved closer so that she could listen.

The radio said, 'What she told you about Dimitri and all that might be true or it might not.'

'D'you think her mother is in on it?'

'Ask her.'

Teresa said desperately, 'I don't *know*—that's what I don't know—I don't know who I can trust any more anywhere.'

'Me, you can trust me,' Thorne said.

'No, you can't,' said the radio, 'he'd shop you if it was important. Just as you'd shop him under certain circumstances.'

115

After a pause it went on, 'Maybe her mother is an agent—maybe she is too. You know the length they'll go to, to plant some one successfully—look at that poor sod they set up for her to shoot. Nobody would ever use her for a job like the one she was on if she's what she says she is; it's mad.'

'There was nobody else,' Teresa said. 'Really. Also there was Middachten handy.'

Thorne said to the radio, 'I have senses that you don't have, you said so. And I think she's on the level.'

'For God's sake, man, on whose level? What level? Look, you're the king pin Isoworg agent at the moment. You've won Hank and hold Towers, so you have the key to Pierre's secret. You've caused mayhem. You're dynamite. And here you are falling in love with her, saying she's been duped, that she's on the level. Has she *acted* like a dupe since you've known her? Do you *like* dupes? You know damn well the only reason you're carrying on like this is because she's an original—a blade—a pretty, brave, compassionate, amusing, steely, demanding *eminence grise*, and she fascinates you.'

Teresa and Thorne looked at each other, hearing this. He shrugged. Then he stood up. He went over to the window. The wind blew icily. London was covered in withering blobs of snow, with wet depressing slates and roads between them. He hung the radio round his neck and went on talking to it as he turned back from the window to the kitchen. He put the things in the oven and some plates as well to heat up.

He was saying, 'Where's the brain laundry and that turd, Towers?'

'15 Montague Street, home of Dr. Bonarjee, hypnotist.'

'I'll be there in an hour. Monitor my 'phone when I'm gone.'

'I already do.'

'Now then, what about Hank?'

'Big stuff, very big stuff.' The tone of the voice excited Thorne.

'How big? Tell me.'

'The boffins are freaking out, man—freaking out all over. When we publish this information, we'll also set out what I explained to you about the complications and the part that we could play. It'll be very carefully worded—the effect should be very interesting indeed.'

116

'When will it go out?'

'We'll be printing tomorrow, so a couple of days. But then the really big question comes. Is there a big plant somewhere which has already progressed a long way beyond all others in the direction Hank's discovery points? If there is, where is it? Who does it belong to?'

'And that's what Towers knows?'

'Yeah.'

'Hell, the oven's too hot.'

'Wild duck ought to be at one hundred and fifty degrees.'

'How d'you know I chose the duck?'

'Oh, for Christ's sake, I know what you've got in the fridge, you told me, and I knew you'd choose the wild duck because you're like that, and one hundred and fifty degrees is the setting for it.'

Thorne chuckled.

'Right now,' said the voice, 'you're about the most wanted person I can think of, so watch it when you go to Montague Street.'

'Okay. Have I got time for a shave and a shower before the duck is done?'

'Yes.' It switched off.

Thorne shaved, showered, dressed, and scarcely spoke to Teresa. He was absorbed in the possibilities his voice had triggered in his mind. They ate in silence, and finally he was ready. He said, 'Bolt the door when I'm gone, if you feel like it.' He was looking through the spy hole on to the landing.

'Aren't you going to say goodbye?'

He didn't answer.

'What have I done?'

'For God's sake, what's *anybody* done?' He opened the door and went out.

When he reached the hall of the flats, old Buzzacott came bustling out for a chat about the weather. Thorne could see a hard-looking character walking busily past on the other side of the street. He chatted to Buzzacott for a few moments, and then left by the service entrance. A mini driven by a girl with her skirt up round her waist and a huge dolly bag in the back was just about to pull away from the kerb. She caught his look at

117

her legs, he opened the door.

'Let's drive right into Buckingham Palace.'

Her eyes sparkled. 'Let's do that thing.'

She let up the clutch, nearly breaking his neck. 'Sorry.'

She turned round a couple of corners, babbling away about his cool, until he jumped out and shot down the steps of the underground.

Chapter Ten

Dr. Bonarjee talked as fast as a print out from a computer, in staccato phrases.

'Not beating about the bush, Mr. Thorne, I'm here hypnotist, shallow pentathol there in that jolly old syringe, so to say. Mr. Towers just nicely, thank you very much. You're the missing link, no offence, corner stone, detonator, catalyst, what you will. Let's go.'

'He'll be glad when it's over,' Thorne said cryptically.

'By golly, yes—oh yes—never know anything about it neither.'

'Either.'

'Eh?'

'Skip it.'

'I've been right through his life with him—all piped away to Isoworg—know him inside out. Oh very good. Yes. Come along.'

He took Thorne into the other room. Towers was strapped into something resembling a dentist's chair, apparently asleep.

Bonarjee changed gear; his manner was now very cool and authoritative as he began his routine with Towers. After a time he said, 'You will feel no pain in your hand,' and he drove a needle in and out of the skin adroitly as though he were tacking a hem.

He went on, 'I have a friend here,' with a nod and a wink to Thorne. 'He is sitting behind you, he is your friend too, your friend. You want to tell him something, he will ask you and you will tell him the truth.'

Thorne began to speak quietly, taking Towers through the events of the evening at Lunar Mews; got him to describe how he had seen Pierre come up out of the basement and stagger into the 'phone box. He got him to recount how he had gone into the 'phone box and taken the piece of paper from Pierre.

He said, 'On it was written "Eleven T.T.," that's the Eleven Town Trip, isn't it? What was the remainder?'

And Towers said, 'Eleven T.T. and then repeated the letters: gdnrddeuxc&hydxm.'

Thorne said, 'Thank you,' and he went out. Bonarjee began talking to Towers. Thorne shut the door. He switched on his little radio and said, 'What's all that mean?'

'It's it—it's it,' the voice almost shouted, and it excited Thorne.

'It's what?' he asked sharply.

'Pierre says it's a piece of cake.'

'Pierre's dead.'

'Only from your point of view. It's like I said, one country, one team *was* going Hank's way—all I can add is that the plant's vast. It's the most closely guarded secret I know of, it will probably be able to put Hank's discovery into action in a very short time indeed.'

'D'you know where it is?'

'Yes.'

'Where?'

'Can't tell you that ...'

'... but you said—'

'... I'd always tell—'

'... the truth except—'

'... about people's identity—'

'... in case—oh, I see ...'

'... exactly; in case they got you in and washed you like we did Towers. Same now. They'll know you washed Towers and boy, will they be after you.'

'So I get lost?'

'Correct. But man, oh man, is this big stuff. This one country will get free power in a few months. We're going to hammer this in the world press (though of course we won't say which country)—point out the dangers—point out how only a very special organisation could cope with the problem. Then, when the time is right—when they've solved the problem—you'll go in, get the final details and we'll give them to the world.'

120

'But the world will still be years behind.'

'Not that far. We'll have been coaching the various techniques along tactfully in various places as well as we can, and then your information, when you get it, will contain all the technical engineering data, plus the scientific data, necessary to build a duplicate plant. The importance of the Isoworg method will be indisputable. The effectiveness of Isoworg as a means of inter-national, or rather supranational, dealings is already becoming apparent.'

Thorne let these big ideas run round inside his head, thinking how happy this evidently made his alter ego—if, that is, it were capable of happiness. Then he said, 'What about Teresa?'

'I took her out.'

'What?'

'I 'phoned her for you, sent a chopper to land on the roof, took her to the lab. There'll be ructions for you about the chopper landing on your roof.'

'The lab?'

'It's very safe. You'll see if you go there.' There was an infinitesimal pause, and then the voice added, 'I like Teresa.'

Thorne didn't answer, he was perplexed. Finally he said, 'How long must I wait?'

'God knows—weeks—months—till it's time to jump. Go to ground, get lost, like you said.' The voice clicked off.

Bonarjee came in, chattering vociferously. Thorne said sourly, 'D'you know what you sound like?'

'No, my man, what?'

'Overtalk.'

'What's that?'

'Skip it. How are you going to deal with Towers?'

'Easy—oh easy as nothing. I can talk him away any time I like.'

'Yes, but then what will he do?'

'He'll be damn surprised, I tell you—oh my God, yes. Look, see here. Pocket tape recorder. It's got my voice going through the waking up routine. I take this wallah on to Hampstead Heath when it's dark, sit him down under a tree, switch on the recorder, and bugger off. He wakes up, damn cold, ho-ho.'

'I wonder if it'd be better to kill him.'

121

'Probably.'

Thorne grunted and picked up the 'phone. He ordered a taxi and waited. Bonarjee went on jabbering about how clever he was. Thorne wondered what he was going to do. There was nothing for him to do. All the racing, crazy urgency had suddenly stopped. He felt sick. The taxi came and he told the driver to drive him round Hyde Park.

The snow lay about in deep patches. But it was heavy and slumped down in the hollows wetly. The Serpentine was still frozen but was already covered in puddles. His feet grew cold, he became more and more depressed. He knew he was subject to depression—recognised the familiar temptation to relish it and slide deeper into a black mood, as though some kind of casque of melancholy pressed upon his skull. He knew that this was a part of his character, yet he still couldn't do anything about it. He knew the fits of depression always took some particular form and wondered what form this one would take. Finally he told the taxi driver to go to Kensington and stopped at random at a small hotel.

The room was cheap and ugly and it smelt. He sat in a chair.

The next morning he read in the paper, 'Doorman brutally killed.' He read on. Buzzacott's name had been Oliver; he had left a wife and two children. He was at a loss—the depression deepened. Finally he went out and had his hair cut; bought strange clothes, heavy glasses; changed his walk.

That night he spoke to his alter ego. It was bubbling with excitement about Hank's papers which had been despatched all over the world. He switched it off.

During the next few days he bought all the papers, listened to the radio, joined the other people in the T.V. lounge. Reactions were chaotic. As his alter ego had said already in Bonarjee's flat, the importance of Isoworg as a supranational body was loudly recognised. Students all over the world were jumping on this band waggon before you could say 'pot'. At last they had something to join and wanted to join it. This coloured the judgment of otherwise reasonable journals, caused them to fall back on the old clichés that idealism is commendable but impractical, that computers are inhuman and dictatorial. This found fertile ground among the telly viewers, who liked to seem shrewd and mature to the others there.

On Friday he read that Bonarjee's mutilated body had been taken from the Thames. On Sunday one of the weeklies said, 'Competition has been man's driving force from the cave to the moon. We are indoctrinated with it from the first moment that we try to walk like Daddy or keep up with the Joneses. It is impossible to imagine, far less predict, the effect of removing the competitive stimulus from the struggle for knowledge.' He wondered what the hell the writer thought he was talking about.

The Times said cautiously, 'From the varied reactions of world opinion it may be possible to draw one conclusion; Isoworg is, potentially, an instrument for change.'

Hooray, muttered Thorne and turned the page. He was confronted with a photograph of the woman doctor who had examined and loved him. She had been tortured to death. He flung the papers down. He went up to his room hating himself, life, Isoworg, everything. He tried to think of something to do. There was nothing to do. He sat on the chair and did nothing.

During the days that followed he slipped deeper and deeper into depression. It pressed down upon his mind, numbing him. He began to get the feeling that the enemy was everywhere all around him, and would kill or destroy everything that he touched —Oliver Buzzacott, the doctor, Bonarjee—and that he was the instrument of their destruction.

He hadn't shaved. His clothes were crumpled and he found he hated to eat regularly. He felt as though he was some kind of monster, greedy and senseless, that had to be fed with people, their lives, their happiness.

He lapsed into the habit of hour-long conversations with his alter ego, listening to his own cool reason, the reasoned patience. He felt it would drive him mad. And all the time the memory of Teresa haunted him, now true, now false, now his lover, now his betrayer. At last he could stand it no longer and knew that he must go and see her.

He knew his own car would be watched, so he rang a friend who dealt in high performance cars, and spoke to him for a little while, asking for a slight modification. When the car arrived at his hotel he looked to see that the modification had been made. He found a small switch had been loosely taped to the steering column. He checked and found that it worked exactly as he had prescribed. Half-an-hour later he was moving down the M.1., working the Jensen Ferguson Formula up to its top speed of about one hundred and forty.

At Hemel Hempstead he turned off to find the village of Potten End and the location of the Isoworg lab. He found an airfield disused since the war, and saw that it had been refurbished. The hangars had Isoworg printed on them, as did a jump-jet gleaming outside.

He was directed to a blockhouse on the other side of the airfield.

When he got to the door, it opened automatically. He found himself in a short passage. The door shut behind him. In front were three doors. One had a lighted sign saying, 'Enter here.' He did so. Two men in white jackets had him covered.

'Up.'

He put them up. One man took his gun, frisked him and put the gun in a box.

'Undress,' said one of the men.

He did so. His clothes were put tidily in the box with his gun. His identity was flashed through the circuit. He was probed and had his teeth examined for any kind of gadget that could harm personnel or equipment. He was given yellow cotton trousers, yellow shirt and soft shoes, a note pad, biro, camera, and mini tape recorder.

'What for?'

'Spies,' said one of the men, bored.

Thorne left the cubicle and took the lift downstairs. When he got out he found himself in a minute reception room. The receptionist was pretty. A notice on her desk said that her name was Linda Jowitt. She said, 'Sorry about all that mallarky. It's just so that nobody can try to sabotage us. From now on you can do exactly as you like in this place, anything at all.'

So he leaned over and kissed her.

'You should shave.'

'I know.'

'Do you want a guide?'

'Yes, you.'

'Sorry, I'm receptionist today. Here—' She pushed towards

124

him a list of people with their various qualifications. At the bottom, under the heading, 'General P.R.', there were three names, and one of them was Teresa Stanley.

'I'll have her.'

'You already have,' Linda said quickly.

'Did she tell you?' he asked incredulously.

'No, you did.'

'Me? Oh, I see what you mean. Good God, will it tell?'

'If it wants to, if it thinks it's okay.'

He looked baffled. If she knew this sort of thing, what didn't she know? How much did each member know about the other? His mind raced at the possibility.

He opened his radio circuit. 'Have you done Teresa like I was done at Carter Hill?'

'She wouldn't.'

'Why?'

'Why do *you* think?'

'Damn.'

'Yes.'

He shrugged. 'I want to know about Linda Jowitt.'

'You must be with her.'

'Yes.'

'You want to know how many men she's been to bed with?'

'Nine,' said Linda quickly.

'I think she said nine,' said the radio. 'More probably two.'

Thorne switched off. 'Like to make it three or ten?' he asked politely.

'Any time,' said Linda.

'I'm going to shave.'

'There,' Linda said pointing.

For no reason and quite abruptly the helmet of gloom lifted.

When he came back, there stood Teresa. She put her arms round his neck and kissed him.

'You knew it was me?' he said.

'I told her,' Linda said.

'Oh yes, of course,' and he wondered who else might be visiting the lab and whether they too would know of his arrival; and he wondered what action might be taken and whether any-one would be sent in to follow him or be waiting for him when

125

he left. The idea of complete non-secrecy which existed and was fostered in this place was still alien to him.

Teresa said, 'Thank you for getting me in here.'

'Me?'

'Yes.'

'When?'

'When you rang me up.' She looked puzzled.

'Oh yes,' he said.

'What do you want to see?'

'The whole thing.'

She moved away in front of him, her skirt swaying. They went through a door into a gallery. The gallery ran round a large central room that contained some big appliances.

'You don't know what it's all for, do you?' he said.

'Not really.' She pointed to a wall telephone. 'There's that. Or one of the scientists will take you round and give you a complete file to take away.'

'You're more talkative.'

'I like it here. I'm a prisoner. Dimitri will realise that, so Micky's safe too.'

'Any Russians here?'

'Lots.'

'Where?'

'Where the information comes in.'

'Why? We mail it to them anyway.'

She chuckled. 'Yesterday one of them told us we'd left one of their top secret places off the list—said it by mistake.'

'What happened?'

'They laughed. Then they had a row.'

They walked on.

She showed him all over the lab and finally he said, 'Let's go and see Hank.'

She went in front of him down a narrow pasage. He looked at her hair and at the way her slim silky legs swung from the hips. He thought of her hot mouth on the Zuider Zee and of the taste of her in bed. He felt that his mistrust in the middle of their affair had been like the suspicion in the middle of a gourmet meal that perhaps one is being poisoned.

She said, 'I talked to your alter ego.'

'Oh?'

She didn't turn round but went on, 'Ask it about me—all about me.'

'Why?'

'Just do.'

'It likes you.'

'Yes, I know.'

He thought that, since it and he were one, she could perhaps 'seduce' it. The whole range of possibilities inherent in the alter ego situation had suddenly taken a new turn into quite unmapped areas. As these ideas poured brightly into his mind, he said suddenly, 'If we can all talk to each other's alter ego, the possibilities are amazing. It'd be total communication. We'd be out of the old suspicious rut of human relationships. It'd be a renaissance for the soul, a transmogrification of destiny—follow that for a phrase,' he said joyfully. He was so exuberant that he took her in his arms and put his hand up her skirt.

She said, 'Do you want to here, on the floor in the passage?'

'Yes.'

'So do I—I'm like that—I'm your kind of girl. Remember that—always,' and she pushed him firmly away and walked on. He realised all the things that he had told in bed to the girl at Carter Hill were available through his alter ego to Teresa—anyone—if the alter ego chose to tell, and then he realised that it would choose to tell exactly as he would. The implications kept his mind busy as they walked on.

Finally they came to Hank's room. Thorne looked at the time. He'd been there nearly two hours. His arrival would certainly have been noted and reported. He wondered how soon he would be able to identify a tail.

Teresa opened the door and Hank looked up. He had changed. He came forward, grinning and holding out his hand. He still had a dressing on his nose, where plastic surgery had evidently been done.

'Goddam, Thorne, it's good to see you.'

He was more relaxed, seeming to have acquired some humour, some humanity, some ease.

'Christ,' Thorne said suddenly. 'You were a virgin and now you're not.'

'Christine, of course!' Teresa said giggling.

Hank looked at her and blushed and stamped his foot, then swore at length in Dutch. 'It is this place, you understand. It is permissive.'

'You look happier.'

'This is a happy place.'

The door opened and a girl assistant came in. Christine's hair was curly and yellow, almost like a Dutch national headdress. Her eyes were bright blue, her legs as taut and promising as her figure.

'Wil je en lekkere kopje koffee hebben?'

'Ja graag,' Teresa said sitting on a table.

Hank said, 'I have been given already Christine to help me.'

And Christine looked pleased with the help she was so obviously suited to give.

'I'll get the coffee,' she said.

Hank said excitedly, 'Already also I have had a meeting with Professor Harris—*me* talking to Harris—fantastic.'

He was standing in the little room with his arms behind his back, leaning forward, springing as always from one foot sideways to the other, flicking his feet up behind him at each stride.

'And already the thunder starts,' he said.

'What thunder?' said Thorne puzzled.

'The results from publishing my work,' said Hank. 'People will come here from the whole world, you understand, to find out...'

The door opened and a huge Chinese stood squarely there in his yellow suit. Thorne just had time to marvel at the fact that anybody had had a yellow suit ready on hand big enough for a giant of his proportions, when he opened his mouth and his teeth seemed to burst out from behind his lips.

'Dr. van Hockeren, please.'

'Yes?' Hank said, still springing from one foot to the other.

'You show me your papers?' said the Chinese.

Hank pointed to the filing cabinet, still practising his skating. 'Fantastic,' he said to Thorne. 'In a few weeks we will have built a small prototype of the appliance.'

The Chinese, turned on the recorder he had been given, pointed

128

it towards the others and started rummaging in the filing cabinet.

Thorne drew their attention to the recorder and said blandly, 'Of course, one secret in this place that *is* a secret is the intelligence side of it.'

'What d'you mean?' asked Hank.

'Surreptitiously the Chinese directed the recorder more accurately at Thorne.

'Well, all that stuff about the assassination of Mao Tse-tung.'

'What had he done?' Teresa asked.

'He was caught red-handed by a purity guard smoking Lucky Strike, listening to the Beatles and reading *Lolita*.'

Christine came back with the coffee. Thorne politely took a cup over and offered it to the Chinese. He saw that he was looking at Hank's papers upside down.

'What is plasma?' Thorne asked him. 'I'm not a physicist.'

'Ionised super-heated gas,' he replied, his Chinese intonation making it sound as though he had learned it like a parrot.

'That's a kind of iron suppository fart,' suggested Thorne helpfully, and the Chinese nodded cunningly.

'What's muon meson injection?' Thorne asked him.

The Chinese drank. 'Very good coffee,' he said.

Thorne smiled and leaned a little closer to look at the papers, so that he touched the man. He was like granite. His fingers made the cup look like a thimble.

There was an instant's pause. But it was enough and Thorne moved away from the man with the killer hands, knowing who would follow him out.

So the alter ego was right. They were watching to see when he'd jump. He was angry. Nobody followed Thorne. Thorne was nobody's prey. The anger made him cold. It spread through him, forcing out all other considerations.

'See you again, Hank,' he suddenly said, and left.

Teresa, amazed, followed him, as did the Chinese. The anger, at the affront of being followed, made his body feel lazy with implacability.

In the hall by the lift he stopped to say goodbye to Teresa. They looked into each other's eyes but there was no communication. He seemed to her to be withdrawing into a person quite unfamiliar to her—to be a stranger again. Sorrowfully he reached

129

out and touched her hand. She held his fingers for a second. Then he got into the lift and went back to the changing room. The Chinese had preceded him.

Thorne was looking forward to getting outside. He had no plan. He felt on top of the world. He'd fix the bloody Chinese properly. As he walked towards the Jensen F.F. he saw the familiar teeth bristling behind the wheel of a Mercedes S.L. 300. He waved. The mouth stretched a little wider, so that a few more teeth slid into view, as though something monstrous was being born. Thorne smiled grimly and drove off. He drove in a normal manner for about half-an-hour, heading for a stretch of road where he had once nearly killed himself. As he neared it, he drove faster and faster. He found that the Chinese, determined not to lose him, was in fact getting a little closer on each corner. He felt certain he was doing this by watching the Jensen's brake lights and then braking fractionally later. Nothing could suit him better. Then he turned sharp left on to the chosen piece of road.

It consisted of a curving beech avenue about two miles long. At the end of it the trees of the avenue continued straight ahead, flanking a cart track, while the road itself surprisingly turned sharp left.

He took the Jensen up through second into third at one hundred and ten, and then accelerated as the curve of the avenue tightened until he could feel the car lying over on the last ounce of tyre adhesion. As the superchargers whined up to their top note at one hundred and forty, he took up the switch taped to the steering column and flicked it. It cut out his brake lights. He was now just approaching the sharp left-hander. He stamped on the disc brakes, he felt the car squat down on to the road and did a heel and toe change into third. With the fourwheel Ferguson drive the car gripped the road like a leech, cornering at a speed impossible for a conventional car. He saw in the mirror the S.L. rush madly up behind him. He touched the accelerator, swung the wheel hard left, overcooked it a bit, took to the grass, all four wheels grabbing at the ground, fought her back on to the road again and drove away.

The S.L. was in real trouble and had to take to the cart track at about one hundred. Thorne turned his head to look. The grey

Mercedes went bucketing up the track like a Dinky toy, jinking this way and that. Then it must have hit something because amazingly it suddenly shot out between two trees, and Thorne could see one of the front wheels rocket twenty feet into the air. A door burst open and the very wide, low car amazingly did not turn over but spun, and then went backwards into a hedge and stopped.

Thorne began singing the *Marseillaise* very loud. And the engine seemed to be chortling with him as he prowled away towards the M.1. He switched the brake lights on again, pleased with himself.

He didn't care who followed or watched him. They could do as they liked. Now they had his permission. Whenever he wanted to be rid of them he could. As the alter ego had said, they would simply keep tabs on him and wait till Isoworg decided it was time to jump. In the meantime he wanted to be himself, uninvolved, solitary.

He went to Switzerland to Grundlewald for the ski-ing. There were women but he didn't want women. He grew tired of the ski-lifts; of the rich who took a helicopter to the Jungfrau-Joch and skied down; of the signs saying 'keep right'. He left and went to Norway. Here he could make his way mile after mile across the snows and all the time he knew why he wanted no women but just to be alone in the snow. Because it was in snow and ice— in the pattern that the blown snow had laid upon the world— that Teresa existed for him. So one day, ski-ing there on the roof of the world, he said to his radio, 'I want Teresa ski-ing here next to me tomorrow'. And it was so.

She said, 'If Dimitri concluded I was on holiday with you— think of Micky. I'll only stay a couple of days.'

Apart from that, they did not speak of such subjects. She found that his enthusiasm was unlimited. Everything that there was to do had to be done; at once. They were towed on skis behind galloping horses, a net stretched between the traces to catch the flying snowballs. The horses had caulking on their shoes for grip.

'They look as though they're on tiptoe,' she said.

He persuaded the horsemen to give them long reins instead of acting as postillions, then they raced each other. She, being lighter, won. She wore a fur parka and would turn and smile the fierce smile and swing and crack the whip in the bright, icy air, and shout at the horse as though he was a personal friend.

They hired snow-scooters and raced each other across frozen lakes in and out of patches of reed, so that the brittle stems cracked and the brown bulrushes would suddenly be snapped down by their passage. They danced and skated, ate, drank, sang and made love, and then she said she must go back. He felt she had been snapped away out of his life like a flattened bulrush.

He drove her down to the airport in the car that he had hired. They were silent together, he was morose. In the lounge among the people he saw her head turn, just a fraction, and then turn away again. But he looked and caught the eye of a man in a grey suit. The man turned away. Thorne registered a weedy frame, thin clever face, black hair, widow's peak; and then he was swallowed up in the milling crowd.

'Who was that?'

'Who?'

'The man you looked at.'

'Thought he was Ivan, friend of Dimitri—it frightened me—but it wasn't, thank God.'

He wondered if she'd tipped them off or whether it was a coincidence or whether she'd been followed. He considered keeping her with him, rejected the idea. He scarcely spoke again and soon she went through into the departure lounge.

Spring had come to the valley. As he drove back up towards the snowy fields and the hotel, he looked at the grass and flowers appearing as though just now created for the first time in their complex beauty from the piles of featureless snow, by the sun's power. He considered what to do about the man he felt sure was Ivan. He didn't want to allow anyone secretly to follow him; he wanted to get whoever it was out into the open and force an issue of some kind, so that he would know where he was.

That day he remained in the hotel. Once he thought a very tough-looking man was eyeing him. But he was so bundled in ski clothes and a huge Norwegian sweater—so many people were tough and outdoor types and dressed the same—that it was hard to be sure of his suspicions.

The next day he got up early and returned to one of the runs that he liked the best. The track led through a forest. Here the snow lay thick on the boughs of the fir trees, making them look like a million acre Christmas card. The sun was bright, the shadows sharp. He felt fit, compact, in command of himself and the situation. He forged his way steadily up the long track through the forest towards the top of the hill. He rested when he reached the top. He thought about Teresa but he was accustomed to his suspicions and they did not weigh on his mind or produce any new ideas. He knew he hadn't been followed up here. He wondered if he had been mistaken about Ivan and about the man in the Norwegian sweater. Then he started down the run.

He was nearly at the bottom, nearly out of the forest, when the track twisted sharply and he had to go into a violent turn. As he straightened up two men raced out of the trees on either side. They flung themselves into jump christies with him sandwiched between them. He felt something strike his arm.

When he came to, he was weak and sleepy but content. He examined himself all over. He was unhurt. He searched his pockets. They were all empty. Then he felt something inside his anorak and realised it was his pencil. Presumably they had missed it and in any case a pencil wasn't much good to anybody except that this one also had a small torch at the top. He took it out and shone it round. He found that he was in a very small room with no windows. There was some old lino covering the boards, a rat-eaten mattress and cushions, a few cardboard cartons and other junk. Indeed, it seemed to be a junk-room. It smelled damp and old.

He got up and tried the door. The floorboards shifted and creaked in the old house. The door was not only locked but bolted top and bottom on the outside. It was heavy and extremely solid. He sat down again on the floor to think. The men had worn goggles and it had all happened very quickly. Nevertheless, their appearance tied up with Ivan and the big man in the Norwegian jersey. Presumably, therefore, Teresa had tipped them off—presumably.

He examined his arm where he had felt some one strike it. He realised soon enough that a compressed air injector had been used to put him out instantly. He had no way of knowing for how long. He sat and thought calmly and grimly about his predicament.

It was not long before he heard footsteps creeping down the passage. When the door opened, admitting a little dim light, he found himself looking at a pistol held by the man in the Norwegian jersey. The man looked extremely pleased with himself and, waved the gun jauntily, he said in Russian, 'Come on.'

Thorne stood up. 'Your flies are undone,' he said.

The man's eyes never left Thorne's face but he fumbled about like a schoolboy, so Thorne said, 'Christ, you'd believe anything,' and shoved past him. The man was muttering about reprisals as they walked down the passage. The walls, Thorne noticed as they passed various doorways, were exceptionally thick.

'Old barracks, is it?'

'Something like that.'

'You don't know when your flies are undone and you don't know where you are. What day is it?'

'Tuesday,' the man said involuntarily, and then added, 'Shut up,' and gave him a vicious jab in the back that made him gasp with pain. However, he had learned that it was still the same day. They passed a few doors which were open. Through one of them Thorne could see a window. All the glass was broken. He got the impression that they were one floor up and, since the light was low, it must be evening. They turned into a bigger passage and at the end of it the man opened a door and shoved him in. There was one rickety chair, a suitcase and two men standing by the window across the bottom section of which a blanket had been hung. One was Ivan the other was on crutches. He was plump, with a pudgy face and curly hair.

Before they had a chance to speak Thorne said, 'Where's Teresa?'

The man with crutches said, 'That's one of the things you're going to tell us.'

The moment he spoke Thorne recognised the voice of Dimitri. He had heard it that first night in the basement flat at Lunar Mews when Teresa had been inside splinting his leg. He remained silent, wondering how to use this. The door was locked behind him. Dimitri spoke quickly and well, hobbling about on his crutches. He ended by saying, 'Dr. Bonarjee volunteered the fact that Canton had a message, that Towers got it and repeated it to you, he even remembered most of it. You will tell us what it means.'

'I don't know.'

Dimitri smiled. 'Of course not—but when we do to you what you did to Towers, perhaps we will find out.'

'Isoworg doesn't have secrets. I'll tell you anything you ask, you know that.'

'You did get the message out of Towers?'

'Yes.'

'What was it?'

'llTT, that's the Eleven Town Trip, then gdnrddeuxc&hydxm.'

'Yes, that's what Bonarjee said—what's it mean?'

'I don't know.'

'But Isoworg knows?'

'Of course.'

'And didn't tell you?'

'No.'

'Why not?'

'In case this sort of thing happened.'

Dimitri felt in his pocket and produced Thorne's radio. 'What's this?'

'Radio link.'

'To Isoworg?'

'Yes.'

'Here—ask what it means?'

Thorne took the radio, being careful not to smile, opened the switch and said, 'Dimitri here wants to know what Pierre's message meant.'

'How the hell do you know who I am?' Dimitri asked angrily.

Thorne shrugged. 'I know lots of things,' he said, and turned up the volume.

His voice said, 'Tell him he wets his bed when he's drunk.'

'You wet your bed when you're drunk,' Thorne said quickly.

Ivan laughed and stopped abruptly. Dimitri's eyes narrowed. He looked past Thorne at the man behind him and nodded. Instantly the pistol was brought down on his shoulder, his legs

135

were kicked from under him, and before he could roll clear he'd been kicked heavily in the back. He lay there.

'Get up,' said Dimitri.

He got up slowly. Through his pain, he looked at the man with the gun measuring him up.

Ivan said quietly, 'Don't waste time.'

The radio was now talking in Russian, listing all the discreditable and contemptible things that it knew about Dimitri. Furiously Dimitri turned it off. It went on bleeping in an irritating manner. But the things it had said about Dimitri seemed to have given Ivan a new station and new importance. Going to the suitcase he said, 'I can make him tell anything he knows.'

Thorne said, 'You don't need to waste the worker's drugs. I told you I'll tell you anything.'

Ivan paid no attention, and a few moments later Thorne was held down on the floor and the injection given. Eventually Ivan talked him back to normality and the pentathol gradually began to wear off. Thorne found that they were arguing amongst themselves. Dimitri was for shooting him at once, and ordinarily he would have been obeyed. But now Ivan said, 'You want him out of the way because he knows too much about you.'

'Our orders are to shoot them at once.'

'This one might be useful. I'm not going to shoot him without confirmation from Moscow.'

'How the hell are you going to get that?' Dimitri asked nervously.

'I'm going out now to telephone.'

'Tell them I said to shoot him now as instructed.'

'Of course,' Ivan said obsequiously. He put on his coat and left.

'Did I say you were a prince's bastard under the dope?'

'Shut your bloody trap.'

'And that you went to bed with your pants on?'

Dimitri lashed out at him with the crutch, but Thorne dodged it and laughed. 'Why does Teresa work for you?' he asked.

Dimitri began shouting. 'Because she likes it! Get him out of here! Get the mother fucking son of a bitch out of here! Take him back into the lumber room till Ivan gets back, and when you've put him there come back here. I want a witness when

136

I talk to Ivan.'

When Thorne heard the key turn and the bolts go home, he put his ear to the door and listened to the footsteps receding. He knew he didn't have very long. He knew the walls were thick and soundproof. He knew he couldn't smash the door because of the noise that would go echoing down the corridor. He couldn't reach the ceiling. There were no windows. The only thing remaining was the floor, and the floor had loose boards and the house was old. There was just a chance. He rolled back the lino and felt about. He found a place where two boards had originally been butted together end to end. Over the years they had shrunk and he could get his fingers in. He pulled one up fairly easily. The noise of the nails coming out was not great. He bent them down flat to the boards. He looked at the joists. Sure enough, as in old buildings, they were larger and therefore further apart than in modern buildings. Below them was the crinkly dusty surface of the lath and plaster ceiling of the room below. He wondered what that room would be. He pulled up another board. They were old-fashioned nine inch boards, so two were enough. He very carefully propped the roll of lino against them and then, standing up, he began stamping on the lath and plaster with his heavy ski boot. It gave way at once. In a few moments the hole was big enough to look down. He shone his torch. As far as he could see the room was empty. He put his legs through, sitting on the edge of the hole. Then he grasped the joist and lowered himself down.

He had jammed the boards carefully against the lino and now, holding the joist with one hand, he could just reach far enough so that, by pushing the roll of lino back an inch, the boards were freed and he could coax them down. As soon as they were back in place, the lino rolled over them. The weight of the lino and boards on his fingers was not important. He eased his fingers to the edge of the joist, holding the torch in his teeth, and dropped. He landed on a stone floor and shone the torch round. There were racks on the walls and the room had a familiar smell. He recognised gun oil and realised the place used to be an armoury. Armouries were kept locked. He flashed his torch to the door and stepped across to it. He turned the handle and began to push. Very slowly it moved. Light flooded in. He smiled to himself grimly and looked out.

137

There was no snow but bushes and trees grew all around the derelict building. Presumably they had brought him here because the deserted barracks was a convenient place, and they were in a hurry.

He wanted to get Dimitri and beat some information out of him about Teresa, and he owed the other man a lesson for the kicks. He slipped out, found the front of the building and using the cover of the bushes made a careful examination of the surrounding country. In the slanting light of evening he could follow the road as it wound away towards a small town on the edge of the fjord about five miles away. But he could not see very much of it. He wondered how long it would be before Ivan got back. He turned his attention to the barracks. He realised the building was not really a barracks, more probably it had been a hospital taken over by the German troops during the war.

He found a side entrance, went in past the usual piles of excreta and the drawings, and moved up an iron spiral staircase. At the top he could hear voices and stopped to listen.

Dimitri was saying, 'Go down to the front and wait for Ivan. I'm going to have a little word with our friend.'

The man began to argue. The argument went on for some time, and then Thorne heard a car. He didn't wait a second longer but raced down the stairs, dashed round the building to the front and, hiding in the bushes, saw Ivan get out of the car. As soon as he was out and had entered the front door and could be reckoned to be up the stairs, Thorne slipped out of the bushes and into the car. The key was still there, the engine hot, the drive had two entrances. He was away.

He drove as fast as he could make the car move down to the town at the fjord, got his bearings and set off for his hotel. Arrived there, he raced up to his room collected passport and money, back to the car and set off for the Swedish border.

As he approached it, he kept his eyes peeled for the railway he knew must cross it at this point, and at the next town he left the car in a side street, walked to the station and took the next train over the border. He stayed on it until it reached Stockholm.

He phoned Isoworg, made arrangements for a new radio, money etc., and took the next plane which happened to be going to Paris.

138

He phoned Isoworg from there and found that his alter ego had anticipated this move. It told him to go to the Hotel des Saints Pères in St. Germain des Prés and to go to room No. 9. When he opened the door of No. 9, Linda Jowitt looked up from a copy of *Paris Match*. He remembered her behind the reception desk at the lab and said, 'D'you want to make it three? Or more?'

'I only brought you a new radio link,' Linda said sadly. 'I'm forbidden to spend one single unnecessary second with you. Goodbye.' She kissed him and left. He thought maybe his kiss was a kiss of death and sat very still in the room until he heard her drive away.

He stayed on for a few days. He went out sight-seeing to the great pictures in the Louvre, to the murk and sordity of Notre Dame. The memory of Linda made him ponder the question of her conversation with his alter ego and he called her up via their alter egos and speculated about the developments of communication in this way. Suppose, they said, in the future everyone had an alter ego from birth; what would that do to a child's growth? And if people were to talk to each other's, what would that do to human relationships? There were other even more fascinating, more immediate potentials. But swiftly the fun of pursuing this with Linda died and his mind was full of Teresa again.

All this time the effects of Isoworg's first major action built up. He watched the papers carefully. They enraged him. One day he could stand it no longer and called up his alter ego. 'Listen,' he said, 'it's just what you'd expect. Statesmen are shuffling their bloody awful clichés—starting off with words like, "While", or "Albeit". Christ, how I hate them. Listen,' and he read in an oratorical tone, ' "While committing the whole of my political integrity and, I feel safe in adding, the hopes of the vast majority of the men in the street to an unequivocal, nay fervent, prayer that this strange new phenomenon may at last point the way to a solution for the perilous problems of this troubled world; *nevertheless*, I think it only prudent to draw attention to its more damaging and dangerous implications" . . . etc.

'And then this—oh God, listen: "Albeit far from me to denigrate by a single word the noble potential, nevertheless I say,

139

if these be men of integrity, let them come out into the open ..." '

'Where,' said his voice, 'we can have a chance to destroy them.'
It went on, 'Everyone knows we've got the edge on them—knows
I know where to send you to grab the secret of the big plant
application, so's to tell the world. They're working like hell to
beat us to the punch—may even co-operate against you and do
a deal amongst themselves afterwards. I'm just waiting till the
minute's right, and it won't be long now.'

The next day Thorne hired a car and drove to Brittany.

In Brittany it was spring—spring of washed skies and boisterous
seas hurling themselves in bright rollers on to the rocks and
shattering into leaping spray. Thorne stayed there until one day
his alter ego told him to return to England and go to a house in
Wimbledon.

In Wimbledon the door was opened by an old young man
wearing an heirloom-type knickerbocker suit and slippers. His
teeth and the whites of his eyes were yellow. He said, 'Come in,
young fellow. Care for a gin?'

'No thanks.'

'Don't mind if I do, I suppose?'

'No.'

And Knickerbockers poured gin into a glass, diluted it with
about a pint of water and shuffled about.

The living room was long, low, heavily curtained, book-lined,
shambolic, busy. Lying about were felt boots, photographs of
South Russia, pipe ash, cigarette ash, dirty glasses. Pages torn
from books and marked in red pencil were pinned to the walls and
mantlepiece. Books were piled on the floor. There was a beagle,
lying with its hind legs turned back flat on the carpet. The man
moved in and out of the debris like a gentle old rat who knows
his maze.

The first thing he said was, 'Know why you're here?'

'No.'

'Ask your what-not.'

Thorne opened the link. 'Well?' he said. 'I'm at Wimbers—now
what?'

'Okay. I'll tell you.'

'About bloody time. Gdnrddeuxc&hydxm, right?'

'Mmm. Pierre says group them like this. Gdn. rd.'

140

'What's that mean?'

'Golden Road, and for Pierre that means Samarkand.'

'How far's Samarkand ...' Thorne interrupted.

'... from Ashkabad?' His alter ego completed his thought, and added, 'Five hundred and twelve miles by rail.'

'Right, Samarkand.'

'Deuxc gets grouped to deu xc means Deuterium ex sea, hyd x m means hydro electrical power ex mountains.'

'Big deal.'

'Well, listen. It was exactly as I guessed. There is a big plant which is proceeding in the same direction as that in which Hank made his breakthrough. It's near Samarkand. It's fed with Deuterium from the plant at Krasnovodsk on the Caspian and with huge quantities of electricity from the enormous hydro-electrical installation in the mountains above Samarkand. That's why the Russians wanted Hank so badly. Of course, they got all his secret stuff from us, just like everyone else, though they didn't realise that they would beforehand. Anyway, they clamped down the tightest security seal that's ever been heard of even in Russia. Man, oh man, do they know what kind of a lead this'll give 'em in world economy. Now I've got two operators there, Jakov and his daughter, Natasha. They say they know very little, but from straws in the wind they think a fusion reaction has been sustained and electricity generated, but they only think so. However, that is the crucial thing. They say that now is the time for you to go.'

'And what's the brief?'

'The brief is that this time the information you get has got to be complete. It isn't the physics of it, the theory of it, it's the technology, how to build an appliance that will work, that is important. So you've got to get information so complete that other countries could, in fact, build a plant and build it quickly. If it isn't complete, the situation would be difficult to predict, even for me, and I'm good at making predictions where thousands of factors are involved. You see, if you try and fail, Russia will forge ahead and have *exactly* the weapon a communist country most dearly wants, namely a weapon to wreck the economies of a capitalist world. It's God's gift. On the other hand, all the secret services will know where you have been, so they'll be after

141

it. They might try to sabotage it or even to bomb it. And you can think of the consequences of that. Whereas if you do your job properly and we publish your findings then other countries could build a plant in a reasonable time and so the danger of Russia having this economic weapon and the danger of somebody being tempted to bomb it would be much less. Incidentally, the plant is inside a mountain. They may have a tail on you and let you lead them to it and try to beat you to the snoop or grab you afterwards. They may even co-operate, like I said earlier on, in doing this and then do a deal or a double-deal with each other afterwards.'

'Christ, what a hornet's nest!'

'Yes.'

'You'll be briefed where you are. Don't go out. When you're ready and I'm ready, you'll jump. It won't be long.' And the link went dead.

Thorne was already more or less bilingual in Russian and during the next few days he practised the local accent with the man in the knickerbockers and imbibed information about the Samarkand area.

During the briefings Knickerbockers would switch on a tape recorder and then shuffle about his maze, drinking gin diluted in pints of water. He talked fast and indistinctly about the city, the surroundings, people, jobs, way of life, and the nomadic Towbitz.

'Ride like bloody centaurs, I tell you. Tough as blazes. They even play Baskashi if they get the excuse.'

'What's that?'

'Dates from the time of Genghis Khan.' He poured more gin and padded about the room, telling of this hell-raising, primitive contest between tribes of the horsemen he admired and in a strange way loved as well. Then he went on to speak of their fierce independence and of how they kept it by doing certain tasks for the government. He spoke tersely about their formidable prowess with women.

'Maybe s'thing to do with th'height they've developed at— radiation of the hormones or so'thing,' gabbled Knickerbockers, shuffling about the room. They never bloody well stop—got cocks like cabers—local women have a special attitude to 'em—

reminds me of Greek myth. Privilege to be had by some God chap bundlin' down from the heights of Olympus—if you can stand it—kind of arsey-turvey kudos if you can—see what I mean? See? Young birds'll dare each other even. Oh yes, and about local loyalties to the Kremlin, better explain how that goes, its cockeyed.' And he went on punching out advice, names, people, places. And each night Thorne played back the tape, poured over maps, memorising the information, the surrounding terrain, escape routes, communications, customs, formalities.

One day Knickerbockers produced a small, fly-blown menu card. It belonged to a restaurant in Samarkand called in Russian, 'The Cavern'. He put some brown oil paint on Thorne's thumb and after a few experiments pressed the thumb print on to the menu.

'A girl called Natash'll tout for you with this in the bazaar every day at twelve-thirty as soon as she gets the word. Put this in your left lapel.' He gave him an ordinary pin.

His cover story was prepared. He would be Piotr Feodossiev, Soviet adviser in agricultural pesticides to the Persian government, now returning from Teheran. He would have two huge wooden boxes with compartments containing his 'insecticide samples' and an atomiser, for demonstration purposes.

Two pills were inserted beneath the skin under his arm, one an emetic, the other an evacuant. He was given a camera, microfilm and other accessories with Russian markings on them, and practised their use. He was given a small capsule in two halves, and an adhesive to stick them together after he had put the microfilm inside.

His papers were ready. He had been stained brown and sunlamped, and then one day he left Wimbledon and a car took him to the airfield at Potten End. The jet landed him near Teheran. He crossed the frontier at Ashkabad.

Having passed through the frontier control, he stood for a moment looking at the featureless modern buildings. In his head was the address of Teresa's mother. He wondered in which direction it lay; wondered about Teresa, where she was, what she was doing at that moment.

In almost every direction the land stretched away for ever like the sky. Being an islander the feeling dwarfed him. Where was

Teresa? Where was he? They were lost; continents and lies had lost them to each other; he turned and asked the porter who had his wooden cases where to catch the train to Samarkand.

Chapter Eleven

When he got to Samarkand, he looked with distaste at the squat skyscrapers, from which blank windows gazed in rows and tiers. Between these monuments he saw proletarian gardens. Plants, bushes, flower beds had all been chosen and combined, arranged and set out so as to achieve a uniform proletarian ugliness. Where there were no gardens and no skscrapers, there were slums. He headed towards them and found an ancient, creaky hotel and took a room. An old man helped him upstairs with his boxes, dumped them heavily on the gritty floor and went away. The ceiling rafters had rosettes carved in the wood. The wooden stairs leading down were narrow and uneven, and the smells coming in through the window were the only nice things about the place. Animal dung, garbage and diarrhoea, smell the same all over the world and are reassuring.

The next morning he went to the bazaar wearing the small pin in his lapel. The bazaar was cold, bright, windy, full of movement, shouting people, animals and flapping merchandise. Old crones sat with braziers under their skirts. A teenager shaved the head of a kneeling client. Men passed him carrying bales of skins slung on poles between their shoulders. Camels grunted and cried. Yaks, with gigantic loads swaying on their backs, were led about by women with bare feet. Up on top of the loads he saw a chicken or a child, tied down.

Through it all two influences threaded and crossed. One was the suited cosmopolitan Russian, and the other was the tribesmen. The tribesmen wore baggy trousers and soft boots, slouchy as a cavalier's but made from a patchwork of coloured leather. They wore sheepskin jackets with the long wool hanging in crimping rats tails, and sashes with knives or swords or whips stuck in them. Some wore crimson blouses with high necks, and most had furry caps above their hawky faces with the wild, wild eyes. They came from a world of movement, horses, camps, high altitudes and bitter winds, where the air is so clear that a mountain twenty-five miles away looks as though you could walk up it in a morning. The spirit that can survive such humbling blazes in the eyes.

Thorne walked amongst them. He enjoyed the movement and the sharp air filling his lungs. He smelled the smells, dodged the yaks and camels and loved every moment as a good axeman loves the moment when, stripped and chilly, he squares up to a great tree with a sharp axe.

Sometimes he caught the eye of a tribesman and grinned. Their responding grins were sudden and pleased as though, within Thorne's exterior, which they despised and feared, they had suddenly recognised something worthy and therefore amazing.

Then another pair of eyes caught him and darted to the pin. She was cheeky and swift. Her face was not very weather-beaten. She was touting for a restaurant. She moved in and out of the stalls flourishing a menu, praising the food. Her skirt hung in pleats from hips that switched from side to side as she walked with a springy step, running two paces, sauntering three. And her suppleness was like a gymnast's who likes movement for its own sake.

The face that she turned to him was high cheek-boned, her eyes shone; her mouth was only just not laughing.

'Kebab, saffron rice. Very cheap, sir.'

She gave him the menu with the thumb print on it and with a flirtatious look over her shoulder she switched away. He moved past a stall selling root vegetables, damp and earthy. He felt them, looked disdainful and moved on. With his earthy thumb he made an impression next to the original and caught up with the girl.

'Excuse please, this menu. Between what hours?' he asked.

She looked at it, comparing the thumb prints carefully.

'Now,' she said, 'you will be welcome now.'

The restaurant was dingy but clean, and by the time he arrived she was already there, wiping table tops. The room was empty.

'Eating room in back,' she said perfunctorily.

He went through a fly screen, and then through a door which

146

led him into a small room furnished in the style of old Russia, poor but cosy and perfectly commonplace. In the far corner at a desk sat a man of about fifty. He had watchful eyes and a quirky mouth. He got up and came towards Thorne, who realised instantly by his walk that he was the girl's father. His handshake was so quick and violent Thorne was not surprised at his words.

'I'm Jakov. Got a drawing here—plan two—the quicker the better. Message for you. Sent about midnight. "Towers squeezed Knickerbockers".'

'How did you get a message?'

'Radio same as yours of course. They didn't want to call you in case there was anybody near you.'

He had raised the top of the desk, reached inside, taken out a map and laid it open.

'What's the message mean?' he asked.

The girl came in and locked the door behind her.

'Means they know I'm in Samarkand. That's all Knickerbockers knew. Depends on their intelligence what they can make of it.'

'They'll know you've jumped,' Jakov said. 'So it'll have to be tonight. You ready, Natasha?'

Natasha came and stood beside them. She was a girl who sweated easily and so she smelled; a healthy female smell. She said, 'Yes, I'm ready.'

Jakov shot a glance at her, then at Thorne. 'Look,' he said, irritably jabbing at the map, 'this is the plant. Vast. Cavern in mountain hollowed out. Only one entrance. Small. See how entrance lies back in this curve of mountain face, eh? Eh?'

'Yes.'

'Like a crescent, eh? Mass of barbed wire across from each point of crescent—blockhouse at gate through centre of wire.'

'How many guards?'

'Two patrolling outside the wire, two in the blockhouse. Four men do a six-hour stint. There are other security people inside, of course.'

'Where's the intake for the air conditioning?'

'There,' he pointed.

'Why are you in Isoworg?' he asked flatly.

147

'Because I'm a Taoist.'

'Tao—the way of Laû Tzu?'

Jakov looked grudgingly pleased and held Thorne's eye for a moment.

' "Do not ask whether the Principle is in this or in that, it is in all beings" ', Thorne quoted at him.

Jakov nodded. For a moment his hard eyes softened, he glanced at Natasha and he said, 'Heaven arms with pity those whom it would not see destroyed.' Then briskly he turned to Thorne and added, 'For the moment—here in this benighted country, benighted world even—it seems to me Isoworg is "The Way". Satisfied?'

'Yes.'

Jakov returned to his map but Natasha said, 'All former people weren't decadent princes like Gagarin. Real Russians were like my father.

Thorne stood very still. He felt she had been instructed to mention Gagarin. By whom? Why? 'What do you know about Gagarin?'

'Not much.'

'Where does he live?'

'Ashkabad.'

'Alone?'

'No, with his daughter and mistress and great grandson.'

Thorne's heart leaped 'with his great grandson' she had said Thorne looked from one to the other. They betrayed nothing. 'Tell me about them.'

'Why?' asked Jakov.

'It is better not to know why.'

'Very well. I met Gagarin's daughter, Carla, once only.' He paused, looking at Thorne so that the subject of that meeting might reasonably suggest itself to Thorne. Then he went on, 'Now I know nothing except that the child's mother is said to be a nymphomaniac who takes drugs and is used as a free whore for party members on duty in London and Amsterdam, and that is why it is better for the grandmother to keep the child here. So it is said.'

'Is that all?'

'Yes.'

148

After a pause, Thorne said, 'Where's the air intake?'
They bent over the map.
'Where's it visible from?'
'Only from the blockhouse.'
'Do you know the rate of flow of air through the plant?'
'Of course,' said Jakov irritably. And he explained what was to be done. The cave containing the factory was pear-shaped, the stalk being the entrance passage. To save boring through hundreds of feet of rock at the front end, one gigantic fan had been installed at the end of this stalk. It vented into natural fissures in the rock. The necessary amount of nerve gas could be introduced through the fan during a period of a quarter-of-an-hour. It would take that amount of time for the gas to spread to all parts of the factory and to become effective.
'How big is the whole plant?' Thorne asked.
'About a quarter of a mile long.'
Thorne whistled. 'What sort of plans have you got of the inside?' he asked.
'Bad. I've added what I can.'
Half-an-hour later Thorne knew as much as Jakov about the inside of the plant.
'What are they actually trying to do in there?' Natasha asked.
'Contain tremendous temperatures up to one hundred million degrees.'
'Why does the place have to be so big?'
'A magnetic field up to seventy thousand gauss requires miles of condenser banks—gigantic transformers—a space for the Tokomak, etc., magnets and windings.' His mind raced with all the knowledge he had had crammed into him in the last few weeks.
Jakov said, 'You've been well briefed. Describe it—see if it ties up.'
'The Tokomak is probably about fifty feet high, Hank thinks, and about five hundred feet across. It's shaped like a bangle, a hollow bangle.'
'Like this,' Natasha said holding out her wrist with a bracelet on it. 'Only the metal part is fifty feet high and hollow, and it's as though my wrist was five hundred feet through. Is that what you mean?'

149

'Yes.' He took the bangle off her wrist and made two circles with the thumb and index finger of each hand, so that the tips of all four digits were together in the centre of the bangle. The bangle itself ran round through the two circles he had made. 'And this is a gigantic electromagnet,' he said, pointing with his nose to the two circles that his fingers and thumbs had made. 'And furthermore all round the bangle there are coils of copper wiring.'

'What happens?' asked Natasha.

'First they pump out the hollow Tokomak, make a vacuum, put in a little puff of Deuterium gas, and then let drive with the colossal electrical jolt. The idea is to cause the nuclei of the Deuterium atoms to fuse together and spring apart and in doing so to release energy. When this happens the gas turns to plasma and it must be constrained within an electrical field inside the bangle. If it whips and touches the walls, it won't work, so the electrical field has to be very complicated to hold it still. The point is that when you've got the theory right, as apparently Hank has, it's still a very difficult piece of engineering to make the materials and to build a plant so that it will give results which the theory has predicted, in order for the working of it to be effective.'

'How do you get power out of it?' asked Jakov.

'When the fusion occurs, there is a colossal surge of thermo-nuclear power, like a mini H-bomb, for a micro-second and then it diminishes, and then happens again. Now, this surge of power within an electro-magnetic field happens thousands or millions of times a second, and it is similar to the movement of a bar magnet inside a coil, and as you know that is an ordinary way of generating electricity. Now this electricity could be taken off and used.'

'But,' said Jakov, 'what we're after is all the technical specifications for building the bloody thing—the quality of the copper—the thickness—how it's joined—all the technical data?'

'Yes.'

'So it's a question of getting the right files?'

'Yes. I'll recognise them when I see them, I've been shown what to look for.'

'Good job somebody does,' Jakov said.

There was a pause. Then Thorne said, 'There is one thing—

150

how do we fix the sentries?'

Natasha sighed. 'They're Towbitz,' she said and paused.

'Go on.'

She seemed at a loss to know where to begin. At last she said, 'Well, in modern Russia you're either a worker or not, and they're not—they're nomads.' She shrugged. 'So the department for "former people" is being *humane*. They can go on being nomads if they do *some* useful task. Being guards is one of them.'

'Why guards for nomads, it's sedentary?'

'They've been guarding their camps every night for thousands of years. Now their pride's involved in being better than anybody else at guarding the plant. That makes them keen, so does the fact that, if they fail, they'll lose their status as nomads; and if we succeed, they'll fail.'

'But if they're stuck there as guards, they aren't nomads anyway.'

'The tribe splits up and takes it in turns. Half of them are free in the mountains now.'

He thought about this. Then he said, 'I liked them—in the bazaar. . . .'

'I like them too,' Jakov interrupted. 'Get on girl and tell him how we plan to fix the bloody sentries instead of maundering on the way you are.'

Natasha said, 'Among the beatniks. . . .'

'Beatniks in Samarkand?'

'It just means they write poetry and like sex and say so.'

'Seems reasonable. I like it myself.'

'Among the girls the tribesmen have a reputation.'

'I know about that.'

'The beatniks have a dare that if a girl can stand up to being had by one of them she's proved herself. Some girls will actually go up to them and ask them to do it because of this.'

'And do they?'

Her eyes sparkled. 'You bet.'

'What's this got to do with tonight?'

'You'll see.'

When they had got everything settled, Natasha showed Thorne the back way out.

'Come and have a drink,' he said.

'Where?'

'In my room.'

She put her arm through his and he could feel the rhythm of her stride as she kept easy pace with him.

'What's your job—real job I mean—do you have one?' he asked.

'I worked in a circus.'

'What at?'

'Equestrienne—like standing on the rosinbacks, cantering round, shooting out electric light bulbs.'

'Some shooting.'

'Also I did trapeze work—fun—like *real* fun.'

'Here, do you do it here? In Samarkand?'

'Oh no. We come from Georgia. So did the Gagarins.'

He didn't respond to this. She went on, 'We came here some months ago simply for this. It will be the last thing we will do.'

'Why?' he said, as they ducked under an archway out of the narrow street into one much narrower.

'If it works, dozens of people will be killed in the reprisals. We could hardly escape. Since I will die anyway in the next twenty-four hours, this thing has got to work and you have got to escape.'

'What d'you mean, you'll die?'

'I feel it,' she said matter-of-factly.

'One of us must escape,' he replied.

They walked on. Soon they reached his hotel and went up to his room. They didn't talk while they were in bed. At a certain point she said, 'This time we needn't trouble to be careful,' and as a bribe to the gods he came inside her and she smiled. Afterwards he felt calm and intent. Natasha turned her young outdoor face to him, she looked happy.

'I'll be able to keep my mind on what we're going to do now,' she said grimly.

Jakov brought the truck for them at midnight, and Thorne loaded his gear inside the back under the canvas canopy. Here he found cylinders of compressed air and three gas masks. These had walkie-talkie units built into them. They tested them and

152

then drove off. The town ended abruptly with a wall which ran uphill to the right. The wall was pierced by a gateway. Beyond lay the open country. They went about a mile, crossed a small crossroads and then the newly built road led through a deep cutting and wound its way up into the contours of the hills.

They drove up this road for an hour and saw nobody, not a light, not a house, not a thing. They had picked a moonless period and the night was very dark.

Jakov said, 'The only danger is that sometimes the tribesmen go and visit their friends to play pranks on them. Their camp's not far. It depends on how much they have been drinking.'

They timed their arrival well. Even as the headlights picked out the blockhouse, they could see the sentries changing over.

The new ones immediately patrolled off in opposite directions, and so the truck came on fast. When it was about ten yards from the gate it stopped, and with much giggling Natasha got out. Her father egged her on. She walked quickly forwards, still giggling and constantly looking over her shoulder, wiggling her hips. She got to the door of the blockhouse, opened it, giggled some more and said, 'They dared me—I've come to be—, like you know, by a tribesman, you know.'

Thorne heard the patrolling sentry on the right turn at the end of his beat about seventy yards away. He saw the man in the blockhouse come to look at Natasha, laughing good-naturedly—roisteringly. Jakov revved the engine loudly. Thorne saw a look of incredible surprise come over the sentry's face, saw his knees crumble, saw Natasha step over his body as her silenced gun recoiled again in her hand.

Her father said softly, 'Mine is in range, is yours?'

'No,' said Thorne. 'Say something.'

Jakov shouted out, 'Brought one of the girls up, crazy bitch—some of them dared her.'

A big laugh from the sentry. 'Oh, girls,' he said, 'can't you do it yourself then, you poor eunuch?'

'It's the mystery,' shouted Jakov.

'Three,' Thorne began counting.

'She'll be a different girl afterwards,' said the sentry still coming closer.

'Two,' said Thorne.

153

'Let's go and watch,' the sentry called to his friend.

Thorne said, 'One—shoot.'

They pulled the triggers simultaneously and leapt out of the truck and rushed to the men. They were both dead. They picked them up and carried them into the blockhouse. Natasha had cut the 'phone wires and she and Jakov took the long sheepskin coats and caps from the sentries and put them on. Then they began patrolling up and down to look like sentries in case anybody should come, while Thorne drove to the air intake and backed the truck up to it.

From his 'insecticide' suitcase he took the thin glass cylinders of nerve gas and placed them in a steel container. He screwed the compressed air cylinder to the bottom of it and the atomiser to the top. He pressed the plunger which would smash the glass cylinders inside. He poked the jet of the atomiser up to the huge intake fan and turned on the compressed air. He flashed his torch once as a signal and looked at his watch. Then, taking his camera and his gas mask, he went to cover the main door in case anyone should try to escape. He knew enough about the nerve gas to believe that nobody would.

A quarter-of-an-hour seemed a hell of a long time. He thought of that stupid great fan pushing the nerve gas steadily into the plant and the nervous systems of the people. It would lay them out for several hours. He thought of Natasha and her circus-girl's body and of Teresa's body in comparison with it.

Then the fifteen minutes were up. Natasha and Jakov were walking towards him. They all put on their gas masks and Thorne slung the camera and its accessories over his shoulder.

They went in and fastened the door behind them. Bodies sprawled gawky and useless while the vast automated plant hummed on. They began their search with Natasha in the administration office, Jakov in the plant manager's office and Thorne in the chief engineer's room. After a few minutes Natasha joined her father, and together they marked up on a plan the areas of possible interest and struck off the rest. They joined Thorne in the office of the chief engineer. It was functional, every inch put to some use. There was a big knee-hole desk, maps on rollers on the walls. The chief engineer was crumpled at the foot of them.

154

Thorne said, 'Can't find any reference to the bloody Tokomak anywhere.'

'Have you tried his general correspondence file?' Jakov said.

'Haven't got to it yet.'

Natasha started looking for it and Thorne said, 'Jakov, get into the security office, find the book these sods keep on everybody. See if you can get a reference to it there.'

Jakov went out. Thorne began to get the panicky feeling of trying to do everything at once. He said, 'There's nobody at the switchboard, it can't be long till somebody 'phones and the gaff's blown.'

'You can't get here quicker than two hours.'

'Except by helicopter,' he said.

'Anybody'd be out cold in four-fifths of a second after entering. Here, this looks like something.' She read out, 'Re Isoworg's publication.'

'Who to, quick?'

'Minister of Science, Telex, last month.'

'What's it say?'

'Interim report, application of Hockeren's theory in Tokomak 4, promising. Fusion chain sustained. Muon meson injection satisfactory and improving stability in plasma core. Success in sight. Message ends.'

'Crikey,' muttered Thorne, 'that's it. Tokomak 4. Did you hear that, Jakov?' he said into the w/t mike.

'Yes.'

'Find out who works on No. 4, where the files are, where it is and then come and collect us.'

As he spoke he noticed a huge map of the Soviet Union hanging on the wall. He whipped out his camera and photographed it, because the markings on it suggested to him sites for future appliances. While he was doing this he noticed that behind it there was something else. He ran the map up, and indeed, behind it there was a plan of the factory. It was easy to locate Tokomak 4, but more important were the names of the appliances associated with it, because next to each one was a number in a circle.

'What do you think these numbers are?' he asked Natasha.

She came and looked. 'It's unusual for them to be in Cyrillic, mathematicians use Arabic.'

'Let's get round the bloody room and find a filing system which uses them.'

He ripped open the top drawer of the big green filing cabinet, then the next and the next. As he did so he glanced at his watch; it was ten minutes since the exchange went dead. If they didn't find something soon, they were bound to be caught. He left the filing cabinet and started on the drawers of the big knee-hole desk. The second drawer down was a dummy containing a suspension filing system. It was indexed in Cyrillic numerals. He flipped through the numbers associated with No. 4 on the plan. Each one was empty.

'Jesus—somebody's been here first.'

'Can't have—the files must be just out with somebody else.'

He looked again at the first empty file. Inside was one slip of paper.

'Listen,' he said. 'Files Nos. 24-32 with Dr. Benjamin Weistein.'

'Benjamin Weistein,' said Jakov on the w/t, 'just got to him. He's our man. He built the thing. Two doors from where you are. I'm coming up.'

They ran out into the passage and into the office of the German-Jewish scientist. He was sitting at his desk with his head resting on his arms in front of him.

'Having a kip,' Thorne said. He found a similar dummy drawer to the one in the other room, took the files out, swept everything including Benjamin on to the floor, saying in English, 'Down, Benjy, down.'

He took out the first file and began to read it.

'Plasma—condenser banks, amps, ohms, surges, gauss—yes, this is the scientific part of it.' His eyes darted round the room. 'Oh Christ, look at that—that'll be the engineering bit.' He pointed to a gigantic filing cabinet and jerked open one of the drawers.

'Look.' He took out working drawings and showed them to the others: side elevations; plans; machine drawings; and the appropriate specifications.

'How much film have you got?' asked Jakov grimly.

'Thousands of exposures.' They stared at the task, silent, crushed.

Thorne bulldogged the camera to the desk, plugged the flash into the desk light. He took the first sheet, focussed the camera on it and then sellotaped a ruler and a blotter on to the desk so as to give him guides to put the ensuing sheets into. He clicked the camera.

'Right, next,' he said.

'It's a duplicate,' Jakov said, and pulled out the next and the next and the next. 'Five copies of each,' he added.

'That's better then,' Thorne said looking at the ten deep drawers in the filing cabinet.

Jakov and Natasha got a system going. The files whizzed from the cabinet on to the desk and thence to the floor. The concentration of the three was electric, they scarcely spoke, each trying to find a way to do the job faster.

Three-quarters-of-an-hour went past. The eye pieces on Thorne's gas mask were beginning to steam up.

'Sod it, I'm steaming up.'

'Me too,' said Jakov.

'We'll make mistakes.' Thorne stopped and took out the anti dim equipment from his respirator case. Then he took several deep breaths, pulled off the respirator and, holding his breath, went meticulously through the drill for anti-dimming the eye pieces. The blood was pounding in his ears, his chest was heaving by the time he had finished. Very carefully he put the respirator back, pinched it tight round his face to expel the air and then, with relief, blew out a great lungful and sucked in a fresh one.

Jakov had done the same. Natasha, whose eye pieces had not steamed up, had gone out and down the passage and now came back and said, 'I could hear some one banging on the outside door.'

'How long will the gas last?' asked Jakov.

'Another hour at least,' he said and slid the next drawing on to the desk. 'How much longer here?' he asked.

'About ten minutes,' Jakov said. 'Then we've got to do the physicist's file we found at the beginning.'

Thorne added, 'And then we've got to do the appliance.'

157

The room was in chaos. The four duplicates of each drawing and specification lying around Jakov's feet and the others after they had passed under Thorne's camera tossed away behind him. Thorne's hands flew, the light flashed, and flashed, and flashed.

'Right,' Jakov said, 'that's that. Now the other file.'

But Natasha had already started on it and was taking out the pages and giving them to Thorne, who was photographing them. They finished that file in seven and a half minutes and Thorne, unclipping the camera from the desk, said, 'Do you know the way to the Tokomak?'

'Of course,' Jakov said crossly.

When they reached the main 'corridor', Thorne was baffled and would have stopped but Jakov knew what he was doing and kept going.

The 'corridor' was thirty feet wide. It ran the whole length of the plant so that it was about four hundred yards long. Down the edge was a narrow walk-way. Next to the walk-way was a moving band and beyond that another going faster. The fact that these and the walk-way and the walls were brightly painted gave a carnival atmosphere to the bodies flopped out and moving to and fro on the bands.

By running down the fast moving bands they aggregated twenty-five miles an hour and covered the distance in about forty seconds. They skipped back on to the slow band, thence to the passage and took the express lift down.

'How long before the gas clears?' Natasha asked.

'It'll be clearing up near the front very soon, but there'll still be pockets of it even there.'

'How long do you need here still?' Jakov asked.

'No idea.'

The lift stopped and they raced down an enormous hall. Suddenly he saw it and stopped. It was indeed as Hank had predicted, but seen close up its dimensions and complexity were awesome. All around were the huge blocks of condenser banks and other apparatus. Thorne began photographing—long shots—medium shots—close-ups. As he did so he was saying into the w/t, 'Find the control room.'

A few minutes later Natasha called and directed him. He found her in a semicircular room with windows and a vast console upon which dozens of gauges flickered or stood impassively still. He looked at them closely. Some of the calibrations were extremely small and fine, as were the descriptions alluding to their significance. He realised that he would have to get very close for them to make any sense. When he had plugged up the flash attachment, he moved the camera in closer and closer, adjusting the focus until he reckoned the calibrations and lettering would be legible. He measured the distance of the frame on the panel and said, 'Be sharp and nip round marking the panel up into frames this size.'

She found a chinograph pencil and, using the side of a box containing magnetic tape for the computer as a straight edge, she went round dividing up the panel into rectangles as he had described. They could hear Jakov panting into his respirator through the w/t.

Thorne said, 'Jakov, by the time I'm finished it'll be about thirty minutes since they began hammering at the door. They may be in when we reach the front.'

'That's right,' said Jakov.

Then Thorne finished. He took out the film and put it carefully into the capsule that he had been given to receive it. Then he stuck the two halves of the capsule together and put them carefully into his pocket.

He dropped all the camera equipment and said, 'Let's go.'

They went back to the top floor and as they reached the moving band Thorne said, 'Take it easy. You can't shoot if you're panting.'

At the front end of the plant they went to the spiral staircase and listened.

'Doesn't sound as though they're inside,' Thorne said.

'If they were they'd keep still,' Jakov answered.

'There are no windows,' Natasha said. 'We can't see what's going on outside.'

'Lying up for us,' Jakov said.

'Maybe gone to get gas masks, left a guard on the door,' Thorne said.

They took the lift to the ground floor. As it went down, they stood inside with drawn guns. Thorne told them what to do. When it stopped the doors opened automatically. Thorne went out straight, the other two on either side, all balled up and rolling, guns ready, eyes darting. They stood up. There was silence. Nobody there. They moved towards the entrance area, backs flat to the walls. When they got within sight of the door they saw four unconscious bodies.

'Towbitz,' Jakov said. 'Must have ridden out from their camp like I said, found the dead ones and come on to investigate. Gas must collect here.' He paused, thinking. 'They'd have had a mate outside watching. He'll have gone back to the others and they won't tell a soul. They'll turn out every man that can move and get up here and fix the job themselves. They'll be waiting for us outside.'

They stood in the towering plant where a power, unmatched except in the sun, was to be harnessed for man, and Thorne said, 'Do the Towbitz drive?'

'Unlikely. Why?'

'Then they may not have moved the truck.'

'So what?'

'Where are some tools?'

'Like what?' Natasha said.

He told them. Jakov knew and left them. He returned in a few moments and Thorne took them to the duct where the great fan sucked in the air. There was a vast black plastic tunnel carrying the fresh air into the plant.

Thorne said, 'We've got to turn out the lights.'

'Wait then,' said Jakov.

It seemed hours before first one and then another light went out. Finally the darkness was absolute. Jakov re-joined them by the light of his torch. Thorne found the wire that took the power to the electric motor in the centre of the fan and cut it. Then he cut a way into the plastic wind tunnel and worked his way up to the fan itself. It was about ten metres high. When he got up to it, he could see out quite well and beckoned the others; in the fresh air they took off their masks.

Natasha said, 'The wind's got up—it'll make it hard for them to hear us.'

'I can't see anything,' Thorne whispered, 'except the truck, here, right under the fan where I left it.'

'Wait till our eyes get used to the dark,' Jakov said.

160

They stood in silence, waiting. Outside were the Towbitz waiting for them. The wind whined remorselessly.

Jakov said, 'Natasha.'

'Yes, father?'

'The Russians; in the north, when the wolves chase their sleigh ...'

'Shoot a horse for them to feed on,' she interrupted.

He grunted. After a pause he said, 'Two horses would hold them longer than one.'

'Yes, father.'

They waited while the fan blades moved idly round, and he said again, 'Natasha.'

'Yes, father?'

'As I said, Isoworg's not just another way, it's more different than you can imagine. It is "The Way".'

'Taoist,' she chided him gently.

He smiled slightly but he did not answer. Then urgently he said, 'There! Horses! Men! By the gate, on the other side of the wire. Others on our right by the main door. I can't exactly see them, I just know they're there.'

Thorne said, 'Does the truck start easily?'

'Yes, starts first time, only good thing about it.'

'Natasha and I will lie up in the canopy and give you covering fire. You go like hell at the gate.'

'Mark you,' said Jakov, 'they won't want to kill us, they'll want to take us.'

'Why?'

'To punish us for what the Party will do to them.'

'Some punishment it'll be too,' Natasha said. 'Every man in the tribe will rape me for a start—that's a convention.'

'Often wondered what happened at conventions,' Thorne said.

'Well, we're better dead than finding out,' said Jakov, and Thorne began clipping the wire mesh. When he had cut it down both sides and across the bottom he bent the first fan blade up to a right-angle. Then the next and the next until enough were out of his way. Then he took the cut mesh and bent that up too.

They could see nothing and hear nothing. For all they knew their every movement was being noticed, and they would be climbing down into the arms of the Towbitz.

Jakov went first. He inched himself silently on to the canvas canopy of the truck, found a small hole and sniffed. He knew that he could smell a Towbitz in a place like that by the rancid butter and sheepskin. His nose told him nothing, so very carefully he lowered himself into the truck and thence into the driver's seat.

He sat there straining his eyes and sniffing the wind. He loosened his gun and moved it to a better place. He felt Natasha's weight land on the canopy and then Thorne's. He felt them wriggle to good positions and lie still. He listened to the wind. He switched on and waited till the petrol pump stopped ticking. He put the truck in first gear, keeping his foot on the clutch. He eased off the handbrake and she stood still. He put his foot on the accelerator, wished that he had arranged a signal with them for what would be a very sharp start, and turned the starting key.

The engine roared right up the scale and at peak revs he let the clutch in with a bang. The wheels spurted and they leapt forward. The engine screamed till he whipped it into second and headed for the gate. The next moment the front of the truck hit the barrier pole across the entrance, and it rode up the bonnet, smashed the windscreen and jammed the steering wheel. A horseman came alongside, and Thorne shot him dead. Then there were others.

'Christ, accelerate, man!' he yelled at Jakov. 'We'll do it if you accelerate.' Then the rock wall was racing at them. Natasha shot another and Thorne another. A sword flashed and Natasha rolled too late. It did not take off her shooting arm as it was intended but it cut it deeply.

Jakov was half on the bonnet, straining at the baulk of wood. He freed it, swung right to miss the rock wall, and settled back into the driving seat. A man galloping alongside now lunged at him with his sword. Jakov could not dodge in the space and the scalding sensation of a blade biting into his neck told him instantly that he was badly hurt, as he lunged the truck at the horse, which went down with a sickening crunkle of bones booming on the tin body of the truck. Natasha shot another with her left hand and her last round. Thorne, his gun now empty, turned round on top of the wildly accelerating truck and

162

saw the last of the horsemen spurring his horse madly. The frenzied nodding head of the horse was just behind them. The rider kicked his feet free from the stirrups, vaulted them up on to the sides of his saddle, crouched a second for balance and launched himself at Thorne. The truck lurched. Thorne fell underneath the man, whose thumbs in a second were on his eyes, until Natasha split his skull with the butt of her pistol. Thorne rolled clear and pitched him over the side. Seeing the blood on Natasha's arm, he was about to speak when Jakov switched the lights on and Thorne glimpsed a corner coming at them with a sheer drop on its outer side.

'Ready to jump!' he yelled, even as the brakes went on.

The gravel slithered under the wheels. Jakov pulled the wheel over. The back end slewed round. He gave opposite lock and it rocked back on to the other point of balance. Thorne and Natasha were nearly flung off; Thorne's hand came away sticky from the grab he made to save her.

'You're wounded.'

'Yes, but Papa's worse.'

'How do you know?'

'Christ, he drives bloody well.'

Thorne drew his knife, ripped open the canopy and dropped through. Natasha followed him. He dragged Jakov from behind the wheel and took his place. By the time Natasha had got him laid down in the back he was quite limp. He pulled her head down to his face, 'Remember, it *is* the way.'

'Yes, Father.'

She cradled his head and their blood flowed together freely.

Thorne handed her a first-aid box. She sat still. She knew her father would bleed to death because she had put her cold fingers in the wound in his neck and felt the hot blood pumping fast. Therefore she laid his head on her thigh and put a thick pad on her own arm from the first-aid box and bound it securely on. Then she put her hand inside her father's windcheater to feel his heart, but it had stopped. She sat there for a little while in the rush of icy air that came through the broken windscreen. She took his gun and ammunition and put it in the big pocket of her windcheater. She rested her hand on his forehead, curiously cut off now by the death of the man who

163

had given her life and who had *always* been there. Then she remembered what he had said and she tipped him over the back of the truck into the middle of the lonely road for the 'wolves'.

She went and sat next to Thorne. They turned to each other, looked a moment and did not speak. She watched the headlamps slashing out over the precipices into the eyeless night and raking round to spotlight the cliffs of the next corner.

Thorne had got the feel of the truck and was drifting it easily through the bends, converting the power intended to haul a load, skilfully through the gear box, into speed.

Natasha did not speak. She took Thorne's gun and re-loaded it carefully. She gave it back to him. She re-loaded her own. She slipped the catch on her father's gun, took out the magazine and pressed her finger down to gauge how many rounds he had fired. She topped it up with four, emptied the breach and put back the magazine. She gave the extra gun to Thorne because her right hand was practically useless.

The air which had blown over hundreds of miles of mountains came in through the broken windscreen and threatened to freeze them to a point where they would stiffen up and be unable to function. He had shut the side windows and turned on the heat, and now he said, 'Is there a canopy screen rolled up behind our heads?'

'Yes,' she said.

He heard her groan and gasp as she turned in the seat to find a way of getting it down. At last she did so and secured all the tabs. The effect was that the cab filled with hot air from the heater and formed a cushion driving most of the cold air over the top.

'This road goes round the contours in a loop,' she said. 'Horsemen can cut across so they'll attack us again.'

'Where?'

'Just outside the town.'

'The first crossroads we saw coming up?'

'Yes.'

They drove on. Natasha thought of her father lying crumpled in the road. She thought about Thorne. They did not speak for about fifteen minutes. Then Thorne said, 'Headlights— coming towards us—going like hell.'

He switched off their own lights, jammed on the brakes. The truck juddered to a halt. He leapt out and rushed forward up the road. Natasha felt too weak and too glad of the peace to move.

Thorne ran round the next outside bend and chose a spot with care. Then he got down in the deep drainage ditch on the left and waited. The driver of the oncoming car would be on his side and he knew exactly what he intended to do. He crouched, measuring the approach of the car by its light and noise. He heard the driver change down to take the corner round which he himself had just run. He watched the edge of light and darkness as the car raced up the hill towards him. The instant before it came level, he leapt up and began shooting at the uniformed driver. He got off three shots. Then the car accelerated and, as if deliberately, hurtled over the edge of the precipice.

The flashes into which it burst with a bang blazed up crimson and reassuring, and he ran back to the truck without a second glance. Natasha smiled at him. She felt warm now. The heater worked well when no cold air was blowing it. She spoke softly to him; drowsily.

'Well done, darling.'

He drove off. 'Sleep,' he said.

He went on down the mountainside and it grew light. Finally he came to the straight piece of road where it passed through the cutting. The rock wall on either side seemed to be sheer. In the bleak dawn light he could just see that there was a road block by the crossroads at the bottom, with about two hundred horsemen clustered about it. He slowed right down. The block was solid; there was no way round.

He said, 'Do you see what's ahead?'

'Yes, darling, I see.'

He knew that the Towbitz would want to take them alive in order to exact their own kind of vengeance and would therefore attack at once before any officials arrived. He decided that the steep cutting would be the best place to welcome them, as they would only be able to come at him in twos and threes. So he stopped the truck. 'I have a plan,' he said.

'There is no plan, my dear love.'

'I have a plan for me.'

'And I shall take off my bandage and bleed to death.'

He could think of no answer to this. After a time he said, 'I'd better shoot you or they might ...'

'No, I'd rather be raped by my enemies than shot by my lover.'

He let this idea slide about in his mind. He could not think about it.

'Take off your bandage then,' he said, 'but only when I tell you.'

She nodded. She was already weak from loss of blood. Lassitude made her loving. It was nice to be with him; she held his hand. With the other hand he took the capsule out of his pocket and swallowed it.

'Do they all have guns?' he asked.

'None. It's forbidden. Only the sentries, and Father and I fixed those.'

They waited. Finally the Towbitz made a decision and two detachments of horsemen left the main group and circled out to make a pincer movement on him. He slipped out of the truck and wriggled underneath it with all three automatics.

He believed the steep sides of the road cutting were too sheer for a horse and he therefore expected them on foot. But he had reckoned without the total recklessness and fury of horsemen like these. Before he knew what was happening there was a thunder of hooves, and they came over both edges at once like buffalo driven by Indians. They rolled and tumbled and slithered. Horses fell upon the horses in front, their hooves breaking the riders' bones. But the front horses took the brunt, and in this way some, from behind, miraculously arrived at the bottom intact. Not many arrived intact but enough. The angle was now impossible for Thorne to shoot, and he slid out from under the back of the truck with a gun in each hand. He shot four. Others already hurt made off upon their lamed horses. Then two came racing along the road as he stood by the tail board. Both were slung down from their saddles, trying to put their horses' necks between them and his bullets, but this didn't work very well because the space was too confined and they had to come straight at him. One horse, out of control, plunged

166

right up inside the back of the truck, crushing the rider's skull on the steel frame of the canopy. The other raced past. Thorne shot the rider and then for a while he was unmolested. He grabbed the loose sheepskin coat of the man who had killed himself on the canopy frame, and put it on. Then he took his long boots and his hat, his sword and his dagger. He stowed his guns in his windcheater underneath the fur coat. While doing this he considered Natasha—no, she couldn't ride, she was too weak. No, she didn't want him to shoot her. It was a crazy loyalty. He sprang on to one of the horses that was not lamed, and felt its whole muscular quivering body leap like a spring as he dug in his heels.

'Now,' he yelled at Natasha. 'Now take off your bandage.' And she didn't answer. She was already asleep.

And then he was flying down towards the road block preceded by the only two survivors who still had horses that could go. He jumped the horse over the ditch in the bad morning light and raced out past the cluster of horsemen. He hoped that he would be able to skirt them by a sufficient distance for them not to recognise him. He left the choice of terrain to the horse and galloped furiously. But there were boulders through which no horse could pass, and these forced him down towards the tribesmen on the road. They spotted him and suddenly he heard the blood-chilling Towbitz yell. Now they knew they'd get him. He on a horse like they. Now things were right and their wild exaltation pierced and rung the air. Desperately he lashed at the horse's withers with the ends of his reins, but the curve of the hills turned even more sharply to the road. He could hear them heading along it to cut him off and the others were gaining behind him. Then there was the grey city wall in front of him, which he had seen earlier, and it forced him to turn even more directly towards the road.

Those who had taken the short line were now speeding along the road to the gate through which he, Jakov and Natasha had come this morning in the truck and they would be there at the bottom of the hill waiting for him. He was thus galloping furiously downhill with the wall on his left, one group of his enemies behind and the other waiting for him at the bottom. He saw the lights of a vehicle coming from the city, moving

167

towards the horsemen; he saw that it was a police-type armoured car.

He glanced at the wall, saw that as the slope went down it got higher. It was now or never. He flung his weight on the reins, the horse's quarters slithered under him. The group behind shrieked louder. His horse just came to a halt. He stood in the saddle and vaulted on to the wall.

His pursuers were following suit. He leapt down from the wall on the other side and found himself in a very narrow cul-de-sac leading down into the main road. He spun round, drew his gun and dropped the first horseman to appear on top of the wall. The other side of the cul-de-sac consisted of a factory with a few small doors. He raced to the first of these and tried it. It was iron and as solid as a rock. He was on his way to the second when the armoured car came roaring up the narrow cul-de-sac, effectively blocking it from the horsemen who were following.

At the same instant about a dozen tribesmen came over the wall together. Instinctively he opened up with both automatics but a thrown knife struck his wrist. Some one landed in front of him and drove at his head with a sword hilt. He ducked. He heard the stutter of a machine gun from the armoured car, saw a couple of Towbitz fall, and then some one got him on the head with something that he never saw.

Chapter Twelve

Natasha opened her eyes dreamily, in no pain. It was dark. She felt warm and contented. She felt a dull ache in her shoulder but recognised that it was well bound up. She knew she was in a bed of some kind indoors—a bed of straw or shuck, because she could hear it rustle. Next to her somebody was breathing heavily.

For a while she wondered about this. Then fear fell upon her because she was not dead and therefore all horrible things were still going to happen. She became aware of a small pain in her good arm. She moved her bad right arm over and felt on the inside of her left elbow. She felt the adhesive tape fixing a slim pipe to her arm, and recognised a blood drip.

So she wasn't with the Towbitz. And yet she certainly wasn't in a hospital. Suddenly hope and joy flowed through her and the adrenalin surge was so fast that it left her head aching and heart pounding. Thorne had come back and rescued her. He had her shacked up somewhere to mend. She put out a hand softly in the dark to the person breathing, knowing now who it was. He muttered and then the breathing changed.

'Who is it?'

'Natasha.'

'God, my head. Where are we?'

'Don't you know?'

'No.'

'Oh Christ!'

'What?'

'Oh God!'

Pause.

'I've got a blood drip going. We're being looked after.'

He put his hands up to his head and felt the other bruises on his body. He came to the conclusion that he must have been kicked. He stood up cautiously on the palliasses lying on the floor and felt around him. He found the wall and leaned against it. Then he felt through his pockets; all were empty. His hand was about to dart to his armpit when he thought of infra-red light. Instead he chafed his arm and felt the reassuring presence of the two pills inserted under his skin. He could see a window with a few chinks of light coming past the wooden shutters.

He fumbled around the room until he came to the door. He tried it. To his astonishment it opened, and the next moment he was blinking across a small shuttered room with one light bulb hanging in the centre. Sitting on a chair tilted back against the opposite wall, looking at him, shaking his head wryly, was Towers.

They looked at each other. All the blood abruptly drained from Thorne's head and he dropped forward on to his hands and knees, letting his head loll down to stop himself passing out. He heard Towers saying, 'Surprise, surprise!' He saw a figure moving over from the side of the room. Thorne looked up and stared at the oriental face for some time, feeling that it was familiar. When he spoke, Thorne recognised him by his bristling teeth.

'We have about one half hour to get it. You tell us quick,' said the Chinese.

Thorne grinned at Towers and said, 'Busy, isn't he?'

Towers got up. Hell, he's a big man, thought Thorne, and wondered if there was any way of getting him and the Chinese to fight each other. He began to churn this over in his aching head as Towers came towards him with his funny little steps, his toes turned in and his thighs touching.

'For a limey you did damn well. Hear me say that? Isoworg's filth. I'll tear you to bits any time; any time at all. But sure as shit you did a damn good job.'

How to turn this sincerity to account? Thorne wondered. How? How?

'Suppose that's why you fixed up Natasha?'

'Yeah.'

'And old dragon's teeth here didn't approve?'

170

'Too right.'

Thorne rolled back his tongue and flung a gob of spit accurately into the Chinese's face. The effect was immediate. He took two strides, gathering himself to kick Thorne's head off, and ran into a back-hander from Towers that would have decapitated anybody else.

From Thorne's position on the floor it was a splendid sight because the Chinaman's legs came on and went straight up into the air so that he fell flat on his back with a tremendous crash. But even before Thorne had started to laugh, Towers had sprung back like a panther and had them both covered. The Chinese didn't move.

'Thanks,' Thorne said. 'I'm a gonna, and where you're a gonna you give way to temptations like that. I know it's stupid.'

'Where is it, buddy?'

'That's the bugger. The bloody camera didn't work, it was all for nothing.'

He climbed slowly to his feet and stood swaying more than was necessary. He sighed dejectedly and went back into the other room and shut the door. In a few moments he heard a sound as the Chinese came to and the row started.

Feverishly he picked at the skin under his arm, took out the nearest pill, crushed it in his teeth, swallowed it, flung himself into a corner, drew one of the palliasses over his head and shoulders. The emetic worked immediately and he vomited quietly. He covered it with one of the palliasses, took the capsule, washed it in his mouth very carefully, cleaned it and wiped it. He listened desperately for the sounds outside and heard Towers' nasal barking voice obviously talking from behind a gun. Then he went to Natasha.

'You've got about ten seconds to swallow this capsule.'

Before he had finished speaking she had taken it and put it in her mouth.

'My mouth's too dry,' she said guiltily.

He heard her gagging on it in the dark. He said, 'Wait,' and crawled round the room like a lunatic, feeling everywhere. He found a niche and in a niche a pitcher. He put his fingers in the pitcher and felt liquid. It was water, old but not bad.

He took it back to her and she swallowed the capsule. Thorne

171

put the pitcher back and then returned to her. He lay next to her and listened to the voices outside ...

'Okay, then so I'm only the boss when I've got the gun. But get this, nobody tells Jan Towers what to do, but nobody. So from now on I'll keep both guns, and wherever you go you'll have one of 'em pointing right at you.'

'This cannot work. Thing we do more important than us. I apologise. Stupid to kick him till we have film. Now you apologise and we do good work.'

'Oh shut up, you grinning ape, and get in there and bring him out and we'll work on him. Methodically. He'll tell.'

'Listen,' Thorne said to Natasha, 'I can't get out of this one. They're huge men. I know them both—tough as hell. I've already made them squabble. I aim to make them fight. If that succeeds we'll try to get away. If not I'll promise to tell them where the capsule is if you may go free. I'll demand proof of your arrival on the Persian side of the frontier by Ashkabad. Then you 'phone Isoworg.'

The door burst open and the Chinese came in and said, 'Come out here.'

Thorne got up and went.

Natasha lay back, trying to keep calm so that she could assimilate the blood drip. Common sense told her you can't have blood transfusions when your heart's going like mad.

'Sit down, limey.'

He sat at a table, slumped forward.

'Now listen,' Towers said. 'This bastard here and I don't believe the camera didn't work. You're too damn good an operator. You'd have checked the mother fucking thing in the first place. You've *got* those pix, and you've hidden them. Now I'll tell you something else too. Doesn't matter if I have 'em or anyone else has 'em, your outfit will give 'em to us in the end—that's the whole screwy idea, right?'

'Right.'

'So save yourself the agony of holding out on us.'

'I'm not holding out on you.'

'Oh yes, you are. So Chinky here and me's gonna beat the information out of you.'

Thorne said, 'Chinky said you only had half-an-hour before

172

the Towbitz'd find you—right?'

'So what?'

'I didn't get my pictures—that's true. But if I was lying I could hold out for half-an-hour and you know it. So you can't win.'

'So what?'

'So let the girl go before the Towbitz get here.'

'Why should we?' asked the Chinese.

'For the same reason you got her the blood drip,' Thorne replied. 'To save her life.'

'Towers did that.'

'Yeah, and only to make the bitch strong enough to work on in case we wanted to,' Towers replied.

'Balls,' Thorne said experimentally.

'You mean he wants her for self, eh?' suggested the Chinese.

And then Thorne remembered the run-down on Towers that he had been given after Bonarjee had finished with him. Carefully, sneeringly he said, 'He doesn't like women—he's the other sort.'

'What did you say?' asked Towers menacingly.

The intensity of his reaction gave Thorne confidence. 'You heard me,' he said. 'You like little boys—that's why they kicked you out of the C.I.A.'

The Chinese mouth burst open in a grin. 'True this...?'

Thorne said trenchantly, 'We washed him clean when we had him in and then we told the world. Everybody knows about Jan Towers. Boy's name was Dwight Brown, little coloured boy. You buggered him and when his Dad came for you, you killed him.'

Towers had stood up, his face was white. He moved towards Thorne slowly. Thorne could see a strange convulsive movement in his neck causing his head to shake slightly to one side, as though he was trying to look over his shoulder. His face was red in two bright patches on the cheek bones and white round the mouth. Thorne looked at the Chinese and realised that he had noticed this too. He wanted the Chinese to understand everything.

Thorne said, 'That's why he went double with you Chinks. He'll kill you and go back and say, "Please, Uncle Sam, does a

173

big coup like this make it okay for an American C.I.A. agent to bugger a little coloured boy *once* and shoot his lousy black father?" Now he's going to kill me for that, you idiotic Chinese. He'll kill me even before I can tell you where I put the pix.'

Towers was very close and quite oblivious of the Chinese. He put his gun in his belt, and his next movement was so swift it took even Thorne by surprise. Towers' hands were around his throat.

The karate blow that the Chinese aimed at Towers' neck just failed to lay him out or kill him, but the pressure on Thorne's throat relaxed for a second and he broke the hold, swung the chair and smashed the light in the shuttered room. He blundered into Natasha's room and got her to her feet. He slipped out the drip, broke it off, doubled it over, pressed it over the place; then bent her elbow up on it tightly.

The two men were at each other; Thorne and Natasha moved round the wall to the door. Suddenly there was silence. Thorne opened the door. It stuck. She wriggled through but the fact that it stuck delayed him. A body hurled itself against the door slamming it shut, and there then began the wildest, weirdest fight in the dark. His intention was to keep himself in front of the door if need be until he was beaten to death. Towers' intention was to kill him. The intention of the Chinese was to prevent Towers from killing him but also to prevent Thorne from escaping.

Thorne began to work to a plan. He identified the Chinese and manoeuvred him to one side so that he could get out of the door. He ducked and parried, remembering Towers' voice. Suddenly he ducked and flung his shoulder against Towers' stomach driving him back. He bounced back himself, wrenched the door open in such a way that as Towers hurled himself forward he shot through the door and down the stairs. Thorne shouted in Towers' voice, 'The bastard's got out.' The Chinese came forward to follow and Thorne pushed him down the pitch dark stairs on top of Towers, where they rolled together trying for a death hold.

Thorne slipped back into the room, jammed the door with the chair, went out through the window on to the flat roofs and finally got into a street.

174

He had no money, no passport, no gun. He ran desperately, twisting and turning in the hope of finding Natasha. But she was nowhere to be seen. Finally he enquired and found the road with his hotel in it and went up to his room.

He had hidden a second gun and his case was there with plenty of money in it. He took them and put them ready. He cleaned himself up as fast as he could and put on his business man's suit again, with the passport and papers in the pocket. He took his money and his gun and went downstairs. A man sat in the hall on a wooden bench. He looked oily and constipated and was reading a paper.

'What do you want?' he asked.

'A taxi,' Thorne said.

'You haven't paid the bloody bill yet.'

Thorne began to take out some money. The constipated eyes looked relieved. He shouted for a child and sent it in search of a taxi. Soon Thorne heard running steps which he assumed belonged to the child, but a woman rushed in breathless.

'It's the Towbitz.'

'You're always on about the Towbitz ...'

'Oh, shut your stupid face—they've taken a girl.'

'Suppose you wish it was you—what girl?'

'I don't know the girl.'

'Who saw this?'

'Me! I saw it about fifteen minutes ago.'

'Ha! And I thought it was real for a moment.'

'It is real.'

'You and the Towbitz. We all know why you're so interested in them.'

The child came back with a taxi. Thorne got into it and it moved off. He fought down his racing urgency and told the driver calmly that he wanted to have a tourist's look at the tribesmen's camp. When he reached it he got out and examined it carefully. He realised they were making ready to leave. He drove back to the town.

Chapter Thirteen

Towers and the Chinese had eventually gone in pursuit of Thorne. It was Towers who finally located his hotel and began asking questions. He heard the story about the girl taken by the Towbitz and that Thorne had gone off in a taxi. Towers offered so much money to speak to the taxi driver that he appeared grinning in about two hours. By that time the Chinese had re-joined Towers.

'Where did you take him after the camp?' Towers asked the driver.

'I dropped him in the central square.'

Towers said, 'That means the girl's got the pix and Thorne's looking for her.'

'But ...' began the Chinese.

'There are no buts, you yellow bloody shitbeetle. Thorne wouldn't rescue a *girl—just* a girl.'

'You mean he is like you?'

Towers looked at him narrowly. 'I'm going to kill you for that. But not right now. No, because he's a professional and pros don't risk pix to rescue girls. I wonder what the hell he's doing.'

The Chinese said, 'First we get back into smart clothes, otherwise police ask questions—look at us.'

'Okay then, we'll go to the bazaar. That's where any news'll be circulating.'

Thorne had arrived in the square and gone at once to the bazaar. The place was seething with excitement; the police were everywhere. He moved about incuriously among the stalls, buying here and there a Towbitz outfit. When he had it all, he went into a public lavatory and changed. Then he went and bought a horse and rode out towards the camp.

He was nervous. Something was happening and he did not know what. He looked round at the hills covered in shale and barren of any living thing.

He rode off into those hills to a point where he could keep watch on the camp. They were nearly ready to move. He kept still, watching.

What haphazard malfunction of his personality had made him think, back in the dark room, that she was more likely to escape than he? Fear of Towers and the Chinese? He must have been mad to think she could escape in the state she was in. He had turned her out into the street for certain capture just because, for a while, he had given up; his spirit had surrendered.

Desperately in need of advice and help he took out the little radio, and then the shattering fact fell upon him that it had got broken in the fight, that he was cut off. In his present state the effect on him was terrible; he felt deserted and fear gripped him. He tried to pull himself together, tried to adjust to the situation, telling himself that even his alter ego could not work fast enough to help him in this predicament. But all the same the loss demoralised him and he sat looking at the camp in loneliness and despair. His mind raced with thoughts about an armoured car—but where the hell from? Towers must have got hold of one, high-jacked it presumably. It was too late now. He thought of helicopters, of hovercraft, of friends, of diversions, of everything, and no possible solution occurred to him.

It was obvious why they were getting out. They would head into the mountains and re-join the other section of the tribe. Then they would have the advantage over those who would bring retribution.

At last they were ready to move. The horsemen first, the yaks second. The sound of animals' feet and jingling harness came to him in the clear air. No word was spoken as the cavalcade, which had changed little since the days of the great Khan, wound away into the bleak hills. Thorne let them go, certain he could follow their tracks.

He tracked them all day. As it grew dark, he realised he would have to get closer. He had seen a lone horseman riding rearguard. He judged he was getting nearer to him in the dark. Soon he heard the sound of water and proceeded steadily, hoping they would approach it to a point where its sound engulfed them. They did. Soon he was riding beside a foaming torrent. It drowned all noise. He drew his gun, screwed on the silencer, kicked his horse into a gallop. Suddenly, in front of him on a bend, he caught sight of the rearguard. He kept going to make sure of him, and the plop of his gun was lost in the sound of water. In a second Thorne had caught the other horse. He changed his cap and coat with the man he had shot, tipped him into the water and mounted his horse. He turned his own horse round, hit it a terrific belt with the tribesman's whip, watched it gallop off in the direction from which he had come, and then turned and rode after the tribe.

Now he felt he could with safety ride close enough to them not to lose them.

All night long they rode steadily forward, trotting often, sometimes cantering. Thorne realised that the baggage train had gone a different way, and that he was following only the horsemen. He wondered why. It seemed that escape from the authorities could not be the only motive. He thought they were covering about six miles an hour, and nearly all the time they were climbing. At one point he thought somebody dropped back, perhaps to relieve him or speak to him; indeed, he thought he heard a voice, but then the rider seemed to change his mind.

Dawn came fourteen hours later and he reckoned they had made sixty or seventy miles and had climbed about fifteen thousand feet. He knew that in this area there were no roads at all.

Soon he realised that the front of the caravan was preparing to halt, and he dropped back. He rode up the side of the mountain until he reached a covered vantage point and stopped to watch. He saw that they had reached the camp of the other half of the tribe.

The sun was rising on the wildest terrain he had ever seen. In every direction rolled the peaks of mountains utterly barren since the beginning of time.

The blazing sun seemed so hostile here he could not believe it would, later on in the day, make children sneeze at thatched windows in West England coombs. The idea reminded him of Crediton in Devon: birthplace of St. Boniface, murdered at Dokkum the home of Teresa. Teresa, Natasha. Isoworg. He stared across the barren land.

He saw that the camp had been made at the top of a precipitous slope leading down some hundreds of feet into a wide, smooth, glacial valley that stretched in each direction. To his left, about a mile away, the valley appeared to be blocked by a rock fall. To the left of this again there was the river, which deepened into a gorge at about the point of the rock fall, separating the right hand side of the valley from the left.

The horsemen breakfasted and still he waited. The sun climbed into the sky. Breakfast finished, the tribesmen were moving about, preparing for something. They were choosing fresh horses from those that were in the camp. Then half a dozen riders urged their horses over the precipice and slithered down into the valley. As they cantered out on to the valley floor, he watched them.

One of them rode out to the middle and dismounted. He beat a stake of some kind firmly into the ground and tied a cord to it. The others had ridden out and planted flags in a great circle. Thorne wondered why, and then in terror began to understand.

Baskashi.

Chapter Fourteen

Baskashi, banned now in the Soviet Union, is as old as the history of the Mongol peoples. Mongols are horsemen and warriors, fearless and cruel. And Baskashi is for horsemen, warriors, fearless and cruel.

Two teams of anything up to forty men oppose each other armed with whips. The whips have a short handle and eight tails. Each tail is tipped with metal.

A goat is tethered in the centre of a valley. The teams ride down a precipice. They gallop at the goat, lean out of the saddle, take it up and try to gallop round the circle of flags with it. The opposite side will beat them with the whips on the face, on the neck, anywhere. The horses will kick at the head of the man as he stoops out of his saddle to pick up the goat. That was what Knickerbockers had told him about Baskashi in the room at Wimbledon with the beagle on the floor among the leather books and the old smells.

His horse flung up its head and pricked its ears, looking back the way they had come, but Thorne did not notice, because at that moment somebody was led forward and flung upon a horse.

It was Natasha. The rider led her horse down the precipice and out to the stake in the middle of the valley. He watched in horror as, instead of a goat, Natasha was taken down and her ankles were tied with cord to the stake. Her wrists were lashed in front of her. Dozens of riders were now assembling on the edge of the precipice. All were silent.

The air was cool, the distances vast. Thorne sat on his horse, watching the negligent elegance which co-ordinates the myriad movements of horsemen preparing to move. He felt detached, as though he himself were involved in some kind of ritual. He rode down to the camp. They saw him. They did not seem surprised. No one spoke. A few murmured as they made way for him. The horsemen were fully assembled by the edge of the precipice and turned to face him. He could identify their leader in the centre and rode towards him. He stopped

The leader said, 'We knew you would come.'

'Put me in her place and let her go.'

'No. We know of her ruse with the sentries.'

'How?'

'One lived—for a little. She deserves this.'

'This is the place—' Thorne gestured—'for Baskashi?'

'You know about it?'

'A little.'

The leader thought for a moment. 'You will ride Baskashi. We will beat you to death.'

Thorne looked him in the eye. 'If I win and ride her round the flags, she will be mine and go free.'

The leader looked surprised.

'You have two teams,' Thorne said, 'I have no team. Surely it is fair, one Englishman against eighty Towbitz?'

Perhaps it was his contempt, perhaps it seemed better sport that way; at any rate, the leader nodded.

Thorne said, 'You have fresh horses, so must I.'

'Bring him a horse.'

'No, I will choose one.'

Somebody started to speak and the leader cut him off. 'He is alone,' he said.

Thorne rode among the scrubby horses and saw nothing to his liking. Then, away behind one of the drum-shaped tents, he saw something and rode over. It was a magnificent stallion, bigger than the others. He himself was heavier than the short stocky men. The stallion was unsaddled, eating hay. He got down and began to take the saddle off his own horse.

The leader got in ahead of him, raising his whip. 'That is my horse,' he said, 'even I would not ride that stallion in a Baskashi.'

'Are you afraid of me that you grudge me a good horse—up to my weight?'

181

The man said nothing, and Thorne saddled the stallion, doing it very carefully and well. The horse was eating and would be blown out. When he got going the girths would work loose and Thorne needed a very tight girth; above all else, the girth must be tight. Suddenly he brought his knee up as hard as he could into the horse's belly. The horse gasped, emptying its lungs and Thorne snatched the girth tight. He did not look at the leader. A moment later he mounted and rode back towards the others They made a line between him and the precipice He stopped in front of them. They said nothing.

'A whip?' Thorne said. 'A *good* whip.'

There was a shout to his right as someone threw him a whip. Even as he caught it, he intercepted a glance between the leader and another so that he guessed there'd be no formal start. With a great cry of 'Natasha' he clouted his horse over the rump with the whip so violently that it plunged through the line of riders and he was down the precipice in front of them all. He raced out over the flat plain. There had been one rider left at the bottom. For a moment he galloped alongside Thorne. His horse's head was by Thorne's knee. It was stationary there, both horses travelling at the same speed. He saw that its throat lash was loose. With a quick movement he grabbed the poll piece, wrenched it forward and downwards taking the bridle completely off, and swung it round with a terrific back-hander to catch the rider in the face with the heavy bit. The horse slowed down and veered away.

He saw Natasha stooping in a fruitless attempt to unfasten her feet. At just the right moment he slowed his horse and screamed at her, 'Put your arms round my neck.'

He came alongside and bent his head. Her bound wrists were flung behind it. He bore back and up with all his strength, hoping to God the stirrup leathers would hold and the girth not slip on the freshly saddled horse. The momentum of the horse twisted and cracked every muscle and sinew in his neck and back. Then the pressure was off. Her knees flew up and the other riders were on them as she swung her legs over the horse's rump behind him. He had time to cut her wrists free and she took the great Towbitz knife and freed her ankles. During that time blows were rained on them from the whips.

182

Then he could feel her astride the horse behind him and knew she was laying about her with the bridle he had collected. He beat off people right and left and headed for the flags.

Hands stretched out for her. He beat them off and then he heard her cry for the first time.

'Oh no, oh my God!'

He looked over his shoulder as the whole horde thundered across the plain in shouting confusion, and saw two tall men with swords flashing cutting their way through the others who were only armed with whips. He knew that swords and firearms were not allowed in Baskashi and remembered too late how his horse had earlier looked back down the trail when he had been watching the camp from the hillside.

Towers and the Chinese forced their way alongside. Thorne could see no way of beating them off since either could decapitate him if he wanted to. The beating Towers was taking from the rest would have deterred or blinded anybody else but him. Suddenly Thorne felt Natasha move. She got her feet under her and was about to spring on to the horse of the man on her right.

Towers dropped his sword and grabbed her arm and pulled her back. The man on the right had grabbed her leg. The Chinese joined Towers and took the other arm and a Towbitz took the other leg.

Thorne, with swear words pouring uselessly out of his lips in his impotent horror, slowed his horse as Natasha's screams grew in frenzy. She was lifted over his head as he ducked, so that she lay across his pommel. He struck out right and left. There was no time to get his hand inside all his clothes to reach his gun. The melee was incredible and the riders split in all directions. Her torso was now across his saddle-bow and then it happened. Like a nightmare that he could predict but not control, her arms were torn from her screaming, screaming trunk. Then the Chinese swung his sword on her head and killed her. And the next second Thorne saw him blinded by a blow from behind, that wrapped the steel thongs around his face.

With every ounce of strength Thorne aimed and dealt Towers a similar blow, saw him drop his reins and cover his face, saw his eyeball out upon his cheek. Then Thorne was racing down the valley and the Towbitz were not following him.

He saw one group surround the Chinese, beating him to death; another group surrounded Towers. Then he saw that Towers was shooting and the group momentarily dispersed. Towers' horse, its unbuckled reins flying, took him over the small river and raced off, Towbitz following him uncertainly. The river widened into a gorge, separating him from Thorne. Towbitz were galloping after him, slung low out of their saddles. Suddenly Thorne realised that half a dozen men had collected themselves and were pursuing him too.

He knew that carrying her torso as he must, as he must, as he must, he had no chance against men nearly as well mounted and initially smaller and lighter than he.

Desperately he drove his horse at the huge rock-fall, which from here seemed to block the lower end of the valley.

And the six horsemen gained on him.

The fact of what had happened with Natasha made it impossible to think. Her blood and tendons, her smashed head, her body, were still with him. He found that his jaw was quivering as if for tears or nausea; and meanwhile her blood ran down the inside of his thigh as though he'd wet himself.

The foremost pursuer was now getting close behind and Thorne recognised the leader. The others rode as close as possible on his tail. A thought came to him and he beat the stallion harder.

He came to the rock-fall and saw a well-defined trail just wide enough for one horse, twisting and turning between the boulders. He rode into it. His horse flung itself madly from side to side round the bends. Thorne fumbled for his automatic. At last he got it out.

Holding Natasha with his bridle hand, he waited till he came to a straight part, to give him a chance of a decent shot in the narrow track. Then he turned and shot the leader's horse in the head.

The first four horses came down with such a crash that they or their riders were too badly injured to continue the chase. The other two stopped, preferring to help their friends than ride on and certainly share their fate.

Thorne galloped on alone. The gorge which separated him from Towers had become a canyon away on his left. The rock-fall grew less and gave way to the spur of the mountain on his right.

He galloped on and on until the stallion began to roll and wallow in his stride. He slowed down and stopped. He knew what he had to do. He turned and rode up among the rocks out of sight of the trail; then he got down. He laid the torso of Natasha on the ground. The stallion stood still, his legs stretched out in front, hind legs splayed out behind, his neck in a long curve down to his crimson distended nostrils. His flanks heaved in frantic gasps, the sweat and blood poured from him. Thorne stood trembling beside him.

He put an ear to the ground. Nothing. He turned to Natasha and drawing his knife knelt beside her, beside her smashed skull, her grinning teeth. He couldn't control any part of himself any more and was sick. It overcame him and he couldn't stop it. He went on and on being sick and retching completely out of control.

At last he was still, kneeling on the grey shale stones with Natasha. He remained like that for a long time. The sky was cobalt blue, empty and still. The mountains were grey, empty and still. The air was silent, empty and still. Natasha's stump was under his hands—her snarling mouth—her smooth stomach; girlish, as on the other night, she lay under his knife. In that empty place his brain boiled with images and he could not move. He had loved her for an hour. She had said, 'We needn't be careful.' She had said guiltily, 'My mouth's too dry to swallow it.' Guiltily she had said it—guiltily—as though she had failed him. And what had he done to her?

Slowly the silence settled into his ears and he heard it; the emptiness into his eyes and he saw it, until, the objective being clear, it became—in an empty, meaningless way—possible to press his sharp knife into her soft belly. And then quite easily he made a long deep incision.

He wished he knew more anatomy. He remembered gutting rabbits. That would help. He felt sure that would help. Then he tried to estimate where the capsule would be. Twenty-four hours ago she'd swallowed it—he'd kill Towers one day—

Sweet Satan let him kill Towers one day, in great pain. He let his mind dwell on that, he tried to pretend that this was Towers under his knife. She might have voided the capsule already. He wondered if he would be able to recognise her stomach. If Towers had not come along it would have been all right. The Towbitz would never have torn her to pieces. When had she last eaten? The warm, terrible smell of her dead inside hit him and he retched again. He knelt, retching terribly. It had all been caused by Towers. The Towbitz would have stuck to their word. His fingers contracted in a spasm on the stomach, and he found what he was looking for and cut it out.

He held it in his hand. Viscous. Then he stood up. He put it in an inside pocket and got on his horse and rode away.

He put his head down on to the horse's neck and rubbed his face in its sweat. The old, familiar smell of a sweaty horse— he rubbed that old, familiar friendly smell on to his cheeks and mouth to keep out the other smells and the memories of the other smells.

The sky was blue. He tried to canter a little bit, but every stride of his horse said, 'Natasha, Natasha, Natasha, Natasha.' so he slowed to a walk, but the horse was finished. He got off and walked beside it stumbling with fatigue.

Some time during the afternoon the trail descended quite steeply and he came out on to a wide flat valley, resembling the one in which the Baskashi had taken place but much lower.

Crossing it was a small group of people and pack animals. He did not know what the customs were but he knew he must have a fresh horse.

He took a course to intercept them. Very soon a couple of riders came cantering over the plain towards him. When they were close they looked him and his horse over with critical eyes, fitting together the things that could and could not have happened to him. They were young men. They greeted him and, when he replied, they knew that, despite his dress, he was not Towbitz. They exchanged wild looks and rode back.

Some more people came out, obviously senior. They rode alongside him. Finally one of them said to him quietly, 'Baskashi?'

'Yes.'

186

'But who are you?'

'I need a new horse and food.'

They were silent.

He said, 'Are you the friend of a horseman who has ridden the Baskashi?'

He could tell by the shining eyes of the younger ones that they were. But the elders said cautiously, 'It is against the law.'

Thorne looked up at his face. 'I am not of the Party,' he said.

'You speak ...'

'I am not a Russian.'

'By Allah, nor am I Russian, I am Uzbeck. Then what are you?'

'I'm English.'

The elder looked round at the others. He was pleased with what he was going to say. 'I know about the English,' he said, 'they have a king.'

'Was it a good Baskashi?' suddenly interjected one of the younger ones.

'It was the most terrible Baskashi that ever happened,' he shouted. 'It will be talked of for ever around the camp fires and in the mountains.'

He could feel the tears come into his eyes. 'It was not for a goat or a calf.'

They murmured and muttered among themselves coming closer.

'It was for a girl,' he cried out.

'By the prophet.'

'For my girl—I rode against them all.'

'He rode alone.'

He could hear his voice trembling, going up higher, crying out. He could see their eyes envisaging the whole thing, feel their feelings and feel his tears. 'I got her,' he cried. 'I had her on my saddle—she beat them and took the blows for me—look at my back. There is no whip mark there, look, look,' he cried. And he showed them.

'Then they came and tore her from me, but it was not Towbitz, it was others. They tore her from me and tore out her

187

arms like this, like this across the withers of my horse. Natasha!' he screamed.

The tears ran down his face. His high shouting voice bleated in the huge valley, and they rode silent beside him, two or three on either side, their heads high, not looking at him until he was composed again.

They reached the caravan and it stopped.

They flung a rug on the ground for him. They had some reluctance to interfere with his feelings but gave him food and yoghourt and water and they watered his horse. He could not eat. He tried to drink some of the water.

Thorne sat on the blanket. He tried to think. Thoughts swam about but he didn't seem able to tie them together. He could not do any more. He must get away. Natasha. He *was* a monster— he caused things like this to happen to people. Natasha. Madness. He recognised it. Yet any weakness or stupidity now with these people might stop him getting the pictures away, and she would have suffered for nothing. The circumstances all around seemed like delirium in his mind, racing, darting, doing nothing. He must get away.

And all this time he had been looking at the people of the caravan. They were heading away from Samarkand. All the pack animals were fully laden. He asked where they were going and they told him it was a fortnight's journey. A fortnight before they could give information about him. He knew he had enough money to buy what he needed.

He looked at the headman and began putting his lacerated hands inside his clothes. They grew quiet and wary. He took out money in small notes and put it in front of him, laying the whip on it to hold it down. His stallion was a prince among the ugly, serviceable horses around him.

'Will you give me a fresh horse for my stallion?'

This was a procedure they understood.

'Yes,' said the headman.

'And a pack horse and provisions and blankets, for money?'

'How much money?'

He could not think. He sat silent. 'And fodder,' he said suddenly, having forgotten it.

They bargained. Their journey was two weeks and he felt

dimly that amount would see him on his way and asked for it. Later, as he watched them assembling his purchases, one of the young men who had first met him came close and said, 'I wish I had seen that Baskashi.'

'Yes.'

His new horse was led forward. The youth realised Thorne needed helping on to it and moved to do so. Then Thorne stopped. They all watched him stop. The women who were not women, just females necessary for reproduction, watched him, puzzled. He walked, reeling slightly, to where the stallion stood, head down. He ran his hand over the terrible weals. He let his hand rest on his withers, now dry and caked with her blood. It was his last link with Natasha. He wished he had not done it, and he turned and the young man helped him mount.

'Go with Allah,' some said.

'Go with Allah,' he replied, and rode away.

He had got help. Within himself he cringed, he was destroyed; and though his horse walked slowly, he was nonetheless, running away. The horse wound its way up the trail into the hills to the south-west and eventually stopped.

He got down, hobbled the horses, got some blankets, rolled up in them and slept.

And the confusion of delirium and nightmare stayed with him when he woke in agony and set out again so that his journey was a journey both overland and also in his tortured mind. He knew where he was going—he could navigate by the stars. His briefing with Knickerbockers had been thorough. There were no roads, only the desert a few days ahead.

There was the first river. He stripped to his underclothes, waded in and destruction was by icy water. Soaking the clothes off his wounds were the fingers of revenge upon him for what he had done.

The second river wound in a valley with pretty grass. He stayed there for some time. Swimming to teach his body to work again was an act of defiance to enable him to go on being his terrible self. Why did he want to recover? So as to cause more horror and pain.

Then came the days of healing when bodily health, returning, brought glimpses of terrifying clarity through the confusion.

He came out of the mountains to the desert of Kara Kum. He must cross it. The desert identified in his mind with oblivion—a place with no features for his mind—a sensation of meaninglessness. He rode out into it day after night.

In the day the infinite horizon was around him, at night the teeming universe arched above him—all meaningless. If he had not had a goal he would have died there. But he would take the pictures out of Russia, that was certain. It was, however, an empty certainty that mocked him with the grinning teeth of Natasha. He must find some good thing, some sure thing, and for that he had to go to Ashkabad. He had promised, in his own way he had promised Teresa to make Micky safe—that was what the promise amounted to in his mind. If Micky existed— if promises were real—if truth and trust were in the world at all. So he had to go to Ashkabad to be sure about this, to be sure about himself, he had to go there to do one good thing. Implacably, therefore, and empty of all but horror, he rode steadily on over the empty desert and under the empty sky.

As he got closer to Ashkabad he realised that he must force his sick mind to function clearly. As an exercise, therefore, he began to reassemble the pieces of information he had been given about Teresa—her mother and her grandfather, Prince Gagarin. Finally he got it right and worked it over in his mind to impress it clearly on his memory.

Prince Gagarin had had a daughter, Carla, who was Teresa's mother. Teresa and Carla had been staying with him in Russia. While they were there Teresa's husband, Michael Stanley, who was an Isoworg agent, had been killed on a level crossing. Teresa had gone back to Holland on account of this. Carla and Micky, Teresa's five-year-old son, had stayed on. Teresa was the mistress of Dimitri Zoubovitch, a Russian 'diplomat' in London, for whom she also worked. Her 'work' was to snoop on Michael's old friends and acquaintances and tell Dimitri about them and their activities. She claimed that she did not know Michael had been one of Isoworg's political agents and she said that Micky was being used as a hostage to blackmail her into Dimitri's service.

But Teresa's grandfather, Prince Gagarin, had had a mistress, Anya Zoubovitch, the wife of his groom. She had had a child by him named Dimitri. Thorne himself had been captured by Dimitri only a few hours after Teresa had left him in Norway. Finally, what had been the significance of Carla's meeting with Jakov, Natasha's father, the Isoworg agent? What kind of a ménage was he to expect in Ashkabad? What would be the reaction of these people to his arrival, to his intention to rescue Micky—if Micky was real? Was anything real? He rode on over the desert of Kara Kum until one day he saw the low hills in which lay civilisation and Ashkabad.

He rode in through the hills, avoiding roads and even tracks, and lay up out of sight until night. He let the pack horse go in the hills and waited until it was late before making his way to that part of the town's outskirts where he knew Gagarin lived.

Chapter Fifteen

He arrived there about eleven-thirty p.m. The garden was delapidated, timeless, calm under the moon. He dropped his horse's reins and left it cropping the lush grass. The house was wooden, with complicated fretted windows and eaves. In the moonlight it seemed beetle-browed as though guarding something.

By the door was a list of names: Gagarin, Zoubovitch, Gagarin (Rechteren). So far it was true. The prince living with his mistress, by whom he had fathered Dimitri, and with his daughter, Teresa's mother. She apparently had reverted to her maiden name. The door was not locked. He went in silently.

A dim light in the hall showed homely untidiness. Muddy shoes and boots, some very small; old mackintoshes on a coat-stand, again one small one; an oriental chest; wooden stairs with carved wooden banisters, many broken.

He heard voices. He took a breath, put his hand in his pocket on to his gun and opened the door where the voices came from. It was a big room, overfurnished, giving an impression of stuffiness and broken-down comforts; much lived in. An old dog slept by the stove.

Three people looked up. He felt mad, it was unreal, not happening.

He recognised Teresa's mother immediately. The old man, with white hair and beard, looked feeble; his lower lids gapped down redly. The other woman, Zoubovitch, was a fierce housekeeper, held erect from her bell-shaped hips by corsets.

There was silence. And then with the weary certainty of the aged, Gagarin said, 'He is not Towbitz—not even Russian.'

'He has been beaten,' added his daughter, Carla.

Anya Zoubovitch said, 'What's he think he's doing coming in

like that.' Her eyes were hard and Thorne didn't trust her. The other two sat still, silent, waiting.

'What was it we heard on the news from Samarkand?' asked Carla.

'Some provocateurs,' said the woman Zoubovitch, 'assassins, counter-revolutionaries.'

'Ah,' said Gagarin, 'these days an earthquake is counter-revolutionary, so is a flash of lightning. I have been saying that for half a century.'

'They can't help you,' said Anya Zoubovitch to Thorne, 'they've been blown for years, you must be mad.'

He sniggered slightly at the phrase, thinking the whole thing was mad, not really happening.

'For God's sake, talk proper Russian,' Gagarin nagged at Anya, 'not this awful modern slang.' And Carla watched Thorne narrowly, realising that he hadn't spoken, that he wasn't Russian and that nonetheless he had laughed with curious appositeness at Anya's idiom.

She now said, 'Where are my specs? I haven't really looked at him yet.' She reached for her bag.

Thorne sprang at her and ripped the bag out of her hand. Smiling down at her, he took a tiny gun out of it.

'They're on your head, you fool,' he said, and she shook all over with self-deprecating laughter.

'Fool I am,' she blurted out crossly.

To Anya Zoubovitch on an impulse Thorne said, 'Fancy letting her carry a gun like that. Dimitri will think you're a bloody idiot when I tell him.'

Carla sat deadly still and Thorne pointed the little gun at Anya Zoubovitch, watching her. Anya's hand lay concealed among the cushions and covers of the ancient chair. Suddenly she pulled out a gun, not at all ladylike, and Thorne, aiming to shoot it out of her hand, squeezed the trigger of Carla's little gun. There was a click, and Carla said, 'You sodding old bitch.'

Thorne steadily pulled back the breach. The firing pin was all right and there was a dent in the rim of the cartridge. He took the cartridge out and looked at it carefully. Obviously, there was no powder in it; but the woman Zoubovitch hadn't taken it

193

out, it had been done professionally.

Gagarin's hands began plucking at his trouser buttons and he began to whine.

'He's impotent, poor bugger,' Anya Zoubovitch said and laughed.

Gagarin looked miserable and ashamed at the mess he was making of himself. Outside an owl screeched and Thorne was still holding the useless little gun, Carla was still muttering curses, Zoubovitch still pointing her own gun at Thorne.

'He was my lover,' Anya Zoubovitch said surprisingly. 'In my day it was quite something to be sent up by a prince, and he was as randy as a ferret.'

'A stoat, woman, a stoat, and it's not sent up, either,' Gagarin began testily, and then it didn't seem worth it any more and he looked away at the dog twitching in a dream, and said to it, 'Fight 'em, that's right, boy, fight 'em, fight 'em.'

Thorne felt unreality taking over. He wanted to get at the truth about Teresa—he thought he was lightheaded or going mad—he didn't know how to proceed. He pointed to the cartridge —he knew something about cartridges, it seemed a safe topic— and he said to Zoubovitch, 'You never took the powder out of these cartridges. Dimitri had it done for you.' He felt he was on the right track to infer again that she was in collusion with Dimitri. But he didn't know why.

He moved closer, showing her what he meant. She didn't know how to answer and Carla said to Thorne, 'What do you know about Dimitri?'

Then he was near enough to knock the gun out of Zoubovitch's hand.

'Thank God,' said Carla, 'she's only a peasant, she might have shot anybody. Pour us out some tea, Anya Zoubovitch.'

Anya started to cry. 'Dimitri made me—all these years he made me—taught me.'

'Yes, I know,' said Carla off-handedly. 'Pour the tea, woman.'

'Dimitri made you keep watch on Carla?' Thorne asked.

'Yes. How do you like your tea, sir?'

'Anyhow. What did you mean they're blown?'

Carla said in her deprecating manner, 'She's always picking up words and using them wrong, like impotent when she means

194

Father is incontinent, and sent up by a prince; sent up indeed.'

'What is it then?' Anya said crossly. 'All this slang we get from Dimitri and his friends. I never quite know.'

'Why the hell can't they talk Russian?' Gagarin said peevishly, and took a cigarette out of a box, moving wretchedly. 'How long before you clean me up?' he added.

Carla got up and moved a screen round him. Then she turned. 'Anya,' she said, 'come and get on with it, woman, I'll do the tea.'

When Thorne sat on a chair with horsehair coming out of it, the leg broke.

'Bust the chair, has he?' cackled Gagarin from behind the screen.

'Hurry up and get your nappy changed,' Carla said laughing. 'Blown! Blown indeed,' she added to Thorne. 'Still, she's right, can't help.'

'Would you if you could?'

'Depends what you want.'

'Christ, my arse is sore,' came from behind the screen. 'Why can't you get that other kind of cotton wool?'

At the end of what had happened to him—this. Thorne began to giggle—he wanted to giggle recklessly. He tried to hang on, wanting them to tell him spontaneously, without prompting, about Teresa; so as to get at the truth. Carla watched him, as he stood there sniggering.

She said, 'Who are you? Isn't it about time you told us?'

'You tell me what you do to help Dimitri, and I'll tell you anything you want to know.'

Carla looked at him, assessing him. 'I wouldn't do a damn thing to help Dimitri but I have a daughter.'

Anya popped her head round the screen and spat out, 'She's a whore, a capitalist who took her child to live in a brothel full of film stars and royalty having orgies in Amsterdam and London,' and popped it back again.

'I never *had* an orgy, blast it,' grunted Gagarin.

Carla looked at Thorne very straight, and he did his best; but the giggles got him, he was helpless. The tears came into his eyes. He kept trying to stop but he couldn't.

Then Anya whipped the screen away and stood glancing round

195

from one to the other, looking bullied and miserable because she thought she had made another mistake and that Thorne was laughing at her.

For the first time there was a glance of communion between father and daughter, a glance that told Thorne many things, and then Carla said to Thorne in English, 'You speak with an accent, you behave like an Englishman—I think you're English.'

Through his giggles he said point blank in English, 'Then tell me about this daughter of yours.'

'She's being blackmailed to spy for the Soviet.'

'How?'

'Her son is here.'

Something seemed to be singing in his ears; in the sky. 'May I see him?'

Carla hesitated. She looked at Thorne, trying to make up her mind about something. He was English. He had scars. He dressed as a Towbitz. He rode a horse. She had heard about the failure of the Towbitz guards, at the plant, even rumours of a Baskashi. She already had an idea about what sort of a man he was. At last she said decisively to Anya, 'Stay with Father.'

'Yes, Madam.'

Carla got up and led Thorne out of the room without speaking. Nor did she speak as she led him down the passage.

She reached a door and put her hand on the china knob, flowered like a Victorian soap dish. She looked up into his eyes again, trying to decide about him, but the look slipped away and she only seemed baffled and then guilty. She said, 'He is a hostage,' using the word as though there was nothing worse.

She opened the door gently. The room was dark except for a shielded candle. She took it up and, gesturing for Thorne to look, used it briefly to illuminate his face.

He lay on his back, his hands thrown up near his ears. His hair was blond and his eyes seemed large. Thorne looked at him critically, measuring his height. He looked for a long time, wondering what to make of the fact that he did not believe that this was Teresa's child. He wondered if he could ever believe anything. He wondered if the reason for his unbelief was just because he wanted to believe so much. He felt the singing subside and uncertainty return.

196

Smiling—smiling so as to coax truth out of her—he whispered, 'What's his name?'

'Micky,' she said, and he could not be certain whether there had been a pause. She put the candle back and they went out into the passage. True or false? True or false? He did not know.

There seemed to him to be four alternatives. One, she wanted to test him to see if he was in a position to recognise Teresa's child. Two, she was afraid he was trying to abduct Micky and so she was trying to palm him off with another. Three, she wanted to keep Micky here as a hostage because she was too afraid to make any kind of break. Four, she wanted to keep Micky here as a hostage because in fact she was loyal to Dimitri. Finally, could he be sure, merely after looking at a sleeping child by candlelight, that it was not in fact Micky. He stood by the door, head bowed, thinking it all through. But he did not trust his own brain. Desperately he longed for the little radio. He thought about Teresa, wondering if his knowledge of her would establish some point of communication.

So he tried saying, 'If I take him now he will be with Teresa tomorrow.'

'Do you know her then?'

'Yes.'

'When did you meet her?'

'At Middacten, where she was found in the tunnel by Cousin Tom in *flagrante delicto* with his son.'

Carla's short laugh shook her in the same way as did Teresa's.

He tried to think hard about the next question, and then said, 'What did Michael Stanley work for?'

'Isoworg,' she said at once.

'What did Teresa think of that?'

'She didn't know. I never told her.'

'Why?'

'Because Isoworg is dynamite. They kill Isoworg agents like vermin on sight.'

'How do you know?'

'Dimitri told me.'

'What do you think of it?'

'It is the way.'

'Did Jakov or Natasha say that to you?'

197

She jerked her head up very fast and then tried to pretend it meant nothing, saying, 'I've never heard of them.'

'You *did* listen to the news on the radio?'

'Yes.'

'The truth is that Jakov and Natasha and I photographed the inside of the fusion plant in the mountains by Samarkand. They are dead. I have the pictures. Give me Micky and I will take him to Teresa.'

Then she knew who he worked for. She walked nervously about. She found herself standing by the coat-stand at the end of the hall and she said, 'Yes, I knew Jakov. He was interested in Taoism; he used that phrase to me once.'

'You were mixed up with him?'

'Only very slightly, but Dimitri found out.'

She paused. She found a loose button on a coat of Micky's and begin picking at it to get it off.

'I know who you work for. I believe you will understand what I'm going to say. Dimitri wasn't popular with the Party because of being Father's bastard. He was going to tell on me and Jakov, so I seduced him. He's a mixture—not all bad. Then it came out —about me and him—Anya told them I think—and the Party doesn't approve of people sleeping with half-sisters and princesses. He was getting the push gradually.'

'But he didn't tell?'

'No. But things got worse and then Michael was killed. Dimitri was here in Ashkabad. I thought it was a coincidence at the time, now I'm not so sure. Teresa dashed off, leaving Micky with me. And it was then, you see, that Dimitri had this idea. He said if I didn't stay with Micky, he'd tell about me and Jakov. Then he blackmailed Teresa with Micky. He reckoned it would reinstate him with the Party.'

'What would?'

'Exploiting people like us, and her spying on Michael's friends.'

'But you said she didn't know.'

'She didn't. That makes the best agent—of that sort.'

He nodded; it seemed to tie up.

'But he told her—' he stopped and changed it to a question. 'What did he tell her?' he asked.

She smiled wearily. 'He told her he wanted to know about the

198

trendy people—swinging people—all that bit. He likes modern slang.'

The voices were alike and Thorne remembered Teresa using the same phrase.

'What's he like?' he asked.

'Fun. Two-faced. Shrewd. Opportunist. Makes a good diplomat. All the Gagarins were diplomats, but he's got a flaw—he's cruel—and a coward.'

'What did Teresa think about—?'

'Me sleeping with him?' she interrupted.

'Yes.'

'Dimitri's ugly. She never knew *why* I did it, so she hated me—thought I was in with him to keep Micky. It made her sick going to bed with him. She'd kill him if she dared, she's quite capable of it.'

The button came off at last. Carla looked up at him.

He recalled Teresa's sudden changes of behaviour at Middachten and on the Yssel Meer. He understood how she must have wavered between desperate fear for Micky, hatred of what she was doing, determination to resist, fear of doing it badly. And still in the back of his mind he wondered where the truth lay—wondered if, after all this, he could *ever* really believe in her.

He took a deep breath and let it out slowly. 'I see,' he said, and after a pause added, 'Okay, let's go—you too. But that's not Micky,' he pointed.

Carla looked up at him and at last she smiled—just like Teresa.

'Good,' she said and patted his arm and sighed. Then she took down a heavy loden coat and put it over her arm. She took blankets from the chest and put them with the coat on a chair. She beckoned him and they went into another room. There was no light.

'Micky, are you awake?' she said in Dutch.

'*Ja, Grootmama,*' he said almost at once.

'We are going for a midnight drive. You must get dressed very quickly.'

'Oh, what fun!' He struggled up.

She lit the lamp. Thorne came in and shut the door.

The child, who was standing in pyjamas, seemingly knee-deep in the bed, was a miniature Teresa. Tears smarted in Thorne's eyes. He put out his arms towards him and then stopped. But Carla had seen, even as he tried to turn his movement into a gesture towards the other room, saying, 'Who is he then?'

'A playmate of Micky's,' she replied, dressing him, smiling.

Thorne heard somebody leave the sitting room and come uncertainly down the passage.

Carla said, 'She's such a fool, it would be better for her sake to tie her up.'

When the door opened Thorne took Anya by the arm and walked her firmly back to the old man.

'Told you to mind your own business,' Gagarin said, dropping his upper dentures at her wolfishly.

'What do you think you're on?' Anya asked Thorne truculently.

Thorne looked round the room, cut down some of the old-fashioned blind cord and said, 'It'll look better for you both if I tie you up.'

'Well, I never,' she said and muttered away, outraged. As Thorne dexterously bound her to her chair, he said to Gagarin, 'You can pretend to be too senile to know what's going on, can't you?'

'I am. I'm half bats as it is. Tell you what's the cause of it. It's having to live for half your life with some girl you once just poked for the fun of it. It's like being in hell; especially if she can't even wipe your arse without damn nearly castrating you.'

'Then do it yourself, you old idiot, you're not a prince any more,' said Anya.

Surprisingly Gagarin stood up. He was taller than Thorne and it seemed perfectly natural for him to hold himself quite upright.

'I am a prince,' he said. He held out his hand to Thorne and went on in careful, old-fashioned sounding English, 'I do not want to know who you are nor where you come from nor where you are going. I will find out later—isn't it?—that you have taken Carla and Micky with you. Naturally you did this at the point of a gun.' They shook hands.

'Goodbye.'

'God speed,' said the old man in English.

Anya shrugged her shoulders and did not speak. Thorne went out and shut the door.

In the hall Carla was wrapped in her loden coat, a scarf over

200

her head. Micky wore a padded suit, miniature ski boots and a knitted cap with a bobble on the top. He smiled up at Thorne who got the impression he had been told not to talk.

'Have you a car?' he asked.

'Yes, an old Zis but it's quite reliable.'

They all sat in the front and Thorne drove. One of the items he had memorised in Knickerbockers' flat was the detail of a frontier post in the mountains. It lay in a gorge between un-scalable rock faces. The road through it was forbidden and the guard post was only there to cover the river which could other-wise be used as a means of escape. He drove in that direction, his mind busy with the problem of how to deal with it and whether he could get the car through.

They arrived there at about four a.m. It was very lonely. A narrow dirt road led down the gorge. He coasted down the hill as close as he could get. When the car stopped he got out and said, 'Keep dead quiet and wait'. He went forward on foot.

There were juniper trees and cotton-woods and mesa scrub. Clouds came and went across the moon. He saw a wooden hut backed up against the rock wall. Between it and the river were cones of concrete to block the track. He knew that now they must go on even if they had to walk.

He was able to reach the hut unseen and looked in through the tiny window. Two men were asleep; the third sat sprawled at the table. Thorne could not decide if he was asleep or not. He wished he had a grenade. He took out his automatic, screwed on the silencer and crept round the hut to the open door.

He shot two through the head before the third awoke, then he shot the third accurately in the forehead too. He went round the hut, trying to work out a way of negotiating the barrier. None presented itself. At the back of the hut was a lean-to shelter containing firewood and some tools. Among them was a big crow-bar. He grabbed it and ran back to start work on the concrete blocks. But it was hopeless. Just three rows of the damn things stood in his way. He stood staring round, angry, thwarted. Then another idea came to him. He went back to the lean-to and looked it over carefully and then ran back to the car.

Carla said in English, 'Dead?'

'Yes.' Then he explained about the blocks and his idea while

201

he drove back to the hut. He leapt out, grabbed the crow-bar, ran to the lean-to and began to tear it apart. It was badly put together and in a few moments he had dragged one wall section of it free. He brought it round to the blocks and leaned it against them, making a ramp. He went back and fetched the other section. This he laid across the top of the blocks. He made Carla get out to steady the sections and gingerly drove the car up the ramp and on to the top section. He put on the hand brake, very carefully got out, hauled the ramp section round to the other side, put it in place and drove the car carefully down. Then Carla and Micky got in and he drove off slowly down the track, with weeds and bushes growing on it. He hoped it had not been mined.

When they reached the Persian post they found no concrete blocks. Evidently people were not so keen on getting out of Persia. Thorne went into the hut and spoke to the guard commander. He gave him the number in Teheran which he had memorised and waited. A few moments later the commander said they could go, but Thorne—who didn't understand Persian—didn't like his manner and took the 'phone from him.

He said, as he had been instructed, 'Call me on the radio—know what I mean?'

After a moment the voice on the other end of the telephone said, 'Go ahead.'

'Say I've got the pix, Micky and Carla, and I want a plane.'

Then the voice said, 'Gurgan airfield three hundred miles—what is registration of your car?'

'Zis, Ashkabad registration 2002.'

After a pause the voice said, 'Hamid Gajar will meet you first crossroads. He will make 'I's with headlights, you will make 'G's'. Obey him, Get cracking.' The line went dead.

Thorne drove off into the mountains. They drove for an hour. Micky slept. Nothing happened. After two hours Thorne began to worry about Hamid. In this roadless district of high mountains he knew he could not by-pass the T. junction with the main road which would take him west to Gurgan. Therefore, if anybody was going to try to ambush him, that was where they would be. The question was, therefore, how could he tell whether it was Hamid or an ambush in time to do anything about it. Dawn was just breaking when he came to the T. junction.

He saw two Volkswagens there, one facing him, the other pointing west. He slowed. When he came close the car facing him flicked its lights, I, I, I. With a sigh of relief he made G's and drew up alongside.

A man came over, pudgy, unshaven. He looked at the registration number and then put his head in at the window. Thorne had his gun on him, ready to shoot him through the door.

'Toron?'

'Yes.'

'Hamid Gajar. You follow. We stop only for petrol. If anything happens I will flick rear lights, then go like rocket. Before the airport I leave you to get away. Okay?'

'Right.'

'You crash barrier and find Harrier. Can recognise, yes?'

'Yes.'

'Good. Now listen, lady—you jump with boy—straight up on wing. Okay?'

'Okay,' she said.

'Right, let's go.'

'What's he say?' asked Micky in Dutch.

'We're going in an aeroplane.'

'Oooh, exciting.'

While this has been going on two of Hamid's men had changed the number plates on the Zis.

The three cars drove off in the early morning light, Hamid's car in front and the other VW behind. They stopped once for petrol. Carla snored.

Outside Gurgan, just before the road left the mountains, there was a place where it had been cut out of the face of the cliff. Some workmen were out with their 'Stop' signs clearing a small rock fall.

Hamid flicked his rear lights furiously and accelerated. Thorne drew his gun, changed down and followed suit. He saw two tommy guns pop out of the sides of Hamid's car, saw the workmen snatch up weapons before they were mown down. Then Hamid's car lurched and slewed across the road, blocking it. The fire was being returned from the front and all of Hamid's men were replying. Thorne slowed the Zis, put the heavy bumpers up against the light front end of the VW and accelerated. He got it straightened up. He saw some one up in the rocks and took a snap shot. Then the VW got going and with a shriek of metal where the sides were touching, it drove off and he followed, the engine screaming.

Micky had woken up and was jabbering excitedly. In the mirror Thorne saw the other car stop. A man jumped out and rushed up the hill after the man at whom Thorne had taken a snap shot. He hoped they would prevent word of their having got through from reaching the airport before them.

The road to the airport was obvious a long way off. Hamid braked, waved him on, Thorne raced past, saw in his mirror Hamid turn and head off towards a forest to the south. Thorne accelerated down towards the airport road. He raced along it, gathering speed all the time, crashed the barrier at the entrance and dashed out over the tarmac and grass bouncing madly, his eyes darting in search of the Harrier. Then he saw it and headed that way.

'Be ready to jump out, Carla; put Micky up first and then you and then me.'

She threw off the rugs and explained to Micky what was going to happen.

'I can run faster than you, Granma,' he said proudly.

Cars were beginning to race after them. Thorne reached the plane and skidded to a halt. Micky was out like a flash and Carla hoisted him up on to the wing and he nipped inside. Thorne boosted her and bundled in after. Before the canopy was properly shut they were off, Micky chattering excitedly. They were all crouched on top of one another. The jet screamed, the plane lifted and then leapt up and away, banked and went into ordinary climbing flight, the G's pressing them down. The pilot turned and grinned at their predicament and beckoned. Thorne put his ear to his mouth and he said, 'Sorry about the squash, it's all the extra petrol we've got aboard for the trip. Radio etc. there for you.'

Thorne climbed over Carla and looked at the equipment and read the instructions. He couldn't understand them. His brain wouldn't work. He found his hands were shaking. He started again. The instructions were very simple. They said, 'This is your radio link, use it.'

His radio link—his! The tears gushed into his eyes—he giggled. He switched it on, put on the headphones and began gabbling into the mike, incoherently telling his story. At last he steadied himself. His own voice, calm, matter of fact in the headphones, gave him confidence. It began giving him instructions. It gave them slowly and carefully one by one. Slowly and carefully, one by one, he obeyed them. When he had finished the voice said, 'Good. Now there is one small thing.'

'Yes, what's that?'

'D'you see a little yellow box sellotaped to the radio?'

'Yes.'

'Well, here's what you do with it.' His own voice went on explaining carefully. Finally Thorne said, 'Right, I've done that.'

'You will land momentarily at a field outside Paris. Linda Jowitt will drive you to rooms I'm preparing.'

'Why Paris?'

'Shut up and listen. I'll have your stuff there by then, plus your usual radio link. Call me the moment you arrive. It's quiet there and you'll concentrate better on what I'm going to tell you.' The line went dead.

Carla shouted at him, 'What's been going on?'

'We're dining in Paris—there's nothing worth eating in Persia.'

He could see her laughing and it triggered him and he began giggling and he couldn't stop. He felt weak and shaky with giggles.

They reached Paris that afternoon. The pilot took them down in a steep dive, identified the field, eased off, steadied the plane at twenty feet, hovered and landed quickly on his vertical jets. He throttled back and they leapt out and ran in the sandstorm the idling jets created. They had scarcely got the car door shut before the plane was off and vanishing towards Potten End.

Linda looked once at Thorne—once only—and looked away in horror. After that she didn't speak a word.

The rooms were in St. Germain des Prés, not far from where he had stayed the last time. Linda drove through an old eighteenth century coach door which gave into an interior courtyard. From there tatty spiralling stairs led to the top rooms. She described them and gave Thorne the numbers without getting out of the car. Then she drove away. Thorne led the way up. The door at the top opened into calm, beauty and peace. Big windows, open in the warm air, looked out over the gardens. His room led, through a bathroom, into Carla's. She took Micky past him without a word, through the bathroom and into the other room and shut the door, smiling once briefly over her shoulder.

The curtains moved in the gentle air. A pigeon cooed. He went to the cupboard and found there his own clothes and belongings, just as he had been told. He picked up the radio and opened the link. He listened to himself being reasonable, thinking clearly and calmly, deciding exactly what to do.

Finally, his voice said, 'Got all that?'

'Yes.'

'Now listen. You and Isoworg have got such a hell of a reputation that the others might just conceivably not kill you—might try to use you in some way.'

'How?'

'Don't know exactly but the Micky rescue sounds a bit of a pushover ...'

'Like hell.'

'I think it might be part of a plan in which they'd go to *any length at all* to convince you that one of their agents, let's say Teresa, was on the level.'

'Why?'

'Because our resources are building up to be so much greater than their's, their only chance of beating us to the next punch is through conning you.'

'Oh. So?'

'So listen carefully and I'll tell you what to do. I'll go over and over it with you until you're word perfect, so repeat carefully everything that I say because you're practically all in.'

Thorne sat like an imbecile repeating over and over the instructions he was being given.

'But why—why?' he cried out.

'Because,' said his voice, forcibly, 'because I am you and I know what you want, and I'm bloody well going to get it, so do as I say.'

'But I can't—I can't any more.'

For once his voice didn't answer, and Thorne went on, 'Souped up or nuts—I'll be both if I do as you say.'

His voice harshly replied, 'You'll be you, and if you don't do it you'll be nothing.'

Thorne looked round the room. Wildly he said, 'I want Teresa ...'

'... she'll come at 5.30 ...'

'... for her I want ...'

'... Champagne, mimosa—look in the fridge ...'

'... and also a present—I'd like to give her ...'

'... an Australian water opal, it's in the cupboard ...'

'... I want it like ...'

'... like I want it ...'

'... I'm going mad ...'

'... not yet.'

'I can't, I can't,' he cried and he knew the voice was his own will driving him on, driving him past the point where his present resolution would have been broken by fatigue and shock. All the reasons, the explanations were sensible and the motive was there, namely that he wanted to put her to the proof once and for all and trust her as his own woman—but there were still such terrible things that his voice had told him he had got to do.

Finally, his voice said, 'Get cracking. Out.'

Mechanically he began to do as he had been told. He took off the coat, the bloodstained Towbitz coat, and threw it open on the floor. As the other clothes came off, he threw them down upon it. He put his gun next to the bed. Then he took out the capsule containing the microfilm out of his pocket. He held it in his hand, remembering Natasha. He heard the pigeon pleading quietly, 'My toe bleeds, Betty, my toe bleeds, Betty.' He knocked the girders up out of the socket of the bed's foot and turned the foot upside down. He put his dirty shirt under it, as he had been instructed, to catch the pieces, and with the tiny brace and bit which had been put ready in the room he drilled a hole in the under side of it. He slipped the capsule in. He bunged the hole with the plastic wood which had come with the brace and dirtied it. Then he put the bed back, put the shavings carefully down the lavatory, made a bundle of the clothes and put them in the dirty clothes basket. He put the brace and bit away on top of the cupboard, as he had been told. Then he stood still,

207

Naked in the peaceful room.

It was four-thirty p.m. He went into the bathroom and turned on the shower.

The hard needles of hot water drove off him and he saw the dirt swirling round the bottom of the blue bath. When he started to soap himself the pleasure of the amount of dirt that ran out of his hair was hypnotic. He watched it, wondering if he could wash it all away—wondering if there was enough water in all the world to wash him clean.

He shaved for the first time in three weeks, and then he showered again. He felt de-personalised, as though this were not him at all. Afterwards he dressed in his smart clothes, placed his gun in the reinforced pocket holster built into the coat and put money in his pocket. Then he took the tiny radio and the handsome ring box, and pocketed them too. He went to the fridge and took out the Champagne. Carefully he eased out the cork. He felt that he might as readily have squeezed an eyeball up into his palm. He poured the orange juice and bitters into the jug to make the mimosa, and then he poured in the Champagne.

When it was finished, he unlocked the door. He sat in one of the modern black leather armchairs, took a long pull at the mild drink, belched and reached for the jewel box. With great pleasure he looked carefully at the water opal. It was a sphere about a quarter-of-an-inch across. It looked like a pale, honey-coloured soap bubble in three dimensions. If you turned it, the appearance changed. If you had the ring on your finger, you could look at it from different angles and in different lights and it would never be the same but it would always be full of pale golden light. He felt blank and meaningless.

The ring, the mimosa, the waiting for Teresa were all a charade. But Teresa was coming; and they would look at each other at the end and believe.

'Ummm. Thought it'd be you,' blurted Teresa, shutting the door and putting down her case.

He jumped jerkily up to take her in his arms. She looked at him oddly. He stopped, stood nervous, smiling hectically.

She said, 'Oh, what's the drink?'

'Mimosa.'

She poured some; he jerked forward to help her, too late. Still he kept smiling. Now she was here. It'd be all right soon—all right.

'Here,' he said abruptly, and his hand jerked out and gave her the ring. She took it and looked at it.

'Never seen one.'

'Australian water opal.'

She turned it slowly this way and that. Thorne watched her.

'Can't make up my mind if it's nearly silver or nearly gold colour.'

He giggled. 'Who can? Who can?'

'Peaceful,' she said.

'Yes,' he said brightly.

'Happy.'

'Yes. Happy, happy, happy.' He nodded hard to show that he was really with her.

She took a pull at her drink, found a cigarette and lit it. Carefully, she said, 'Darling—um—darling, you look ghastly,' and the tears came into her eyes. 'You've had a very bad time—um? Very bad—tell me.'

'Can't—no—you mustn't know—too terrible ...'

'You did something—what did you do, darling?'

He shook his head. He did not think she had ever called him darling before. 'Something for you—I promised once—twice—remember.' He nodded at her as he spoke. She glanced at him sharply and her eyes were full of an unshieldable poignancy. In the silence an evening breeze moved the curtain; the pigeon pleaded.

The knob of the bathroom door rattled. They both looked at it. Micky came in as though playing a game. Teresa's knees gave way with the shock. She sat down abruptly in a chair, holding out her arms and smiling the little fierce smile, while tears ran out of her eyes. Micky looked uncertainly at Thorne and his face crumpled.

'Aren't you naked?' he said looking at Thorne's face. Then he turned dutifully to Teresa saying as though he had been taught, 'You are my mama.'

'Yes, darling.' She was still holding out her arms.

He went and stood by her knee and she put her arms round him gently, talking Russian.

209

'You were only two-and-a-half when I saw you. Do you remember me at all?'

'I remember your smell,' he said, pushing his nose out. 'Anya said you were bad.'

'She had to say that.'

'Why?'

'Somebody told her to.'

Micky giggled. 'Thorne *was dirty*. We went in an airplane, all squashed, and Thorne barged a Volksey right out of the way—it was a very fast airplane. Thorne said it was the fastest airplane in the world, didn't you, Thorne? Can I have some of your glass, I'm thirsty?'

Thorne poured out some orange juice. He gave it into both Micky's hands and watched him put the glass up to his face and tip his face down and drink with concentration so as not to spill in the smart place. When Micky saw them looking at him, he giggled, which made bubbles in the glass; he got excited and blew more bubbles. Thorne thought he could have sat like that, watching him blow bubbles into his glass, for ever. Teresa sat watching him too.

Carla came in. She and Teresa looked at each other across a gulf, Carla hoping it would be bridged by the *fait accompli* of Micky's return. Carla's eyes were pleading, Teresa's burned with the impossibility of forgiveness.

Abruptly Carla broke into an extraordinary, deep cry and to Thorne's embarrassment flung herself on her knees, clasping his legs and sobbing.

'Oh gracious,' Teresa said sharply in English.

Thorne broke away, went into Carla's room and shut the door. He went and stood at the window looking out. For no reason his brain suddenly started singing a tune. *Sous les toits de Paris.* Under the twats of Paris, he thought, and it made him laugh. It was like the plane again, he couldn't stop it.

Suddenly Teresa came in. 'Standing there by yourself, roaring with laughter,' she said, smiling. 'Dotty.' She shut the door behind her.

He blew his nose and wiped his eyes.

'Tight?' she said.

'No.'

He stood awkwardly. She came over and they stood together.

'Mother told me what happened at Ashkabad,' she said, and he couldn't think how to answer, so he was silent. She went on, 'Then she helped me unpack. She put all my things alongside yours. Seemed funny. She was happy, I think.' She put her arm round him and he smiled at her. But it wasn't right.

He said, 'I've ordered a meal up here.'

'Thought we might go out.'

'Mustn't leave Micky.'

Fear for Micky made her brain work fast. 'Why? Who might come?'

'Well ...'

She stared at him, her mind raced. 'You've got something they want?'

He didn't answer.

'Haven't you?'

He replied according to plan. 'Yes,' he said.

'Where is it?' she asked.

'I bored a hole in the foot of the bed. It's quite safe.'

She was furious. 'But here—with Micky—what the hell—you're *mad*!'

It stung him and his reflexes answered for him. 'They're just as likely to come for him as for it.'

'Oh God!' She banged her fists on her temples. 'Can't I *ever* get away—*ever—ever*?'

'Yes.'

'How?'

He didn't want to go on—he wanted to put his head in her arms for ever.

'*How* can I get away?' she repeated.

'It'll be okay.' He took her hand loosely. 'We stood like this in the lab and couldn't believe each other,' he suddenly jerked out.

'Yes.'

'Awful to be like that.'

She said, 'It's you that are like that.'

'Please,' he said, 'don't.'

She felt nothing for him. Then she remembered the promise

he had kept, how much he had suffered, what he had done. She smiled and kissed his cheek.

'Thank you for Micky.'

He looked pleased.

She said, 'You see, I *was* telling you the truth all the time, wasn't I?'

For an instant his clouded, bewildered face lit up. Then he remembered his alter ego's caution, 'They'll go to *any length*', and the look left him, and she knew that he did not belong to himself. It made her flesh creep and she moved away from him.

They went into the other room. Micky and Carla were solemnly sitting in a pretence of being grown-ups having drinks together. He had crossed his legs and was puffing away at an unlit cigarette, making grown-up faces. Thorne wanted to amuse Micky. Micky was nice. He looked for Teresa's hairspray, handbag size.

'Look, Micky,' he said, and Teresa turned to look too. He picked up her cigarette lighter, flicked it alight and then squirted the lacquer through the flame. It threw a jet of fire a foot long. Teresa and Carla gasped, Micky shouted with delight.

'Again, again.'

'Like Loge,' Carla said.

'Who was Loge?' Thorne asked, giving the spray to Micky and holding the lighter.

'The god of fire—he went "psst" like that, pointing, and flames shot out of his finger tips.'

'Just like Loge,' Teresa said. 'Is it fun, Micky?'

'Will you give me one, Thorne?' Micky asked.

'Yes, I'll get you one tomorrow.'

Thorne gave the spray back to Teresa. Micky said flatly, 'You're the cleverest man I've met so far.'

'Thank you,' Thorne said.

Teresa thought he seemed better with the child.

The evening passed edgily. Thorne seemed to be waiting for something. Teresa wanted to leave.

'Tomorrow,' he said. 'Tomorrow—got to sleep.'

At last they went to bed. But it was nothing.

In the morning she got up early. The room was warm and she moved about naked. She poured him orange juice from the night

212

before and came and sat on the edge of the bed next to him, drinking it.

'What happened to Natasha?'

'Did I talk in my sleep?'

'Yes. Oh Christ,' she said in horror but her look was one of compassion; and then the door burst open and Thorne's reflexes sent his hand darting for his gun and also stopped it as a bullet thudded into the pillow next to it.

Dimitri raced past into Carla's room and Thorne was looking at the scarred face of Towers with a patch over one eye. Inside him everything seemed to have become molten and obsessed. He was aware only of Towers and the implacable will to tear him to pieces with his hands. A pain stabbed in his head.

Towers had banged the door and locked it. In the next room Carla cried out as Dimitri knocked her down.

Towers said, 'Okay, let's have 'em quick.'

The words Thorne had rehearsed with his alter ego came automatically to his lips. In French, because he knew Towers didn't understand it, he said to Teresa, 'Get close to his eyes and remember Loge.'

'What's that?' Towers snapped.

'I told her to put on a dressing-gown.'

'So where are they, or I'll start on her?'

Thorne said, looking at Towers' gun, 'Okay.' He started to get out of bed very slowly and cautiously. Towers' eyes never left him.

'Working for Dimitri, are you?' Thorne asked.

'Just move very slow or she'll get it, see.'

'He'll shop you,' Thorne said as he got his feet on to the floor. Towers watched him. Teresa had put a cigarette in her mouth. The dressing-gown gaped as she moved towards Towers, holding out the cigarette pack towards him. Confidently she said as she approached, 'If I give you the pictures, will you get Micky from Dimitri?'

She came close with the cigarettes. Towers took one. Thorne watched, coiled like a spring. Teresa put the pack back into her right hand, masking the little spray, and raised the lighter with her left hand towards Towers' cigarette. She failed to make it light. She put out her other hand as though to use both hands

213

to flick it more sharply. The lighter worked. A jet of fire hit Towers in the eye and simultaneously Thorne's waiting body unleashed itself in a karate swing with the back of the hand upwards under the nose, to drop him like a sack. In the same movement he reached for the gun under his pillow, and Dimitri said from the door, 'Stop!'

Thorne stopped; his hand had barely reached the pillow.

Dimitri said to Teresa, 'Right, lift up that pillow.' She did so, and Thorne's gun was revealed.

'Chuck it here,' he said. She did so.

'Now Towers'—and no tricks. I've taken the first pressure.'

Again Teresa obeyed him. Dimitri took the guns and put them in his pocket.

'Dimitri,' Teresa cried at him. 'Dimitri, please, please, please.' Her voice had lost all control. It seemed to come from her stomach or her womb.

Dimitri said to her, 'I'm for the high jump unless I get the stuff back to them. Micky'll be a bonus.'

He reached behind him and lifted a big kitbag round and put it next to him. Sticking out at the top was Micky's face, his mouth sealed with sellotape and his eyes bulging with shock. He was wriggling furiously.

Teresa flung herself forward and Dimitri caught her with his fist, so that she was knocked back and sat down hard, shaking her head dizzily. Thorne stood still, watching. He knew he had to do this part well.

'Now,' said Dimitri, 'the film, or I'll start pulling his ears off.'

Teresa was gathering herself to spring at him. Instead she said, 'I'll tell you where it is.'

'Shut up,' said Thorne.

Teresa screamed, 'I won't. I hope he shoots you in the balls.'

'Shut up. Once he has it he'll kill me and take Micky anyway. Don't you see?' He was watching her as though his whole life depended upon the minutiae of her behaviour.

Dimitri took hold of Micky's ear and twisted it. Micky screamed. Teresa leapt and Dimitri's fist, leaving Micky's ear, caught her with an upper cut and she fell back again.

When she could speak, Teresa whispered to Thorne, 'Do something, you sodding swine, do something.'

214

'Where is the film?' Dimitri said.

Teresa began, 'In the—'

'Shut up,' Thorne snapped.

'So you told her,' Dimitri said, surprised.

'I trusted her,' Thorne said.

'It's in the foot of the bed,' Teresa choked up, and to Thorne, 'You didn't even try. That's what you're *for*, and you didn't.'

'Shut up, for God's sake,' Thorne said, watching Dimitri and trying very hard to play it just exactly right.

'I tried,' she said, 'and I'm a woman, and you didn't.' She was beside herself.

He saw a flicker of suspicion in Dimitri's eyes, and then Dimitri said to Teresa, 'Okay, you—you get them out.'

'I don't know—how—where—' She started messing with the bed foot, trembling and sobbing.

Dimitri saw that she'd never get it done. He backed up into a corner, putting Micky in front of him. He pointed his pistol at Micky's body.

'I'll maim him,' he said. 'D'you understand that, Thorne, I'll maim him if you try anything.'

'Yes, I understand,' said Thorne, standing deadly still.

'Now,' said Dimitri, 'stand back, Teresa. Thorne, very carefully, come over here. You do it.'

Thorne, keeping his face wary, experienced in himself a tiny flicker of relief; then, to his horror, he felt his hands begin to tremble quite violently. As he moved across, it seemed that Teresa and Dimitri were somehow a long way off and that everything was happening slowly or not really happening, and yet he heard his voice speaking quite normally. On the floor was Towers and he wanted to get at him. In the meantime he had been told what to do—he had told himself what to do and he had to do it. His sense of unreality increased, he faltered for a second, he didn't seem to know who he was. He had said, 'I have to take the foot board right off,' and Dimitri had said very sharply, 'Stop,' and he had stopped. Then Dimitri had said, 'Teresa, move the mattress.'

She did so, lugging it out on to the floor, covering Towers.

When Dimitri saw that it concealed no weapon, he said to Thorne, 'Right—go on.'

Thorne took out the footboard, turned it upside down. He said, 'I need the brace and bit—it's on top of the cupboard.'

Dimitri said, 'Get it, Teresa, and if there's a gun, then remember I'll get Micky first.'

She seemed unable to think. Thorne was all the time watching Teresa. His eyes were boring into her and he tried desperately to miss nothing; to be certain of something. He was sure she was now in a state of shock—oh God, please—it was a state of shock, wasn't it? Real shock? The kind of state in which she would be past any ability to act; to deceive him.

'Get a chair,' Thorne said quietly.

She did so and handed him down the brace and bit. When he had bored down to the capsule, Dimitri said, 'Now get back over there. Teresa, take it out and give it to me.'

'Please, Dimitri, I entreat you, take it and give me Micky.'

Slowly, almost reluctantly, he shook his head, still pointing his gun at Micky.

'I daren't,' he said.

Thorne was afraid. He knew Dimitri was losing his decision. 'Don't try to jump him, Teresa,' he heard his voice saying, 'he's not thinking straight.'

She shook the bedboard, the capsule fell out. He saw her hand reach out very slowly, take it up and hand it over. Dimitri took it and said to Teresa, 'Now back over to the other side of the room.'

She obeyed him. He raised the gun from Micky, pointing it at Thorne. He was shaking his head at him perplexed.

'Why did you not even try something—for her sake, for Micky—eh?'

Thorne was watching Teresa's face. He was sure that she—Teresa of all people—could never have pretended the look that was there; terror, hatred, so total as that. He forced his mind away from the wonderful possibility. Nothing must spoil what he had to do or it would all have been for nothing. And this was the difficult bit. Thorne very carefully kept his face expressionless, hoping that Dimitri would think as he was expected to think; and he did. Dimitri's expression changed as something dawned on him.

216

'It is empty, this capsule, eh? That's why you didn't try anything?'

Thorne did not speak. He kept his head lowered, trying to keep his breathing regular. Dimitri measured the distance across the room to where Thorne was.

'Turn round,' he said. 'Lean against the wall.' Thorne obeyed him. 'Feet well back, that's right.' Thorne watched him in the glass of a picture.

It was working. Very carefully Dimitri laid the gun down and then, never moving his hands more than an inch from it, very warily he twisted the capsule undone.

It blew up in a flash in his face and Thorne, leaping across the room, knocked his gun aside and crashed his fist into his face. Before Thorne realised what was happening, Teresa had grabbed the gun and was emptying it into Dimitri, screaming at him in Russian. Thorne stopped her, and turned to undo Micky. Teresa grabbed Micky away from him and rushed into the next room, holding him in her arms. Then she banged the door and locked it.

Thorne found himself shuddering so hard he could hardly pull the mattress off Towers. The cauldron in him—the obsession blanked out everything—he was back in the Baskashi with Natasha screaming and Towers tearing her to pieces. And there was Towers, his eye open, gazing at him stupidly, coming round. Thorne was looking down to return the gaze, shuddering, waiting. When he knew Towers was awake, he tried to tell him what he was going to do, but he couldn't find any words, and so, like an animal, he fell upon him. He tore the flesh from his face; then they fought. He was lost in a red mist of obscene exultation. He took out the other eye with his thumb and began to tear at Towers' throat. Then he stopped, his hands clenched on the windpipe, and Teresa came in and found him like that

He remained still, feeling Towers die. At last it was done; and he still remained in the same position.

He didn't know what was happening because Teresa was hitting him in the face as hard as she could.

'You didn't even try—even try—and it blew up and so *everything* was for nothing. Natasha, the whole thing, for *nothing*, you swine!'

The blows steadied him. She seemed to be hitting him slowly

217

and he didn't feel it at all, but he said, 'I sent the real one with the plane.'

'What!' She stopped.

'I had to make Dimitri check, see, and you didn't trust me—you didn't trust me—you didn't trust me.' He said it over and over again.

She stood looking down at him, as he sat shuddering uncontrollably on the bed, saying over and over again, 'You didn't trust me.'

'For what—why—what was it all for?'

'*You*! *I want you*—*to trust*. I want to be certain of *you*. See?'

'But you *knew*.'

'No.' He said the words singly. 'You can pretend *anything*. Except feelings; this time you were *not* pretending—this thing you couldn't pretend and I *saw*. So now I know.' Then he was shuddering again and couldn't do anything else, nor even speak.

Carla came in, holding her head, moaning. Micky was crying— the police were hammering at the door.

He opened the radio. The shuddering made his teeth chatter, he could hardly talk. He jabbered into it incoherently.

'Listen,' said his own voice clearly. 'You're babbling about the police, right?'

'Yes.'

'Tell them Perfus is on his way, I'm just 'phoning him—he'll take care of things.'

Teresa heard this too, and as the police burst in Thorne ran into Carla's room. The police started jabbering at Teresa. She said nobody would speak till the arrival of Perfus, and she kept on saying it. Carla then began talking to them with Micky on her knee, sobbing as she stroked him. Teresa went through into the other room. Thorne sat on the bed holding the radio, still shuddering, gabbling at it insanely.

'What happened?' it said calmly, over and over again. 'Come on, what's happened?'

Teresa took it, said, 'Damn you, I hate you, you've destroyed him,' and then in a madness of frustration, 'You are him. I can't even—can't even—*anything*, can't do anything.'

'What happened?'

'Micky's okay, the other two are dead. How did they know we

218

were here?' she blazed at it.

'I tipped them off.'

She was too astounded to answer. At last she gasped out, 'Why?'

'To lay a trap for them, for Thorne and for you. Thorne taught you the trick with the hairspray, didn't he?'

'Yes.'

'He didn't know why,' Thorne's voice commented drily and added, 'Oh well, so it all worked, and there was nothing to lose.'

'Only Micky and me and my mother and Thorne,' she stormed.

'Yes, only people!'

She knew his voice so well she could hear the wry satirical note, knew there was something else. 'What then?' she shouted.

'You couldn't trust each other at all—in bed—by the fire—in the lab—*for ever*—right?'

'Yes.'

'Now you can.'

She sat shaking her head, and suddenly Thorne said quite clearly, 'I'm going mad.'

'No.'

'I'm terrible—no—monstrous—mad,' and his voice broke. 'And you can't help, you're nothing.'

'Teresa,' said the radio, 'I can't help—you can—that's why you're there,' and it clicked off.

Thorne was standing by a gutter. There was a lump in the gutter to guide the sluicing water.

Then he was by the Seine. People were buying and selling books from boxes. They seemed to be caring about it all.

He was in Montmatre. Lunchers were stuffing napkins in their necks and food down their throats, all caring about it all, while traffic scrambled and marketeers haggled with spite and meanness on their faces, just like him.

Men asked him if he wanted a woman or a boy, or to watch women or boys; or humans and animals, in fornication, fellatio, sodomy or beating each other, just like him, just like him.

He was in Notre Dame—grimy gloom and people genuflecting. He saw them reach for the holy water and cross themselves with a gesture, slick as masturbation, and Holy Church had burnt four million witches, just like him, just like him.

He was in the Louvre—brilliant colours and brilliant techniques. People were being skinned, stoned, shot through with arrows, nailed up or nailed down, scourged, broken on a wheel, dragged behind a chariot, hanged by hooks, having their eyes put out, their genitals torn off, being raped, being burst open, filled up with a funnel, eaten by animals, torn apart—torn apart—arms and legs torn out—like him—like him—for what? And the libraries told him the answer: it was so as to love and understand each other better for the sake of God or Buddha—Buddha who solved the problem of want by saying, 'Stop wanting.' Like the Hindu Goddess Kali living on human sacrifice. Like Red Indians who solved the problem of pain by teaching the braves to laugh under torture. Like Chinese who made a pile of hands and feet as big as a hotel and burned them for days to teach somebody something else. Like Tchaka who marched the flower of his Zulu Impis into a bonfire half a mile long to teach a watching missionary what he'd do with hell. Like Hitler who had used all the techniques and ideas all over again in causing five million Jews to 'die in agony'. Just like him, like him, like him.

And then there was something else you found in the places you visited—which all people visited so as to learn about each others' greatness. You learned about letter boxes for secret denunciations; about confessionals with venal priests; torture chambers to extract secrets, twist truth, change minds.

It was everywhere he went. He couldn't get away from himself.

There were paintings as big as houses, of battles and entrails, and all the time there were celibate men, who were not celibate, holding up two fingers to bless the bowels and the pain and to canonise men who had had their skin torn off or their eyes put out or stuck it longer than the other bloke, because they had poisoned their enemy while God wasn't looking. Like him. Like him.

He ran away—rushed away—but couldn't escape himself. In another place he found tools for chopping people up or bashing them to bits. When it wasn't chariots with scythe blades or men with maces, falchions, bilbos, glaives, daggers, poniards, gisarms, ballistas, it was ships. Galleons with pointed prows and drowning

220

slaves and ironclads with turrets and torpedoes, and now it was in the air with fighters reaching speeds at which man's brain got left behind so that he had to invent electric brains to carry his madness faster and further, into space, to people the universe for ever and ever with fear, guilt and hatred, just like him, like him. And it obsessed man's mind so that atom bombs were built with which to lay the blueprint of insanity upon the genes of life for ever. And this was all there was in the world—all there was in him—in him—in him. Why? There was *no* answer except to break and burn those that didn't agree with *your* answer. His mind was crushed down by the old casque of despair, but this time it numbed even his last will or wish to remove it—numbed even his knowledge of who he was, and he wandered about.

Eventually Teresa found him. She took his hand and led him away.

Isoworg calmly went ahead with its plans. It knew that the fair distribution of cheap electrical power was a weapon as perfect for Isoworg's purposes as could ever have been devised. It was constructive and peaceful and had immediate application to the individual. It was a matter of economics, and therefore politics were bound to follow it. Finally, for all these reasons, it offered a focus for the millions of dissident voices in the world, most of them young voices, a focus around which their disgust and terror at power politics could become effective.